WANTON

BOOK 4

BLENDED

WANTON

Copyright ©2014 Erica Chilson

Wicked Reads
PO Box 29
Nelson, PA 16940

www.ericachilson.com/wicked-reads

Printed in the United States of America
First Printing, 2017
ISBN-13: 978-0-9979899-4-6
ISBN-10: 0-9979899-4-7

A FEW WORDS FROM THE WICKED WRITER

Before I began writing Wanton, I planned on it being more like Wildly Wedded Wife– a novella that strictly focused on the main couple. With WWW, Bethany & Rory were showcased because the readers needed to know them on a deeper level for when they appeared in Wayward, or else it would've looked out of left-field. While writing Wanton, it evolved into something else entirely. My quest for a quickie romance novella turned into a full-length novel that features every single character in the Blended series.

I realized Ginny wasn't some two-bit side character I could quickly write a love story about. Ginny was there *before* the blended family began. She's been pivotal since the beginning, being Camille's sister. Malcolm's sister-in-law. Devon, Kieren, Raven, and Weston's aunt. Sam's childhood friend. Clover's rock. Ginny was the sole reason Clover met both Sam *and* Malcolm, and without that meeting, we wouldn't have the Blended Series. With an unbreakable tie to everyone in the blended family, I realized Ginny was the perfect nexus to foreshadow upcoming events and to voice past wounds.

As for Opal, she's always been an enigma. It wouldn't have done her justice to just quickly write her as some sexy, mysterious woman who Ginny falls in love with– that would lack depth. Opal has deep ties with the blended family: Isis's best friend. Malcolm's lover. Rob's buddy. As well as becoming a very important person in someone's life in a later book.

Wanton is slow-building in the romance department, whereas it's peppered with a massive amount of foreshadowing. I'm not a fan of insta-love, but I do believe in instant attraction– chemistry. It takes time to build a lasting relationship. A foundation of a week of chance-meetings and sex isn't what you build a life upon, but it's a start to a solid friendship. It takes time to develop trust, intimacy, and an emotional connection. No *I love you*s will be spoken, but that doesn't mean the emotions aren't felt.

I'm writing characters in their early forties, and I refuse to cheapen my creation by having them act out of their maturity level. They are professional women, seeking a life partner, and they aren't going to mess it up by moving too quickly. While

Wanton is sweet, humorous, slightly awkward, and a whole helluva lot of hot, my ladies aren't silly virgins.

Wanton is a slowly budding romance that evolves into a quest of sexual exploration between Opal and Ginny. But it also features several other romances. I realize this is odd, since one very young romance is prominent in the book, along with our skittish Triad (Rob, Auggie, and Isis). There is a very good reason behind this: Opal and Ginny were best to voice these particular characters, for reasons you will soon realize. This young couple's voice closes out the entirety of the series. Since it will be a decade in the future, it was necessary to show their beginning, so the readers will appreciate their ending.

As one of my readers, you're just going to have to trust me. Trust that Wanton is not the last time you will hear from Opal and Ginny, just as you've always heard from all of my characters in most books. Wanton is Opal & Ginny's beginning, and they will be at the Blended Series' **THE END**.

I'm tearing up just typing that. Yes, all of the Blended Series has already been written in my head– it's just a matter of getting it out and forming it into novels. I know how the series ends for each and every single one of its characters. *chokes up*

Enjoy!

-Erica Chilson

Orbiting one another's lives, yet never intersecting, a clandestine meeting finally pushes Opal Fischer within Ginny Jamison's path.

In the past, in the present, and in the future, both women make a major impact on the lives of the Blended Family. They worry more about their loved ones than themselves, pushing their needs and wants to the back-burner. They themselves are the only ones in their own path to true happiness, by holding onto the debilitating wounds of the past and refusing to let go of their visions of the future.

Opal's lifelong adage: the sin isn't in the wanting; it's in the taking. Will Ginny be able to make Opal realize the sin is actually in the regret of never taking what you want, what you so rightfully deserve?

Wanton (Blended #4) is a full-length Contemporary Romance novel featuring the slowly budding relationship between two females. Warning: a glimpse into future Blended Series books, with sensually erotic scenes featuring f/f & f/f/m. Wanton is approximately 67,000 words in length.

CHAPTER ONE

Opal Fischer

In the throes of passion, one usually feels blissed out and relaxed, as if everything is right with the world and you have no worries of any kind. As I stand here, trembling and breathlessly panting from my release, my hand tightly wrapped around a throbbing penis mid-eruption, with fingers rapidly thrusting inside my engorged pussy, I've never felt so desolate and lost.

Malcolm's back arches off the massage table as a deep moan flows from his throat. His ejaculate coats my fingers, easing the path of my stroke. My movements speed up, intensifying to draw out his release. Mind numb, I don't feel my body's natural response to Malcolm's expert touch between my thighs.

Colin shouts, his head hitching backward, exposing the column of his throat. The movement shows great trust, because in the animal world, that is an act of submission. Never bare your throat to the enemy. Comfortable in his own skin, happy with our arrangement, Colin's release speckles Malcolm's chest, splashing onto my stilling hand.

Of the three of us, I am the only one left feeling unfulfilled. Satisfaction and relief glow from Malcolm and Colin. My mind is numb, even as my body goes wild, rendering me sensationless. I feel nothing: no pleasure, relief, relaxation. I am left as an empty husk– a void of bitter loneliness.

I can feel Clover's eyes intently, albeit avidly, watching us, digesting every movement we make to file it away for later. The woman makes me feel like a third-wheel during an act I've performed countless times, not that I've ever enjoyed it. Now that we have a willing female, one who enjoys masculine attention, I'm no longer necessary in this equation. Another girl has entered the playground, so I'm thrust out of our sandbox of loneliness. Finally, here is my excuse to abandon our arrangement.

As the soon-to-be Mrs. Mason, Clover is here to stay, and this is my subtle send-off. Cast-off. The only place where two females belong is in my lesbian mind.

Malcolm's fingertips slip from inside me, affectionately caressing my thigh as they go, and then they come to rest upon the edge of the massage table. Guilt infuses me. This was a logical arrangement, but now there is a fiancée waiting in the wings, watching, making me feel like a faithless whore for touching what is hers. Not that Clover is thinking these things. But one cannot stop the flow of destructive internal dialogue from ruining everything.

Numb. Guilty. I fetch the ceramic water basin and a washcloth. After years of giving sponge baths, I slowly and efficiently remove the evidence of my body's secretions from Malcolm's skin, all the while my stomach twists with wretched sickness.

I don't fit here, yet I fit nowhere else, either.

Of the four people in this attic Playroom: two are staring at one, desire glinting thickly from their eyes. The one is staring back at the two with an equal ferocity of lust and hunger. This equation leaves me alone and undesirable, as always.

I did not find it amatory and alluring to have Clover act as witness to our ritual. I realize Malcolm believed the addition of aroused feminine flesh would amp up my pleasure, so I don't fault him. But as we were touching, as I watched Clover fervently watch the men, it hammered home the disturbing truth. Clover wanted them, *not* me. Clover was aroused by them, *not* me.

Colin, Malcolm, and Clover belong here, feeling sated and gratified. While I know I don't belong in this environment, I don't know where I truly belong. I liken the fantasy-dissolving situation to men tossing one dollar bills at a stripper on stage, knowing full and well they will never be wanted in return. It reeks of desperation.

I am not desperate, nor will I be pitied.

As I wash Malcolm's chest, looking no one in the eye, I make peace with the fact that this is for the last time. Whether Clover puts a stop to this scenario, or simply takes my place, it was time for me to vacate anyway. Every week I felt worse, felt less relief than the week before. But more so, I felt worse about myself.

With a respectful nod of my chin to Clover, I make my way to the bathroom to freshen up and redress. I maintain my composure, my dignity. I am a strong woman. As I shower body fluids from my skin, I don't get weepy, woe-is-me, nobody loves me, nobody understands me or gets me or wants me...

I like my life. I am intelligent. I am healthy. I have a wonderful family. I know love. I feel love. I give love. I am happy and content with my lot in life. But there is no crime in wanting more– craving more. It's the wanting that makes us feel alive.

With no dreams to reach or goals to achieve, what are we?

We are our pursuits.

More. Never stop wanting. Never stops needing. Never stop craving and hungering. Never stop dreaming. Never stop reaching.

Never stop living.

"Opal!" Malcolm's piercing bellow echoes in the small albeit efficient bathroom. Juxtaposed to his demanding nature, Malcolm says he respects me, sees me as his equal. Malcolm Mason is one of the best men I've ever met, rivalling my ex-husband, but he is highly contradictory. The man never ceases to boss me around. That is telling, is it not? The only consolation: he does it to both men and woman alike.

I make Malcolm wait while I slowly button my blouse. I then gaze into the mirror as I smooth my short, white-blonde hair to my head, baring every feature of my face: a strong jaw, wide lips, large blue-green eyes, all emphasizing the starkness of my demeanor. With a heavy sigh, I shrug at my reflection and it shrugs back in exasperation.

As I depart the bathroom, I see Colin's stocky naked form haunting the shadows, no doubt waiting for me to leave. Good riddance, right? Malcolm's sitting nude on the massage table with Clover standing between his wide-spread thighs. The way they look at one another, the snap of connection and attraction makes me feel lighter even as it makes me feel lonelier.

I had a man look at me with the same level of veneration Malcolm levels on Clover– he still does and it breaks my heart. As I said, I've known love, but in return, I've never reached the madness of all-consuming passion that Clover and Malcolm display.

As Opal Sage, born the eldest of five children in a conservative Christian home, I've always done the right thing. I minded my elders and led a life of good example for my brothers and sisters. At forty-three years of age, times were different when

I was young. A girl of my upbringing did not have the freedoms as today's youth. My family is very narrow in their belief system, and woman were only allowed so many choices.

My choices were to either become a wife and mother, or a nurse. Those were the only respectful life paths my father set before me. Since I didn't choose a husband from the herd of my father's colleagues' sons, I was sent to college. My father paid for my schooling, and my mother told me college was where you found your educated future husband, one my father must approve. Mrs. Richard Sage finished this conversation by saying I'd be required to be a wife and mother first and foremost, my education and wants and needs be damned. So I defied my parents by going to college to become a Registered Nurse, where I did *not* find my future husband.

I met my best friend at Massachusetts General. Dr. Byron Fischer felt the insanity of love for me. Following the unavoidable path my parents set me upon, I married my best friend. Unwittingly, my act of defiance played into my father's hands. Not only did I marry a prominent doctor, by casting-off the sons of my father's colleagues, I managed to snag my father's right-hand man instead.

I embraced my father's blueprint of *my* life, and made the most of it by finding what little freedom it had to offer. While there was no passion between my husband and me, it was no hardship, either. I loved Byron, cared for him, and wished him the greatest happiness life could bring. In the beginning, *I* was what made Byron happy, and in return, I was content my husband was happy. My only act of defiance, I did not leave my well-earned career the day I said my vows, gaining my father's ire and my husband's unfaltering respect.

Almost seventeen years ago, Byron and I brought an amazingly strong, compassionate, giving and caring human being into this world. My son is my greatest accomplishment. My inspiration. My hero. Not falling into the trap of living his parents' life, Sage has been his own man since birth. It wasn't until he came to Byron and me, telling us something we already suspected, that I saw the strength in living the life you were meant to live, versus the life someone else scripted for you.

Byron, Sage, and I were content for the most part. Byron could sense my restlessness, my drive to continually live by reaching for what fulfils my soul, and he knew he couldn't provide that for me. I realized I was short-changing my family in my quest to continue my great-grandparents, my grandparents, and my parents' cycle of life. Their heavy oppression was strangling my will to survive.

Sexuality is cut and dried, correct? Wrong. I was taught to live a certain way, so I did. Love does not equate sex– a lesson I didn't learn until five years ago. I loved Byron with all my heart, so I had sex with him as a wife should. As a young woman, I was taught by the Church and my parents that sex was bad unless it was for procreation. It's hard to switch off decades of conditioning.

Truthfully, I never felt a spark for anyone, not even Byron, so I didn't realize I was missing anything. The only reason I knew I was gay, was because in the depths of my mind, my fantasies always starred soft feminine flesh, and more often than not, my eyes always strayed toward my girlfriends in high school.

The catalyst for change: my son was twelve when he came leaping out of the closet with a superior smirk plastered on his face. *"I'm sure this is no big surprise, Mom and Dad. I just thought I better let ya know before it spreads like wildfire through school, before Grandma and Grandpa find out. I'm gay."*

My brothers and sisters were grown, so they no longer needed me as a good example of the Sage's way of life, but my son now did. For Sage, I broke the cycle. I left Bryon for his happiness, for mine, for Sage's. I refused to live a life of lies– lies to oneself. I would not live in the shadow of anyone's expectations of me any longer.

I left my husband, my family, my hospital, and my community to give Sage a better life. Not ashamed, I simply didn't want my son to live under the constant scrutiny of my family's accusing glare. Whispers weren't uncommon from my family regarding my son's sexuality. I left because I would not allow my family to use my child as cannon fodder. Sage has the right to live the life of his choosing without being underneath a microscope, as do I.

We moved to Fairport because it had the hospital closest to our old life that would employ me. We didn't want to be far from Byron, but we wanted to be far enough away from my family's stranglehold. When around my parents, I tend to fall into old, destructive patterns. A little over four years ago, we moved to Fairport to reinvent ourselves, and we've enjoyed the simple life Sage and I have created.

New to town, with no prospects for friends, my life changed for the positive one tragic evening. I attended a young woman who just came out of recovery after suffering an ectopic pregnancy, resulting in surgery. I recognized something inside the woman that called to me– an inner strength to survive every obstacle within her path. Isis Mason has been a genuine friend since that day forth.

Friends are well-meaning yet highly intrusive, and Isis is the reason I am in the Spook House's attic after servicing her brother and his best friend, while his fiancée played voyeur. I'm a private person, and I value my privacy. I work, I raise my child, and I volunteer my time. My goal in life is not about chasing my next hot lay, so Isis began setting me up on blind dates. Not only that, Isis influenced her brother and boyfriends to set me up on dates. It was a synthetic, invasive, and intrusive approach to lesbianism, and I hated every moment of it.

When I feel that essential spark, I'll know I've found the one. Until then, don't pester me. I've lived forty-three years one way. I'm not going to change. I may not agree with the majority of my parents' beliefs, but that doesn't mean I should be promiscuous to spite them. Either way, I'd be allowing my parents to control my body by obeying or disobeying them.

The blind date set-ups were insulting. The last time, the time they got the hard-hitting hint, I shouted in a crowded restaurant, *"I'm a non-practicing lesbian. So what? How about I go find a bunch of eligible straight people between the ages of eighteen and death, and set you up just because you share the same sexual preferences."*

Isis, Rob, Auggie, and Malcolm left me alone after my tantrum. They took the hint that my private life is just that– none of their business. I don't need to know who is doing whom, what color Rob's boxers are, or whether or not Auggie puts the toilet seat down after a piss. I don't need to know who Malcolm's second cousin twice removed is, or who their dry cleaners are. My home life belongs to Sage, and Sage alone. Other than Byron visiting my home, only Isis has bridged the gap between friendly acquaintance or Playroom lover to enter my inner sanctum of true friendship. Even Nina, who I spend countless hours a day with, is not allowed in my private life.

My life is very narrow: work, volunteer work, and Sage, with very little thought to friendship or dating. Scared for my sanity, Isis dragged me to the Playroom, thinking I'd find someone who aroused me. Instead, I found a bunch of desperate bi-curious women, and men who were willing to screw me straight. It was not exactly how I dreamed of popping my lesbian cherry. It's not flattering when a woman looks at you like any ol' lesbian will do.

I agreed to Malcolm, Colin, and my unconventional arrangement to get some much needed relief. But, more so, to keep the harping friends at bay. The Playroom was a place for me to visit with my acquaintances away from my sacred space where my son sleeps. They were all at the Playroom, waiting for me to engage them. I may not want to participate, but it made me feel a little bit naughty as I watched, which provided me with a heady sense of defiance against my father without harming my integrity.

My life got easier, happier, the day Auggie gave me Bethany Essex to protect. She was little Bethany Oman back then: sweet-scented, soft and curvy, precious, inquisitive, and intoxicating. Bethany was proof on how I was a lover of feminine flesh. But it was friendship for us. Beth stared at me as I stared at Byron: with naïveté, willing to do anything I asked, even if it was to her detriment. So I didn't ask, valuing her innocence, not willing to snuff out the bright eagerness in her eyes. If Beth had wanted me, I would have passed. I am not a middle-aged man having a midlife crisis with a twenty-one-year-old hottie. Bethany truly is young enough to be my daughter.

I'm not desperate.

With a heavy sigh, I reluctantly approach the love-crazed affianced. "Yeah?" I ask Malcolm. Not wanting to be rude, I tip my head in Clover's direction to include her in the conversation.

"I don't want to bail on my wife, 'cuz this is kinda important, don't ya think? My realtor is waiting for me at The No-Name with some paperwork I need to sign. Can you go get it for me and drop it off downstairs?" Malcolm asks me, and then he turns to Clover with the largest grin I've ever seen. "The seller has agreed to my terms. The house is ours, and the closing date is early next week."

"Holy shit!" Clover shrieks, and then her voice turns dreamy. "Whoa…"

Stung by their mutual delight, and annoyed by being relegated to gofer, I find great insult with Malcolm's rude request. Who goes around dismissing their '*lovers*' by asking them to run errands for them? Whose realtor works on Saturday nights? Who has the audacity to ask a woman who just masturbated them to go drive across town to pick up paperwork, and then drive back across town to drop it off, all in the opposite direction from her home? Who does this while getting you out of the room so he can have sex with his future wife while stroking on his best friend?

Malcolm Mason is the answer to all the above questions. That's who.

I have every right to feel the bitter bite of spite, the shallow inflammation of rejection, and the illogical burn of hurt. I don't display the emotions, but I feel them nonetheless.

"I'll leave it *downstairs*," I stress, knowing full and well the second I leave the attic, Malcolm, Clover, and Colin will engage in their own sensual tryst. "And lock the door behind me."

I transform into one of those women I can't stand: hate-filled with the green eye of jealousy upon them. I give myself the walk downstairs from the attic to the front door to stew in self-made misery, and then I will go back to business as usual.

It's irrational. I feel jilted, slighted, rejected, dismissed, and pushed out of a situation I no longer wanted to be in. I should feel relief that an exit presented itself before I had to voice my own resignation. Malcolm and Colin didn't tell me to leave, not in so many words, but it feels just the same anyway.

Walking softly down the stairs, not wishing to make my walk of shame known, I creep out of the Spook House like a wanton whore. At least I'm not wearing last night's little black dress while holding my high heels in my fingertips, with raccoon eyes and lipstick smeared across my face– not that I've ever been in that situation before. Sage makes me watch too many romantic comedies. I assume their mating and dating rituals are true-to-life.

Out the corner of my eye, a disbelieving view stops me dead in my tracks. The living room is like a sociological experiment gone wrong. Unable to pass, I find myself leaning against the doorframe, playing voyeur.

I'm not the only person in an impossible situation. These three idiots are worse off than I will ever be. It was the glazed-over look in Rob's eye that caught my attention as I was walking by. Huddled up in the chair he claimed as his own, he's clutching a beer bottle by the neck while staring ardently at the sofa.

Auggie's mammoth body is taking up half of the sofa, with Isis's head resting gently in his lap. Foggy-eyed, Isis nurses at a wine bottle, with no glass in sight. There are several six packs worth of beer bottles littering the floor at Auggie's feet.

Eyes closed, Auggie plays with Isis's black locks as she doodles on his thigh with a fingertip. Their movements attract Rob's undivided attention like a hunting cat after a skittish mouse.

The closing of the Playroom to the majority of the Playroomers was an impossible decision for Auggie to make. It was a decision that was necessary, now that the Playroom is housed within the Spook House. The group had grown too large, too quickly, making it difficult to control what went on behind closed doors, while making sure it stayed behind those same closed doors.

With Willow not in the house, Auggie, Isis, and Rob are draining their hidden alcohol stashes. Judging by Rob's empty bottle he's clutching like a comfort object, and the dredges at the bottom of Isis's wine bottle, the Spook House was tapped out before they could even get a proper buzz, let alone drink their troubles away.

In a gesture of affection, Auggie tenderly strokes Isis's cheek with a fingertip while murmuring words I cannot hear. This is a different side to Auggie than I've ever seen. I've seen distraught Auggie, angry at the world at large as he takes it by storm. I've seen in the throes of passion Auggie. But I've never seen the real Augustus Kline– few have.

Being the outsider, the observer, the person who came into their lives only a few short years ago, I'm not blinded by their histrionics or antics. Nothing is more real– raw –than holding the hand of a woman as she tells her lovers their unborn baby is dead. Auggie was in shock before the inevitable anger set in. While Rob had crushed a cellphone in his fist, not even realizing it until he was getting eleven stitches across his palm.

Sage's coming out was my catalyst for positive change. The death of Isis's baby was the catalyst for negative change in Isis, Auggie, and Robin's young lives. Just as Isis can't get me to date, I can't get Isis to see reason.

In public, the three of them stand side-by-side but never touch. In private, well, this is the first time I've seen them in their natural habitat. Unguarded, Auggie gazes down at Isis with an expression of reverence I've never witnessed on a living soul before.

What I saw in the attic between Malcolm and Clover was fresh, something that could eventually bloom into this everlasting love. The look Byron used to give me pales in comparison. Auggie's look of adoration breaks my heart for many different levels: joy that they have one another, and the resulting sadness that they would allow fear to overshadow the gift of their love. Sadness on my part, simply because I've never felt the way they do about one another, nor have I ever had anyone feel this level of admiration for me, and I most likely will never experience either.

Smiling affectionately, Isis turns her face to place a soft kiss to the inside of Auggie's wrist– the tender action catches the breath in my throat.

My stifled sound instantly gains Rob's attention. With the tilt of his rounded chin, Rob gestures toward the front door. I take the hint and leave, knowing I'm intruding on an intimate moment that is far and few between. Only this rejection doesn't hurt me like the last dismissal up in the attic. Knowing that Auggie, Isis, and Rob might finally be on the path to recovery, four years too late, I feel lighter than I have in ages.

"Hey," Rob whispers softly, catching me just before I click the door shut in his face. "You got a minute?"

Instead of answering, I ask, "Are you doing okay?" I gesture to the cuddle party Rob wasn't invited to participate in. Feeling kindred, my eyes roll skyward, toward the attic, where there is a different sort of party playing out that I wasn't summoned to join.

Rob nods his head while slipping out of the Spook House, quietly shutting the door behind him. As soon as the door latches, his smaller fingers are weaving through mine, taking comfort from our friendship. Rob gives my palm a squeeze before drawing me down to sit next to him on the stoop.

Sighing, I close my eyes and enjoy the sensation of the warm June, night air rushing over my face, causing the fine hairs to tickle my skin as it passes. I momentarily feel bad for the realtor who is waiting on me, but that is on Malcolm's head. I'd rather sit here with Rob and talk, or not talk, than run an errand while Malcolm gets off upstairs.

Speaking softly, so his voice doesn't carry, what Rob says doesn't surprise me any. He's the master of evasion. Not wishing to speak of his own troubles, he speaks of those he caused. "I can't believe Nina went through with it today." Incredulity colors his words, as he speaks slowly in a drawn-out cadence. "I can't believe Nina thought Auggie would take her side."

Eyes still closed, I realize tonight is the night for issuing rejections. "I tried to tell Nina," I barely breathe the words. "I warned her." Snorting in disgust, "Nina actually thought accosting Clover at The Bakery would get Auggie's attention– negative or positive, she didn't care. Auggie did exactly what I told Nina he would do, but she didn't believe me."

"I told you so," Rob mocks me in a sing-song voice, more than pleased with himself, and then he's barks a humorless laugh. "I can't believe Nina was so easily manipulated. I feel bad. But, at the same time, I don't."

"Wow," I breathe out, as a trickle of anger weaves through me. "You're quite the chameleon, Robin Prynne. You broke Nina's heart, all the while setting up your own sister and niece to take the fall, just so you could maneuver Auggie into shutting down the Playroom. If I wasn't so disgusted, I'd pat you on the back."

Rob earns himself a dramatic eye roll when he issues himself a congratulatory pat on the back. Completely unrepentant, voice thick with proprietary possessiveness, "Excuse me if I'm more than a little pissed at Nina for never realizing Auggie belonged to Isis and me. Nina did it to herself for being a fucking moron."

"Wow," I snarl, anger thickening my blood.

"Also, I tried to warn Willow in black and white, with easy to understand wording, but she didn't listen. That mistake is on Willow, not me." Pointing heavenward, "Clover was collateral damaged, but the results are better than expected, seeing as how she's currently upstairs with two hot men."

"And lucky you," I sneer. "Auggie and Isis are cuddling." I'm in a foul mood, so I go in for the kill, "And yet you're out here with me, chatting, instead of inside with them, petting and fondling to your heart's content."

Looking at me sideways yet not angry for some inexplicable reason, "No one gets it," Rob mumbles. "Auggie is the first they blame, saying he's this big asshole. Then they all say I'm a slut. But you know the truth. Isis pushed me to the brink. She cut herself off from us after the... FUCK!" Rob whisper shouts while pounding his fists against his thighs. "I can't even say the words."

"I'm sorry." The pain in Rob's voice kills me, but the tormented expression that flashes across his face draws bitter tears to sting my eyes. Voice thick, I can barely choke out the words without shuddering in fear. "Truly. I can't imagine living life without Sage."

Big brown eyes filled with tears, Rob doesn't blink, fearing the movement would break the surface and become a never-ending torrent of liquid misery. "I want a life," Rob admits as if it's a secret he's spilling. "I *crave* a normal life."

"I know you," I say to reassure Rob, rubbing his thigh to push home my point. "You'll get that life, even if you die trying."

"Right now feels surreal, as if I'm living someone else's fucked-up-ness. This isn't how it was supposed to be. This isn't how I was supposed to act. I do bad things to the ones I love. In essence, I sacrifice them to get Auggie and Isis to see the truth."

I offer advice I'm not sure is true, but nonetheless wish it so. "Someday they will wake up, and their blindness will sharpen into clarity."

"I'd never been with anyone else until after that happened." Turning to look at me, Rob holds my gaze with such earnestness, that I have to suck in a deep breath or suffocate from the intensity. "I never wanted anyone but them."

"I know," I whisper. "I know."

"Auggie and I went almost a year without touching Isis or each other. We were starving for attention, affection– *comfort*," Rob stresses in a grave voice. "Nothing we did or said made a damned difference. Powerless. Isis just pushed us further away no matter what we did. So we bluffed to get a reaction out of her, saying if she wouldn't have us, then we'd find someone who would. But Isis called our bluff, and I was so very angry," Rob grits out, sounding tortured. "So, I fucked and fucked and fucked with a vengeance, and each time I felt worse than the last."

To break the emotional tension, I murmur in a rhythmic cadence, "And Auggie sucked and sucked and sucked his way through Fairport."

Snorting like his mini-me, Rob butts my shoulder with his forehead. "Willow was my wakeup call."

"And you've been plotting ever since," I say wryly. "Was it worth it?"

Pinning me with his earnest stare, Rob states unequivocally, "Yes. Because if I hadn't plotted. If I hadn't pushed the Mason boys toward Willow. She'd probably be upstairs in Auggie's bed with his kid in her gut, ruining all of our lives. So I don't care if my sister thinks I'm a monster for siccing a shrieking whore on her at The Bakery."

I respect Rob. Hell, I even like him as a human being. Worse, I've had sex with him… and enjoyed every single nasty, downright dirty second of it with great gusto. But I cannot let that comment stand. "Don't disrespect Nina," I warn in a cold voice.

"Fine," Rob says tightly. "But I don't have to like her."

Finished, deciding I'd rather be Malcolm's errand girl than listen to Rob pout, "Well, as much fun as it has been talking Machiavellian schemes, torturous emotions, and the past with you…" I rise to my feet.

Raising a brow at my obvious dismissal, Rob gets bitter with my rejection. "A few months ago you enjoyed my company immensely. You even let me meet your son."

Blushing, mortified, I whisper, "I was in a bad place, and I've told no one save Isis."

"What a coincidence," Rob drawls out, smirking but he's not amused. "Me too. But now that I need a shoulder to cry on, you scamper off. When you needed a shoulder to cry on, I gave you orgasms, and then made you breakfast the next morning. I even talked shop with your kid since everyone assumes I'm gay, even when doing the walk of shame from a female's bed."

Rob turns into an over-emotional, spiteful, pissy girl when he isn't getting his way, and he wonders why people think he's gay. We don't think he's gay– we think he's a woman. No man acts like the dramatic Robin Prynne, and that's probably why it was the best sex of my life. Mind you, not that I would ever admit that fact aloud.

"I'm not abandoning you in your time of need," I say, trying very hard to keep the sarcasm from my tone. *Time of need*? "Malcolm has me meeting his realtor since he is otherwise engaged for the evening." Aggravated, my voice thickens with anger. "What sort of realtor meets on a Saturday night?"

Rob hops to his feet as if a marionette magically pulled his puppet strings. "Why didn't you say so? Go!" Rob pushes me down the steps. "Hurry!"

"What the?" I shove Rob off me. "Have you lost your mind? What's wrong with you?"

Before Rob can answer me, Willow comes skipping down the sidewalk toward us, happily whistling a tune. "What's up?" Willow chirps as she comes up the front steps.

"GO!" Rob orders again, but this time it's not to me. "You can't be here, Willow. GO!"

Rolling her eyes dramatically, Rob and Willow's resemblance is uncanny. "Dude? Seriously? I've worked for the past fourteen hours. I want to shower and go to bed. Get outta my way."

Rob just points to the cars lining the street. Confused, Willow shrugs it off. "So what? Malcolm's here. He's always here." Rob points skyward. "So what? Malcolm's in the Playroom. Like I give a shit. I'm going to bed."

Rob tugs Willow to the side, so she has a good vantage point through the front window into the living room, where Isis and Auggie are fused at the lips and gyrating down by their hips. "I'll tiptoe by," Willow says like it's no big deal. "I thought we said no sex on the first floor. I nap on that sofa. Eww," she breaths.

I grab the girl's wrist before Rob can break out into a game of deviant charades. "Of course, Rob is more worried about your presence upsetting this evening's living room shenanigans. But I don't want you stepping foot into the house, because I can't imagine how mortified you would feel if you met Malcolm and Clover on the staircase after coming out of the Playroom."

Tiny brow scrunching with confusion, Willow reasons that out. Her eyes flick to the line of cars, noting whose they are. "If Isis is macking on Auggie in the living room, and Clover and Malcolm are in the attic, and you're standing right here talking to me, where the fuck is Colin in this equation?"

"Colonel Mustard in is in the conservatory with the candlestick," Rob deadpans– the ass.

"You're right," I say to Rob, refusing to touch that subject– ever. "I've got to go."

"What's going on?" Willow demands.

Rob, playing everyone like a finely tuned instrument, "Opal is meeting with Malcolm's realtor. Isn't that awesome?" Rob sounds positively giddy, which sets off warning alarms in my mind.

Easily distracted, already forgetting that her mother and two men are up in the attic doing Lord knows what, Willow shoves me and shouts, "Why are you still standing here with us? GO!"

Rob smirks, all proud like. "You guys are idiots," I say in parting, leaving them to bicker about Willow not entering her own home.

It's more like Ms. Scarlet's in the attic, lustfully tied up by the rope, with Professor Plum and Colonel Mustard wielding their wax-dripping candlesticks.

CHAPTER TWO

Ginny Jamison

"Can I get ya anything else, sweetie?" The pretty, fresh-faced server asks me, pot of hot coffee poised at the ready for a warm-up.

Sighing, I reach a fingertip over to my cellphone, swiping it to life. When I see the time, nearly closing in on ten o'clock, I decide to give them another half hour of my time before I head home. "Yes, please… and I'll take another order of fries with mustard."

"Not a problem, Ginny." Desiree's a smart girl for not commenting on the fact that this is my third order of fries, or that I've had a normal girl's weekly equivalent of fat and calories since I sat down.

"Sorry," I offer lamely for camping out in Desiree's booth for the past two hours. I used the table as my workstation for about an hour before I called Malcolm, and then I've sat here binge-eating since he pawned some poor schmuck off on me. Some poor, *late* schmuck, so I'm not feeling too charitable at the moment.

I now know Desiree's entire life history, all seventeen years of it, including the adorable boy eyeing her like a stalker from across the diner. So now I'm back to pretending to do important real-estate-related paperwork so I don't have to make unnecessary small talk, giving the lad an in with the waitress, if he'd only take it. I'm quickly running out of patience and paperwork, and Desiree and the boy are both pretty daft in the hint department.

I'd march over to the Spook House and personally hand-deliver the forms, but I have a feeling I don't want to know what Malcolm is doing to Clover right as we speak. As much as it thrills me that my best friend and my brother-in-law are literally joined at the hips, it pains me even more because I'm left as the third wheel on a vehicle only meant for two. It also annoys me how Malcolm thinks I'm his little bitch, waiting on his every whim. How arrogant of him.

Malcolm's always, *"I want it yesterday."* But in return, we all have to wait until tomorrow if we want something from him. It would serve Malcolm right if I dallied on his paperwork, inconveniencing him for a change. Except I can't teach Malcolm a lesson without short-changing the kids, too.

I just want to go home and get down and dirty with several quarts of Mint-Ting-A-Ling. I dream of sitting on my new sofa, swaddled in my cuddly cashmere throw, with my spoon scooping between my mouth and the ice cream carton, with my laptop balanced on my knee as I one-click a bunch of awesome shit on Amazon. A girl can never have too much ice cream or home décor. My new throw needs a few pillow buddies to cushion my back while I shop.

I reach over again, checking the time, like it wasn't only two minutes since I last looked. I'm self-employed for a reason, because I suck at waiting around. I'm a doer, and if I don't have something to do, I'm an eater. If I don't want to gain another dress size, I'm a shopper. My favorite hobby is to combine it all: eating while buying amazing shit for my business.

Waiting is such utter bullshit.

It's not like I'm not having a bad day or anything, for Pete's sake. My lonely life is staring me point-blank in the face like a bitter accusation. It's like I blinked, and when I opened my eyes, I was almost forty. Where did my twenties and thirties go?

Blink.

Where did all these fine lines around my hazel eyes come from? I thought the extra weight would keep my skin plumped out and wrinkle-free. I found another gray hair hiding amongst the blonde this morning.

Blink.

I now hear a ticking sound that suspiciously sounds like a biological clock. I don't want kids, but the loneliness is killing me. When I'm old, wizened, wrinkly and gray, sitting on my porch drinking sugar-laden tea with my dozen cats, I'll wish I had a grandkid or two to harass. That's the sound of my clock speaking. I need someone to sit next to me, someone to build a life around. While fun, ice cream and Amazon Prime does not make lasting memories.

While watching my family progress forward, evolve, I've realized I'm treading in stagnant water, going absolutely nowhere at a snail's pace. I knew I'd never get married or have children, and it had absolutely nothing to do with my being a lesbian. I have my nephews and niece and Sam and Clover's children, and I *was* happy with that. But one day I woke up, and I suddenly felt old. I felt like life was rushing me by, leaving me behind. It's a real wakeup call when your nephew is bringing forth new life, your other nephew is buying a home for his brother, and the rest of the kids are quickly encroaching upon adulthood. They are a generation behind me, yet they are bypassing me in life experience.

Clover and Malcolm are happy, in love, and I'm thrilled for them. But it's a bitter pill to swallow when you spend your Saturday nights sitting in the shitty No-Name Diner, all by yourself. It's a sad night when you realize you were looking forward to chatting with your brother-in-law about real-estate just so you didn't feel so alone.

Looking back to when I was a very young woman, not much older than Desiree, I don't remember my mother having wrinkles or gray hair. Choking on the realization, I know why. I am now older than my mother was when she died.

Looking down at my hands, I realize I am the last Jamison, and my tiny family dies when I do. My parents are gone, my sister is gone, and I am left to face the world alone.

"Ginny?" Desiree places my order of fries in front of me. The young woman looks fuzzy because of my emotion-blurred vision. "You doing okay?"

Perking up, playing pretend, "I'm great, Desiree. Thank you." I pluck a seasoned curly fry from my plate, dab it in the saucer of spicy brown mustard, and pop it in my mouth. I sigh as I chew, happy that something still satisfies me.

Since I was a toddler, I've been obsessed with food. My grandmother was fixated with how much she weighed, making my bipolar mother even more neurotic. Their quest for thin backfired with my sister and me. We ate when we were hungry, and we ate to spite them. As an adult, I now eat when I feel depressed, bored, or lonely. But I also eat to celebrate.

Because everything is better with food.

My last girlfriend of three years didn't see it that way. I took Sarah out to an expensive restaurant for our anniversary. The woman I thought I'd be sharing rocking chairs, cats, and sweet tea with, said to me from across the table, *"I hate the way you eat. Just looking at you makes me feel like I'm going to get fat by association."*

Sarah liked what I could do in bed, what I could buy her, and how I treated her, but she told me she didn't want to eat out in public with me ever again. From one tasty morsel to the next, I told Sarah to fuck off.

In the weeks that followed, I ate continuously like it was a fulltime job. I'd gained twenty pounds to spite Sarah. Realizing too late, I'd helped Sarah fuck me over more so, not the other way around. In the two years that followed that, it was an uphill battle to lose the weight that was so easily gained. Turning obsessive in an unhealthy way, I lost seventy pounds in total by starving myself with my neurosis.

I became obsessed with food: what was in the food, where it was grown or processed, how many calories… fat… fiber… nutrients. Empty calories. Negative calories. How many minutes of what activity it takes to burn off a banana. The optical illusion of tricking your brain by serving food on big plates, small plates, white plates, and red plates. Weighing and portioning my food. Journaling every morsel that passed between my lips to go down my throat.

All ridiculously unhealthy ideas naturally skinny people tell us larger gals to use, while simultaneously insulting us with that 'last five pounds' they can't lose bullshit, when we have another forty-five, or ninety, or a hundred and twenty pounds to go.

One day I woke up and realized I'd turned into my grandmother. It didn't matter one way or another what size I was. I was miserable being someone other than myself. I told my thinner reflection *"fuck you"* in the mirror. I've regained about forty pounds since. I'm back at the weight Sarah loathed, and I've hovered at this weight, at this size, for the past two years– my natural size.

Life is too short. So now, if I want a banana, I eat a fucking banana. If I want to drink my tea in a short glass versus an optical illusion tall glass, so be it. If I want to eat on a huge white plate in a blue room… No calorie counting in my head. No estimated exercise times. No more journaling. Food is sustenance. You need it to live. My doctor says I am healthy, so I eat when I'm hungry… and when I'm not.

I haven't had a girlfriend since the fat-hating Sarah. I've had dozens of affairs stemming from several hours to no more than a week. The only dining we've done is between our thighs, and I've never had a complaint about the meal I've served.

The din of the bell over the front door draws me from my miserable musings. As with everything in Fairport– the gossip capital of the world –every patron in the No-Name turns their head in unison to see who has entered the door. All conversation ceases, as the newcomer becomes the sole focus of attention.

It takes me a moment to reason out who the newcomer is, having never laid eyes upon the woman before. Tall and slim with angular features and short blonde hair, I'd have remembered this woman if we'd before. Eyes darting around the diner, searching for me I presume, she has an air of authority, like someone you run toward to protect you or care for you in times of danger.

Eyes lighting on the teenaged boy, then the older couple, and then the booths of drunken twenty-somethings getting their grub on before heading out to find more adventure, finally she spots me. With the nod of her head, she starts in my direction like I'm a homing beacon flashing '*realtor.*'

Coming to a stop at the edge of my booth, "Sorry, I'm late," she says brusquely, stating the obvious and not sounding sorry at all. It's more like she's admitting she made me wait on purpose. "Blame Malcolm."

From one heartbeat to the next, I figure out who this imposing woman is. Opal from the Playroom. That's all I know of her, besides the fact that she's a nurse and a lesbian. Malcolm and Isis have spoken of this woman in passing before. But other than that, Opal is an enigma.

I shrug in reply, when inside I'm a stew of '*holy shit!*' Opal is furious with Malcolm, and I was too until I realized he was actually giving me a gift. "Malcolm always wants his shit done like yesterday," flows off my tongue before I can stop it.

Nodding, nary a smile in sight, "But don't expect what you asked for from him until tomorrow."

Shocked, I fall to rest against the booth's backrest. "You know Malcolm Mason well," I murmur more to myself, wondering just how well Opal knows my brother-in-law.

Dressed in tailored slacks and an expensive blouse, Opal's appearance screams of someone with good breeding– meaning appearances matter. It takes her a heartbeat before she remembers that, though. "I apologize for being rude several times over." Opal reaches her hand out, offering to shake.

Smiling privately, I try not to laugh. As the daughter of a cop and a bipolar mother, my middle name is rude, my first name is chaotic, and my last name is messy. It's a good day if I don't drop the f-bomb while dealing with clients, bankers, and lawyers.

"Virginia Jamison," I readily supply as my hand slips into Opal's. A soft squeeze, barely a brush of our flesh. Opal shakes like a man when he shakes a woman's hand, as if he's afraid he will insult her by squeezing too hard. Opal's shaken many a hand, judging by her proficiency.

I give Opal my given name, not wanting gossip and preconceived notions to taint our meeting. Not everything you hear is flattering, especially when it's pertaining to me. I want Opal to see me as the woman sitting in this booth, and have her speak to me freely, not worried about insulting Malcolm because he's my brother-in-law, or think this was some kind of set-up because I'm of her sexual persuasion. Having been put through the paces on many a blind date, I know how insulting that can be.

"Opal Fischer," she replies in kind. Eyes flicking from mine to land upon my plate, "Are the fries here any good?"

"The best," I answer while gesturing for Opal to try some. What she said strikes me as odd. "You've never been in here before?"

Shaking her head no, "May I?" she points at the booth's bench.

"Oh, shit! Where are my manners?" I don't have any, that's where. "Please, have a seat."

Opal slides in the booth across from me, and gingerly picks up the menu. This moment is surreal for me, so random yet feels normal at the same time.

Speaking while contemplating her choices, "I only moved here four years ago. I haven't gotten around to visiting all the local establishments yet. I've been to The Bakery, Salon, and Howe's Hardware so far… and now the No-Name."

Only? Three places in four years? At eighteen months per business, it will take Opal a lifetime to visit Main Street. I've been eating at the No-Name since I could chew. In this week alone, I've frequented no less than fifty percent of Fairport's businesses. My inner shopaholic thrives on contributing to the local economy.

"Beware of anything that isn't fried," I warn. Then what Opal said clicks into place. Mystified, I ask, "Wait. Where have you been eating for the past four years?"

"Only the fried stuff?" Opal muses, and I don't dare tell her it's because it's prepared at Sysco Foods, so therefore it's safe to eat since the cook can't fuck it up. "I mostly eat in the hospital cafeteria and at home. My son eats here with his friends. He said never to get anything green, but I thought he was joking."

Son?

"No one orders anything fresh, so when someone does, it comes wilted, old, and moldy. Stick to the fried shit. The oil is changed every couple of days, so it doesn't taste funky."

While Opal studies the menu, I study her. My estimation of her goes up exponentially when the cut of her blouse is a dead giveaway on the brand. This woman is wearing a four hundred dollar shirt over her braless small breasts. I bite my lip at the sight of her nipples beading against the silk of her shirt. It's sexy in a classy woman sort of way. An insane need to suck and nip at Opal's tits overcomes me. I want to know if she'll whimper trashy words while I suckle at her chest and between her long thighs.

Jesus. I blink out of my lust-induced madness and try to concentrate on something other than the fact that I haven't been laid in six months, and that Opal is exactly my type of woman.

Opal's blonde hair is baby-fine, wispy, and perfectly trimmed in a pixie cut. Nearly shaved on the sides, if Opal mussed up the top, it would give off a sexy edgy vibe. I bet her hair is hotter than fuck all messed up after sex.

I find out Opal's eyes are a clear, blue-green shade when she catches me ogling at her. Tiny, manicured eyebrows knit together in confusion, as if she can't quite fathom why I'm looking at her like she's looking at the menu. Hungry-like.

Ravenous.

I have no shame. I'm don't even blush out of embarrassment or mortification. I simply hold Opal's eyes in challenge, waiting to see if she'll gaze away first or call me out for staring at her tits like a milk-thirsty newborn.

"Are you ready to order?" Desiree interrupts our impromptu staring contest– thank the heavens above. The girl is smiling radiantly at us, happy she no longer has to fear me slitting my wrists with a butter knife. Earlier, the cute kid used my sadness as an in to get the young waitress to talk to him. Loud enough for me to overhear, he had wondered if I was going to off myself at the table– adorable douchebag-in-training.

"Hmm… let's see," Opal nearly purrs, and then the woman's tongue sneaks out to swab her bottom lip, like everything sounds tasty. Opal's driving me mad, because all I can think about are better uses for her licker. Did she do that on purpose? Naughty minx.

Feigning innocence, Opal rattles off, "I would like an order of curly fries, the jalapeno poppers, and the mozzarella sticks… and a Diet Coke. Please and thanks."

Desiree stifles a laugh, no doubt surprised at the order. "What kind of sauces would you like, Mrs. Fischer?"

"Just ketchup, Desiree." Closing her menu, Opal dismisses the waitress with a, "Thanks."

"You've never been in here yet the girl knows your name?" I arch a brow at that. "And who doesn't want Ranch or marinara… or that awesome raspberry habanero sauce?"

Looking thoroughly amused, entertained even, Opal grins at me. If I was wearing socks, that smile would have knocked the puppies right off my feet.

"I'm a traditionalist. Sometimes, if it isn't broke, don't fix it. Ketchup goes with everything, and all ketchup tastes the same. But I do think I'll ask for that raspberry sauce. Sage brought some home last week for our blackened salmon. Surprisingly, it paired well together."

"Sage?" I stare at my fries as they get cold, grease congealing on the plate, and I realize I'm no longer hungry for food. I'm definitely hungry for other things, though, and intriguing conversation seems to be topping the list.

"Sage is my son, and that's how Desiree and I know one another. They're best friends, and he sits in here, keeping the girl company on nights I'm at work." Opal slides everything impeding her view of me to the edge of the table: my laptop and folders. She leans forward toward me– the action catches my breath in my throat –and whispers, "I may have never stepped foot into this place. But I'm observant enough to know most of the town, even if they don't know me in return," she says pointedly.

The jig is up. Opal knows who I am, just as I know who she is. Lovely.

Voice tight with frustration, "Now, the question is, were you in knowledge of this clandestine meeting, or should I only be angry with Malcolm?"

Gobsmacked, my voice quivers, "I really was expecting Malcolm." As proof, I push toward Opal the folder of paperwork Malcolm has to sign and take to the bank. "I guess you've had many a blind date at the hands of Malcolm Mason." Desiree sets a glass of Diet Coke in front of Opal, interrupting me. I pick up my plate, the greasy smell turning my stomach, "You can take this. Thanks."

"Your order will be up in just a moment," the waitress says sweetly as she totes the dirty dishes away.

"More than I can count," Opal twists out, either angry in the moment or at the past– I don't know which. "I know of you, so I'm surprised it took them this long to try to set us up. It would have made the most sense for Malcolm to have sicced you on me first."

Sicced? Like a damned dog?

Blushing, embarrassed for how I look and who I am, I grab at my coffee mug as a distraction. Clearly Opal isn't impressed with me in the least. It's one of the reasons I stopped dating. The women I meet at gay clubs in the city are looking for the same thing I am– quick, emotionless sex. There is no rejection when it comes to something so blatantly honest. My self-esteem cannot handle the subtle nuances of dating. I know who I am, and I like myself just the way I am. But that doesn't mean anyone else will, though.

"Actually…" I trail off. My face flushes bright red with mortification. "I believe they have. Three? No, four times. Malcolm kept inviting me to dinner, which isn't unusual. But what was unusual, was how every time everyone kept mentioning how you were a no-show."

Annoyance flashes over Opal's face, like it's pissing her off that she's going to have to set me straight. "I'd apologize, but I won't. I'm surprised they went that route. Usually they would just invite me to dinner somewhere and ambush me with a double date, or they wouldn't even be there. Just some woman I've never met, thinking I knew who she was and why I was there. It was humiliating, insulting, and invasive."

"Yeah," I mutter, nodding my head. "I believe I met some of your cast-offs." With my overweight crassness, even my own relatives gave Opal first dibs, only fixing me up with the rejects. I guess Opal rejected them all, didn't she? None of them lived up to her impeccable standards.

Not wanting to intrude on Opal's late-night snack, I start organizing my shit– shoving my laptop and folders roughly into my bag. "Listen, if you could just give that folder to Malcolm, or I can drop it off to his house on my way home. I'm sure he will check in with the kids at some point tonight."

I stand from the booth, struggling to get my laptop bag over my shoulder. Folder extended toward Opal, I think the better of it. "Actually, my brother-in-law has inconvenienced you enough this evening. I'll just give the file to Weston. That kid is more responsible than the adults."

Confused by my abruptness, "Virginia? I-I-I… did I offend you somehow? I can bring that to Malcolm. He's probably still at Auggie's."

A scowling Desiree brings Opal's platter of fat and salt. The woman probably ordered all that thinking I'd sneak her food. Sarah always said she felt like she'd have to physically fork my hand to keep me from stealing off her plate.

I turn to a confused Opal, finding it odd that Desiree refuses to leave, and say, "It's just Ginny, actually. Only my grandmother called me Virginia, and I hated the woman."

Desiree, still not leaving, clears her throat like I'm being the world's biggest bitch. But I'm saving myself a lot of heartache and Opal a lot of frustration. This way she won't have to let me down gently.

"Mrs. Fischer would like some raspberry habanero sauce to go with her poppers," I order to get Desiree out of my hair. In a huff, the teenager stalks off. I stand far enough away so Opal doesn't think I'm intruding in her personal space, yet close enough so no one can overhear. "I'll talk to Malcolm. Generally he doesn't listen to me, but now I can *sic* Clover on him to do my bidding. He won't pressure you to see me again."

I pull a twenty, a ten, and some ones from my pocket, knowing it will cover mine and Opal's bills, plus Desiree's tip. I place the cash on the table, setting my coffee cup on top.

Opal's lips move, like she's trying to formulate a reply, but I decide all that needs to be said was said. "Enjoy your meal," I say in parting. I ignore the confusion and frustration that flashes over Opal's features as I walk away.

I make my way to Malcolm's house, where I let myself in and set the file on the kitchen table. No need to bother ten people for such a simple task, even if it makes Malcolm feel more important to do so. I no longer look forward to shopping and ice cream. Even my usual pacifiers hold no appeal after tonight's bullshit.

I want to skin my brother-in-law alive for humiliating me. Being in love has addled Malcolm's brain, thinking we all need the same thing to survive this shit we call life. I'm not thin or gorgeous, and that is most certainly what Opal is looking for in a lover. Malcolm should have known better than to offer someone as perfect as Opal, someone as messy, frumpy, slovenly, and chubby as the likes of me.

CHAPTER THREE

Opal Fischer

I perform my usual Sunday morning routine while I wait for Byron to bring Sage home. My son is with me Sunday morning through Friday afternoon, with Byron having Sage every weekend, and we negotiate the holidays. Byron's analytical mind comes in handy when creating a yearly schedule. Plus, with Byron living a few streets over from my family, Sage is close to his grandparents and aunts and uncles. I, however, don't step foot into the city's limits. I haven't been back since the day I left, going the opposite direction for shopping and necessities.

I'm sure my family is at church right now, praying for mine and my son's eternal soul. Every Sunday morning while I wait for Sage to come home, I do my crafting. It's the only thing to keep my mind off my old life. A part of me could easily slip back into that woman again. The obedient wife. The devoted daughter. The controlling mother. The good Catholic follower. My identity was always tied to someone for some reason, never being about who I am at my core.

Some people paint, some garden, some read, and some make jewelry or fabric crafts. I'm embarrassed to admit that I concoct soap. I'm fascinated by the chemistry of it and the delicious natural scents. After being around the chemical twang of antibacterial soap for the last twenty-five years, I needed the clean freshness of making my own soaps. So I spend my Sunday mornings, as I wait for my son to come home, making gifts for all the people I care about.

Sage loves sandalwood and chocolate coffee scent. Isis is partial to lavender, and scents like fresh-cut grass and linen. Bethany's face lights up for anything berry-scented. Since our one-night-stand, I've been making Rob almond oatmeal because of his dry skin– something I shouldn't have knowledge of, but I do just the same. I even send my parents, my brothers and sisters and their spouses and children, monthly rations of my sweet smelling concoctions.

Usually my mind is free and clear while I craft– *clean*. I may have left my suffocating past, but some of the tenets still stick with me. I never do anything that gives me a cloudy conscience. I like to be able to go to sleep at night, to look in the mirror and like who is gazing back at me, to be able to look my son in the eye and know I'm a good example. But today, but last night, I can't say that's held true.

I've never experienced these emotions before. It's discombobulating. As soon as I saw Ginny Jamison sitting in the booth at the No-Name, I knew I'd been set up, and I was furious. I allowed the emotion to taint my actions, turning me rude.

But when I approached the table and saw Ginny sitting there, I wanted nothing more than to sit down and talk with her, to share a meal. For a few stolen moments, I felt content. Until Ginny looked at me like she wanted me, which confused me to no end. Never had anyone paid me such intense attention.

Ginny isn't some bi-curious woman who wants to use me to gain the favor of the men in the Playroom. She isn't some random woman who was set up on a blind date with me. Ginny is someone in my orbit, intersecting my life through those around me but not truly crossing my path until last night. I was so nervous that I'd mess it all up, that I managed to mess it up anyway.

Truthfully, I've never been a date, not really. Growing up, my entire life was centered on family. I went to an all-girls private school. I took care of my brothers and sisters. I volunteered at church. My only experience with members of the opposite sex were the boys in our social circles who were invited to dinner. I believe that's where my revulsion of blind dates came from. It was more like '*forced*' dating under a microscope. I knew my parents were picking out their future son-in-law, just as how my brother-in-laws and sister-in-laws were chosen for my siblings. Except I was stubborn, which made me a bad daughter, and an even worse Catholic.

Byron was my parents' dream son-in-law, and that was part of his appeal for me: twenty-one years my senior, cultured, educated, and working closely with my father. We didn't date. We never flirted. It's like Byron sensed my affliction, and he was trying to save me from myself. He didn't touch me until our wedding night, and it was nice and sweet and without passion.

Sex was something we did on schedule, in our marital bed, with the lights off. Byron treated me like the woman my parents raised: loved, cherished, respected, and put upon a shelf as if breakable. Only at the hospital did my husband treat me as an equal, a place where most doctors treated the nurses as sub-human. My husband loved me, respected me, and trusted my judgment, but that wasn't enough for me.

So now, when I contemplate how I mucked up last night with Ginny, how I can possibly fix it, I'm so out of my element that I'm at a loss. This is when you need a best friend to go to for advice, but I can't because of who Ginny is to Isis. I'm too private to talk to Isis about her own family. I've never once said a word of what I did with Malcolm and Colin, and I was blunt without going into detail about what happened between Rob and me.

"Yoo-hoo? Mom? You in there?" Sage's voice isn't what draws my attention. His small hand waving in front of my face does. "You're spilling the soapy stuff all over its mold."

Snapping out of it, quickly righting my measuring cup, "Shit," I hiss. "Pretend I didn't just say that."

Sage laughs at me, finding my cussing hilarious. "I go to public school, remember? The teachers say worse than that." I give my son a droll look as I wipe up my mess. "Mom, maybe you should put some soap in your mouth to clean up your filthy language."

"Did you behave this weekend?" I ask as my eyes roll up, noticing Byron standing in the kitchen entranceway with a companion– the companion who led Rob to my bed. My face flushes with embarrassment. Byron and his new girlfriend heard me cuss. Debonair, only more handsome with age, sixty-four-year-old Bryon with his twenty-three-year-old mousy nurse. My ex-husband has a type, and it angers me to realize I was so easily replaceable with a fresher model.

A few months ago, Bryon took great pleasure in telling me he was dating a woman he met at the hospital. He went on and on about Audra's virtues. Whether Byron was trying to make me jealous remains to be seen. Off-kilter, knowing there was no going back to my old life, I went to the only place I felt bad in. Not bad as in evil or sinful, but bad as in naughty. The Playroom was still in Rush, so on a Sunday night, I sat at the bar and got drunk for the first time in my life. That was where Rob found me, and was chivalrous enough to deliver me home.

Stumbling in my front door, still feeling naughty, "Can I blow you again?" I slurred my words into Rob's ear as he helped keep me upright.

Stilling, we were stunned frozen in the middle of my living room with Rob's arms locked with mine. We were both completely taken aback by what came out of my mouth, to the point that I rendered the non-stop talking Rob silent, but only for a few seconds.

"I was shocked— we all were shocked —that you actually did what Willow asked. Hell, I was floored that you seemed to enjoy it." Rob shook me, making sure I was still with him. "I have a cock, did you forget that part of my anatomy?" Rob grabbed my hand and firmly pressed it to the hardening bulge beneath his zipper. Squeezing my hand over him, "You sucked this cock, so I know you know I have one."

"Whoa… what the?" Wearing a pair of pajama bottoms and a confused smirk, Sage found Rob and me in the living room. Caught red-handed, Rob and I tore ourselves apart and skittishly look everywhere but at each other or Sage. "Is Mom drunk? Who are you?"

"Umm..." Looking guilty and sounding confused, Rob turned to me with a bemused expression on his face. "Who am I, Opal?"

"A friend," I giggled, and I swear I hadn't giggled since I was a five-year-old girl.

Perceptive as always, "Ah, Mom's upset about Dad. Well, Friend, I'm Sage." Reaching out for a handshake, my kid did his usual introduction. The one that always elicits a shudder from me. "I'm gay."

I hate when he does that. I don't care about Sage's sexual preferences. I just wished he realized they were private. Sex is private. Telling someone you like boys is none of their business. Straight people don't use it as a greeting upon meeting strangers. My kid always says, "I'm Sage, and I'm gay." It's uncomfortable.

Not missing a beat, sober but chuckling quietly to himself, Rob met my son head-on. "Well, nice to meet you, I'm gay Sage. I'm Rob, and I'm not gay."

Rob's teasing going right over his head, Sage smiled like he knew a secret. "Have a good night. Don't do anything you'll regret in the morning. But, if I were you, I'd make sure I did more than that." Sage swaggered his tiny behind from the living room, disappearing into his bedroom.

"Holy Christ!" Rob mock-shouted. "That kid is your son? That freaking pretty, little cock-tease of a twink?" Pointing at my six-foot-tall body, and then gesturing to where my five-foot-four son was eavesdropping, "Your birth son?"

"That is my child you are talking about," I growled in warning.

"Oh, I'm not... it's not like that." Rob twisted up his face like he was revolted. "I was complimenting you on a job well done, but also warning you. Your kid is going to be T-R-O-U-B-L-E. He reminds me of me, which means he's going to be the aggressor. Soon he'll be running around looking for something he won't want when he finds it. Be watchful. Just saying."

"Don't tell me anything I don't already know. I moved to the most conservative town in the state to keep his ass shut down for business. Good luck finding a lay."

Appreciating the irony of my miscalculation, "Which backfired for you, didn't it?" Rob taunted me. "If you moved somewhere where the gay population is zilch, where the hell are you going to find willing pussy?"

"Subconsciously, I probably did that on purpose," I muttered to myself. "Do you want me to suck you or not?"

Suddenly serious, "Why? I know people pick on me, saying I remind them of a girl. Is that why?"

"No," I replied, sounding just as serious. "I'm a lesbian, but that doesn't mean I hate men. It just means that I want women. Want one as my partner, my lover– emotional and physical."

Cupping his bulge, Rob bit out, "I'm not a woman, goddamnit! These are balls in my hand, Opal. You sucked those, too, remember?"

"I remember being quite voracious and enthusiastic with your manhood, Robin." I gave an exaggerated eye roll that turned into a cascade of drunken giggling. "Being a lesbian doesn't mean I don't want to be penetrated, or that I can't appreciate that you are very attractive as a man. Rob, you genuinely want me, you know what you're doing, and I like you as a person. Plus, my ex-husband didn't let me do it... and right now, I'd rather suck you to spite Byron than anything on this planet."

Hand leaving his crotch, Rob crossed his arms over his chest, and leveled a glare my way. "Why me, though? It's not flattering to be a vengeance fuck."

Recognizing Rob's insecurity and wanting to assuage it, "Yes, you're small, which makes you more feminine, but that's not why. There has always been something about you that has turned me on a bit. Your naughtiness, I believe. But mostly, I'm naturally the aggressor, with no one to pursue. But as you said, you're also an aggressor. When you mounted my face like a madman... the way you took what you wanted from me, it made me feel like a woman."

Stunned, Rob just stared at me with his mouth hanging open. Drink making me bold, I asked again, hoping for a different outcome. "So, may I suck you?"

"No," Rob said, making my heart stutter with bitter rejection. He took my hand in his, confusing me further. "I want to go down on you, and then have sex with you while you're still coming. You good with that?"

Swallowing, gulping down air, "Yeah," hesitantly flowed from my lips. "We're good."

"For the first time ever, I promise you'll feel like a real woman," Rob vowed, and he kept his promise. Repeatedly. And I learned his favorite maneuver was entering a woman as she was in the throes of orgasm, and he always made her come twice– once on his tongue, and once around his cock.

I blink out of the memory, suddenly pissed at Byron. There should be a natural law against bringing your new girlfriend into your ex-wife's home– invading her space with a replacement just a few years older than your son.

Noticing the arc of my vision and the fury I'm trying to bury, Sage says, "Maybe you should rethink that whole not driving to Dad's for the weekend business."

"It's back on the negotiating table," I breathe to my son as I quickly clean my hands on a kitchen towel. Since the day he earned his driver's license, Sage has wanted to drive to his father's for the weekend. Knowing Byron valued their alone time in the car, I put the kibosh to it quickly. Now, I'm willing to compromise for two reasons. One, it would mean I wouldn't have to see Byron every Friday afternoon and Sunday morning, and his little Audra, too. Two, if Byron truly valued his alone time with Sage, he wouldn't taint it with Audra's presence.

Remembering my manners, "Hi, Byron." I give a little wave, refusing to cross the kitchen. "Audra, nice to meet you." Audra is a very young, teacup-sized brunette with huge brown eyes. Innocence and malleability are wafting off her.

Disgusting.

I'm not jealous of this woman in Byron's life. It's not that. The forty-one year age difference devalues Byron in my eyes. Legal or not, adult or not, Byron is a sick fuck, and I don't ever say the f-word. Looking back, Byron was a sick fuck for marrying me, too.

My son, smarter than the rest of us, breaks the tension by amping it up. "Dad, did I show you this pic text I got last night from Desiree?"

"Shit," I breathe again, determined to make profanity part of my everyday language.

Sage, appearing more innocent than Audra, with his sandy blond hair, huge blue eyes, and a slight frame, is more jaded than any adult in the Playroom. Rob was right about Sage being a budding pain in the ass. "Mom went on a date last night with this pretty woman. See?" Sage passes my ex-husband his cellphone, all proud of his mother.

Something wicked flashes across Byron's face before I can interpret it. But even still, I know he's not happy with me. Jealousy thick in his voice, "When did this start? I wasn't aware you were dating."

Byron intimidates me, and he knows it. He's kind and caring for the most part, but there are times when he reminds me of my father, in more ways than one. They are the same age, both doctors, and both have the ability to make me feel cherished, loved, and appreciated. With that power over me, they have the key to destroy me. I married Byron because of his affect, a fact I know despise.

Refusing to fall into old patterns, I explain nothing. I have no need to defend my actions to my ex-husband while his child-aged girlfriend stands in my kitchen.

"Oh, here," Sage says brightly, quickly scanning the gallery on his cellphone for a picture of something. "This is Rob. He really made Mom blush."

"Bloody hell," I add to my repertoire, and blush just as Sage predicted. That picture was taken at breakfast– the breakfast Rob made Sage and myself the morning after. Rob's standing at the kitchen stove in nothing but his jeans. "Sage, you're making me sound like a wanton whore."

Sage flashes me a look of '*just roll with it, Mom.*'

"A. Man?" Byron says slowly, as if he thinks he's hearing Sage wrong. "You slept with a man?"

"It's really none of your business," I say with a shrug. I ignore the lot of them by cleaning up my soap making supplies.

Sounding more angry than incredulous, Byron's voice is sharp like broken glass. "None of my business? This man was in this house with our son. That picture was taken in this room. This Rob character could be a murderer, and he's very young. Practically a boy."

"Rob is six years *older* than Audra, I'll have you know," I defend. "And do I have to remind you that I'm almost twenty-one years *younger* than you, Byron. Really," I gesture toward Audra, "That's fucking sick," earning myself a collective gasp because I've never said the f-word aloud before. "As for Rob being in my house with our son, Audra's been staying at your home with our son, and I don't know her, nor do I think it's my business. Stay out of it!"

"Leave us," Byron orders Audra like you would one's child, and she goes like a good girl should. But Sage stays planted firmly in the kitchen, going nowhere. "We divorced because you wanted to be with women, and now you insult me by taking a man as a lover."

"I don't know, Dad," Sage says from his position at the counter. "It could have been all about you, seeing as how you're old enough to be my *grandfather*."

Taken aback by the bitter resentment lacing my son's voice, "What has you so antagonistic and disrespectful this morning? You're never like this."

Without taking his eyes from his father, Sage answers me. "Proving himself a hypocrite, Dad and Audra are getting married, and I'm going to be a big brother. Dad will be eighty-two years old when my sibling gets out of high school. There is a good chance I'll end up raising the kid when dear ol' dad kicks the bucket while banging his child bride." Sneering, "Thanks, Dad."

"What?" I squeak out, never in my wildest imaginings did I think this would come to pass. "You're joking, right?" I nearly beg Bryon, "Please, tell me Sage is joking?"

"Last night at the fundraiser banquet, Grandfather loved it when I told half of the hospital board how Dad knocked up a girl before marriage. That went over real well at a Catholic hospital function." Sage snickers, but he doesn't sound amused.

"You didn't?" I draw out in horror, knowing how my father must have wanted to murder my son in that moment.

Closing his eyes, Bryon breathes, "He did."

"Yeah, well, they retaliated. Last night after the fundraiser, hypocrite Dad took me to Grandmother and Grandfather's, where I had to listen to how being gay is a state of mind. They said I was choosing to be gay, that it's a phase I'm going through."

"What?" My voice is strangled by my throat. "I took Sage out of that environment to keep him from being indoctrinated by that horseshit." Again, there I go adding more profanity to my vocabulary. I'm slipping. "As a man of science, I thought we were in total agreement."

Furious, losing his own grip on decorum, Byron relinquishes his control over to his emotions. "As a man of science, we are. As a husband, I'm fucking pissed that my so-called lesbian wife fucked a man. Explain that shit to me, will you?"

"I'm no longer your wife," is my only explanation.

Sage, however, offers his sage advice. "Because Mom moved us to Narrow-Minded-Ville, and if some new people don't begin moving into town, I'm going to have to start looking at girls for some attention. Because we aren't animals you study for shits 'n giggles. We have feelings, you bastard!"

Angrier than I've ever seen him, Byron snaps. "I brought you to your grandparents' last night because you shouldn't have embarrassed me by telling the President of the hospital board that you're gay, Sage."

Sage and I yell at the same time, "I *am* gay!" "Get out!"

Exasperated with us, "For the record, I was forced to be with Audra because you no longer wanted me– never wanted me," Byron whispers, near tears. "You'll always be my wife in my eyes, Opal." Turning to our son, "I was embarrassed, not embarrassed by you, there is a distinction. I know you're gay, but there is a time and a place for talk of sex, and as you so nicely pointed out, I work for a Catholic hospital. That is why I took you to your grandparents' last night, to understand how your asinine selfishness is a detriment to your family."

Exhausted, and it's only morning, I sigh, "Just go. We'll talk later when cooler heads prevail. This has been a lot to digest, and Sage is still a boy."

Cutting his losses– his first family –Byron leaves without so much as a backward glance. I tug my son into my arms, squeezing him tightly. "You know when not to introduce yourself like that. It's always for the shock-value. So why did you do that to your father at the banquet last night?"

Chuckling evilly, "I didn't do it to embarrass Dad. I did it to embarrass Grandfather. Dad was just collateral damage. But I don't give a shit because Dad brought Audra into my life. The man was too busy to play with me when I was little. Now he's seventeen years older than when I was born, and ready to settle down and coddle a newborn at the tender age of retirement. Dad will be old enough to be my baby brother or sister's *great*-grandfather."

"That is just so many shades of wrong." I don't know whether or not I want to kiss Sage's sweet face or kick his naughty behind. "Your father needs a psyche evaluation."

"Be prepared," Sage warns, "After last night's bullshit, there is a legion of right-wing Christian Sages preparing to invade Fairport."

"Lord, help us all…" My family is coming to visit for the very first time.

CHAPTER FOUR

Ginny Jamison

After a long afternoon of house showings, Ren's usual infectiously happy attitude is slowly waning into snide territory. "Wow… what a cocksucking shithole." Ren's expanded vocabulary impresses me, and I taught him most of what he already knows.

"Remind me to thank Willow for teaching you so many compound words," I mutter sarcastically. Gazing around the fourteen-hundred-square-foot, two-story fixer-upper, I'll agree that '*shithole*' is highly apt. "Well, I hate to break it to ya, kid. But this, right here, is the best I can do within your tax bracket. It's cheaper than renting, but not by much. But in this economy, nothing is cheap."

Blond eyebrows raised nearly to his hairline, Ren is the epitome of incredulousness. "It's a three bedroom, one bath house for four adults and bun in the oven. I know you've got to be good at math to sell houses, Aunt Ginny."

We're standing on the sidewalk out front of a home that hasn't been updated since before I was born. The aluminum siding was a pea-green that has slowly faded into a color not found on Earth. I'm pretty sure that the building itself is leaning to the right.

Feeling horrible for the boy, I tell Ren the truth. "I've been doing this for nearly twenty years, Ren. This is a shitty time to buy a house if you don't have any money. Banks aren't too keen on lending to first-time home-buyers, especially ones without an established line of credit. If your banker hasn't already told you, then I will. All four of you will have to be on that mortgage. Even with a thirty-year mortgage, which I advise against, you're looking at a hefty monthly payment."

With a Mason sign of frustration, Ren tears at his hair aggressively while walking in a tight circle. "Why advise against that type of mortgage?"

Thank goodness my nephew has me. Ren's ignorance would have gotten him taken for a ride, from not only a shady real-estate agent, but the banker too.

"The longer you string it out, the more interest you pay. The less of a down payment, the more you have to pay interest on. It behooves a lender to lock you into a thirty-year loan with five percent down while promising you low monthly payments, which are all interest. Best advice I can give, go for a fifteen or twenty year, biweekly mortgage with twenty percent down, and then try to pay it off within ten years. You don't want to be lining the mortgage lender's pockets with bonuses. Put that money into your future."

"I thought I was," Ren draws out, sounding like a lost, little boy. "I thought I was buying a house to secure my future. It sounds like you're trying to talk me out of it."

"I'm not, but I want you to be realistic." Gesturing to the shithole, "This is what you can afford. You just turned nineteen. Willow is only eighteen. Neither of you have ever purchased a damned thing, not even a car. Essie is twenty-one with piss-poor credit from a defaulted student loan. The only one who looks good on paper is Devon, and he's doing a stint in rehab. Combined, you're all a shitty investment in the bank's regard, so they're going to take you to the cleaners. Got it?"

Nearly whining, "What do we do, then?"

"Stay at home with your dad," I grumble, and I'm thankful Ren doesn't hear me. "I have a handful of houses you can choose from. Forget about amenities and square footage. We will pick the one in the best repair, with the cheapest monthly payment, the least to insure, and the least in real estate taxes each year… and then we pray."

"You took all the fun out of this," Ren pouts. "Now it's just stressful."

After seventeen years of selling other people's homes, of buying, fixing, and reselling my own, I've been through this hundreds of times. It's never easy to tell an excited home buyer that they can't have that dream house in their mind. I ruin that dream by telling them they have to go with reality. For my nephew, I go with brutal honesty. "You're buying a house, Ren. It shouldn't be easy. It's a commitment."

Striding over to stand before me, Ren looks me in the eyes, silently begging me to fix it. "Tell me what to do. You know the ins and outs better than anyone. Tell me what to do," he pleads, breaking my heart.

Sighing heavily, "I will do my best, but you have to promise to do as I say."

Smiling, Ren's hands reach over to rest upon my shoulders. With his head shaking like an eager puppy, "Anything, Aunt Ginny. Anything."

I blurt out, "Make Devon marry Essie for everyone's sanity."

Hands dropping from my shoulders, Ren takes a large step back as if I struck him. "Why?"

I reach out to Kieren, knowing touch soothes my nephews quicker than anything else. "I don't have any kids, Ren, and I never will. I've prided myself on being the best aunt I could possibly be. Everything I say and do is with your best interests at heart. Do you understand?"

"Yes?" Ren is hesitant, making his acknowledgment more of a question.

"We have a serious problem here. Before I go on, I need you to tell me why you want this? You're nineteen. Stay to home." Voice breaking from a wound that still throbs deeply, "I was twenty-three and still living with my parents, and probably still would be if they hadn't died."

"So would I," Ren admits for the first time. "Grammy and Grandpa would have still been raising all of us, and Mom might still be alive today. Woulda. Shoulda. Coulda. Let's not kick me in the nuts while I'm down, Aunt Ginny."

It's my turn to walk away as I fight with my emotions. I left college and moved back to Fairport when Clover did, only to find my sister in a deep state of depression. Bipolar mixed with postpartum depression is a fatal mix. While Malcolm was working in the city, my parents and I took Isis, Devon, Kieren, and a newborn Raven from Camille, and we had Camille committed for treatment. A few weeks later, a drunk driver killed my parents– thankfully I was at home with the kids. Malcolm came back to Fairport, removed his wife from the facility, and took the kids back. I went through this routine five more times before Malcolm finally stayed in Fairport for good.

I loved my sister, shitty mother that she was. I loved Malcolm, and I knew he'd do his damnedest to be the best father to make up for Camille's failings. With both parents in the home, I couldn't in good conscience keep the children. Everyone would have resented me for it in the end. If my parents hadn't died, I know they would've never relinquished the children once they entered our home. When I didn't fight to keep Isis that last time, she hasn't spoken to me since.

Smothering the regrets of the past, I walk back over to Ren. "Tell me why you want all of you in one house. I will get you exactly what you need, *if* I agree with your stance."

Staring me dead in the eyes, Ren pours his soul out. "None of us had all the attention we needed. Weston and Raven are better off because they lost Mom so young, because they weren't subjected to Mom's bullshit for as long as Dev and I were. If Dev moves back home with Dad, the kids lose all of that attention they deserve. We're already fucked up. I want to give the little ones a fighting chance."

The last time the kids lived with me, Isis was seventeen, Devon was ten, Kieren was eight, Raven was five, and Weston was a toddler. Isis took control of her own life and moved out at eighteen, selfishly leaving everyone behind, but I understood why. The kids' lives evened out after Camille's suicide. I understand where Kieren is coming from. In his eyes, Devon is no different than his mother, tainting their home with his issues.

Devon's drug addiction is just a symptom of the underlying problem, and I can't fault him for his poor behavior. I don't have to like it, though. "What about Devon? I understand what you're saying, but he needs that attention, even if you feel he doesn't deserve it."

With determination, Ren holds my eyes while stressing, "Devon deserves it. He isn't going to fall through the cracks this time. There will be no children taking the attention away so Devon can hide. He is my brother." Voice breaking from a plethora of emotions, "Willow, as much as it kills me to admit, she loves Devon... and Essie, she loves Devon like I love Willow. It won't be like with Mom, where Dad's attention was on us kids, leaving her to harm herself. Devon will have three adults watching his every single move, and we all want what's best for him."

With the nod of my head, "Right answer. Now, if you can get Devon to marry Essie, I'll help you secure a house, even if I have to buy it myself."

Taken aback by my offer, Ren challenges me, "Your turn. Why?"

We've all thought it, but none of us have had the balls to say it out loud. But I do it anyway. "Devon is confused, hurt, and he lashes out as a test. He doesn't even realize he's doing it until it's too late." Ren's face twists up, so I answer his unspoken question. "How do I know? I grew up with the feminine version of Devon, only my sister was even more vicious. Your mother did horrible things to my parents and me in a quest to prove we loved her, and it was never enough. But Devon is a Mason, so once he's committed to Essie, he should level out some."

Facing twisting up in thought, Ren reasons out what I'm trying to say without actually saying the words. We all know if Devon is feeling down, in need of attention, he might seek Willow out to hurt Ren, just to hurt himself even more– to prove to everyone he's the piece of shit he thinks of himself. "You think Dev'll go after Willow to test me?"

It's my turn to become incredulous. "And you don't? Devon tore a pair of your boxers into confetti, and then Rob had to knock him unconscious. You had to handcuff Dev's ass just to get him on the airplane to rehab. What do you think?"

"What do you think?" Ren counters, voice breaking because he knows I'm right.

"I think this is a disaster of epic proportions. But it can be mitigated if you get Devon to concentrate on his kid instead of wallowing in self-misery. Devon will be so involved with the baby, he'll be too busy to take a drug, nonetheless even *think* about taking one. Get your brother to commit to Essie, and he will be obsessive over her like a Mason always is about their *women*. So that will remove the threat of Devon trying to get inside your girlfriend to test you."

Stalking away from me, my honest words hit Ren hard. In a few strides, he's halfway down the block. With an about-face, Ren speaks to me while walking back. "Why not just tell me to marry Willow?" he asks, sounding beyond confused. "The Devon problem would be solved."

"You do that, and I'll castrate your ass, Kieren Ewan Mason," I warn fiercely, and I mean it too. Pointing with every word I enunciate, "Willow is a child. Let her grow the fuck up and make a life for herself. Don't ask her to marry you out of fear."

Furious, Ren shouts the words in my face, "It wouldn't be out of fear!"

Eyes softening, I feel for my nephew, but I won't allow Ren to mess up his life– not even for Willow. "No, but Willow's answer would be– fear of losing you if she said no. When she's ready, you'll know it. It might be next month, or next year, or never. But don't lock Willow into a life she'll regret just because *you* want *her*."

Sneering, Ren eyes me like I've lost my mind. "But you'll lock Essie into a life with a drug addict."

Exhausted, reaffirming my belief that I was not meant to be a mother since being an aunt takes all of my emotional reserves. "We're past that, Ren. Way past that. Kids are a game-changer. Plus, your brother is almost three years older than you. Essie, too. They are adults. They're on the path they will always be on."

"I *am* an adult," Ren mumbles like a child.

"I know," I agree. "But use this time to act your age. I don't want you to regret it later." I change the subject, knowing Ren will argue with me, even knowing I'm right. "Promise me you'll wait for Willow, and promise you'll force your brother to do the right thing, and I'll get you that house."

Tears glistening in his soft blue eyes, Ren is hearing me out. Stark fear crosses his features– fear of the unknowns and how they will affect his future. "Why? If you think this is a disaster, why would you help me? What if I can't fulfill my promise?"

Not answering Ren, not yet anyway. I walk toward my car, knowing this house is not going to cut it. I get into my car, and as I suspected, Ren climbs into the passenger seat without being told to do so. I turn to my nephew, overwhelmed with pride over the incredible man he's turned out to be, hoping my influence was for the positive in his young life.

I feel hopeful, knowing I'm doing the right thing, because I cannot place the weight of a wounded brother on Kieren's shoulders. I lived that way since the day I was born until the day my sister died, and still to this day, I'm carrying the guilt of not doing right by Camille. Epiphany striking, I find a reasonable solution for everyone. A solution that absolves my guilt. I'm finally doing right by Camille through her oldest children, which frees up Malcolm to do right by the youngest. If I'm wrong, it's only money– I'd gladly pay all I have for my nephews' happiness.

Turning over the ignition, I head in the direction of the new house. "Tomorrow morning I'll start the paperwork to buy you the house. You guys can pay rent to me. If it falls through, I'll fix the house up and resell it. As it is, I'll pay Dave to make the house habitable for you guys. *When*, not if, Devon and Essie marry, I'll change it over to a land contract for them to buy it outright with past rent toward the principal."

"What?" Ren breathes, completely mystified over my change of heart. Sounding out of breath, as if his heart is beating in his throat, "Why?"

I stop in the middle of the street so I can look at my nephew instead of paying attention to my driving. It's Fairport, after all– everyone just veers around me, waving happily on their way by. Nosy bastards.

I gaze at Kieren, compassion and sympathy thick in my voice. "Be a goddamned kid, Ren. You're already taking on the responsibility of Devon, worrying about all of this financial bullshit like you're my age is lunacy. Just pay your rent on time, and we're good. When you marry Willow in the future– *when*, not if –buy your forever home. Buy that dream house in your head– that house where Willow and you will raise your naughty brats."

At a loss for words, Ren stares at the side of my face. Checking my mirrors first, I start driving again, heading toward Ren's new home. "The house two doors down from The Spook House and the Pink Taco Hut is where you should live. It needs some repairs. It's a three bedroom: Willow and you in one, Dev and Essie in another, with the baby in the third. My great niece or nephew is not going to share a room with its parents. When you and Willow move out, they can put another kid in your old room."

"W-h-y?" Ren stammers. "Why that house?"

"Location, not amenities. Clover can help with the baby, and the baby will entice Isis to stay at the Spook House– Isis is a sucker for a newborn," I say while smiling to myself, remembering how awestruck Isis was every time Camille was pregnant– only time Isis would stay in the same room with my sister. "You're going to need your father's help with Devon, and knowing Malcolm's a shout away will be less stressful for everyone involved. If something goes wrong, send Willow back to the Spook House and Essie to Clover, and you and Dev can fight it out in your house. That's what's doing. You either do it my way, or you keep your ass at home with your dad."

Overwhelmed, over his head, Ren just stares at me gape-mouthed. The poor kid is scared shitless. He felt hopeless, out of choices. But there is always a choice– there is always hope.

I can read it in his eyes as clear as day. Ren was going to force Willow into marriage, just like Willow's father forced her mother. After living through that disaster, I now know that if Sam had waited for Clover to grow into a woman first, their lives would have been infinitely better. I will not allow my nephew to do the same to Sam and Clover's girl– to do the same to himself.

The circle of madness ends now.

Answering Kieren's earlier question, "Why do I believe you will fulfill your promise, Ren? Because you're a Mason. It's that same belief that has me confident in Devon's future. Devon's child will give him hope– a reason to live. It's your job as Devon's brother to make sure he finds his sense of honor before it's too late."

CHAPTER FIVE

Opal Fischer

"And here I thought my family was pure chaos… I was wrong," I mutter more to myself than to Isis.

With Malcolm and his youngest children visiting the eldest child in an Arizonian rehab facility, it left Clover in control of relocating three homes into one. With Rob and Clover at the Prynne and Webster households, with the help of Willow, Violet, Seth, Essie, and Ozzy running a yard sale, Isis was left in charge of the Mason household.

Isis is in drill-sergeant-mode, amassing a small army of Rush employees to get the job done faster. Rory and Bethany are running around extinguishing '*walk down memory lane*' emotional fires. Auggie's wandering around with his mind in the past and his eyes glazed over with sadness. I've heard more '*John Mason-isms*' today than in the four years prior while volunteering at dispatch surrounded by John's faithful followers.

Auggie is in charge of packing up Malcolm's personal spaces: the master bedroom and bathroom, the basement, and the garage. But Auggie is doing more reminiscing while pretending not to cry than any actual packing. Several times over, I've witnessed Bethany's natural affinity to lend a shoulder to cry on. Her endless patience was a godsend for the rest of us, leaving us to get some actual work done.

The easiest job in the house, yet the most fragile, fell to Beth. When she wasn't playing Auggie's counselor, that is. Worried Weston would freak out if anything of his gets misplaced, I reassured Isis that Bethany was the girl for the job. Beth's analytical mind was a perfect fit to catalog Weston's pristine bedroom.

Rush's staff is busy in the main rooms, clearing out the kitchen, living room, dining room, and the bathroom. That left one of the worst jobs to Rory– packing up Devon and Kieren's disaster of a bedroom. I'd thought to myself how thankful I was that Isis didn't give me that particular job, but I ate my words when I saw the pigsty known as Raven's room.

If a closet could regurgitate clothing, handbags, and shoes, Raven's surely has. As I've folded clean clothing and bagged up filthy clothing, it's reinforced how my parents did more right than wrong in the way they raised me. As the only girl in a household of men, Raven is so spoiled that I doubt she appreciates one single thing she owns. If she did, it wouldn't be littered on the floor like trash, with actual trash, dishes, food, and disgustingness ground into the expensive articles of clothing with their sales tags still attached.

You can tell a lot about someone's personality by the way they take care of the small space they carved out as their own. Weston probably would glow from something as simple as being gifted a piece of chewing gum. West takes great responsibility, pride, and care for the simplest of things. Other than the signs of a recent destructive fit, which Isis explained away as Ren's outlet for mourning Devon's drug addiction, you can tell the boys took care of their belongings. There was just too much stuff filling a small room for two grown men to share in the space. Raven, she's spoiled rotten, and wallowing in it like a pig in a sty. It's not healthy.

When I was growing up, we were affluent, yet we epitomized the word conservative. I had school uniforms: skirts, blouses, and blazers. My everyday-wear was more skirts and blouses. Everything was expensive but utilitarian– meaning it was mix-and-match wear, which would never embarrass my family. In the eyes of my father, the only pants a woman should wear are scrubs. To this day, I still do not own a pair of jeans.

My upbringing has filtered into how I raise my son. No person needs more pairs of pants than the days of the week. I don't care what articles Sage chooses to wear as long as his ass is covered, but he won't have a department store in his closet and dresser.

"Isis?" I say to gain the woman's attention. She is reverently running her fingertips along the flowered wallpaper with a faraway look in her eyes. "Did you buy the girl all this stuff? I just counted twenty-three pairs of jeans with the tags still on. Yet every time I see Rae, she's in the same outfit."

"Huh?" Isis turns to me, surreptitiously wiping a stray tear off her cheek. Her eyes land on the pair of designer jeans in my hand. "Oh, yeah. We'll take them to Revamped, and what doesn't sell, we'll donate."

At a loss, I try to get Isis to answer me. "Why does Rae have so much stuff?"

"Ginny and I–" hearing her name is a jolt to the spine. "Ginny is a compulsive shopper, so most of it is from her. Rae doesn't have a mom, and she won't let either of us mother her, so we buy her shit as a way to make up for it."

"Clearly, that is not working. The pants she's wearing are threadbare, and not because it's the style."

Softly smiling to herself, Isis murmurs as if she finally got a clue, "Malcolm bought Rae those jeans, that's why. He took us all out shopping as a family, and told us to get whatever we wanted. Rae's been wearing them ever since."

"Maybe Raven's aunts need to try talking to the girl," I grumble beneath my breath, but Isis hears me anyway.

"Good luck with that. Rae is practically mute. I'm waiting for her to dye her hair black to match her attitude... oh, wait a minute, it already is," Isis says sardonically. "Rae is her mother's daughter but looks like me– a deadly combination. Raven gets sick of everyone comparing her to us, as if she isn't her own person, so she just checks out."

I hesitantly broach the subject, "How is Rae with Clover?"

Frustrated, on the verge of tears, Isis bear hugs an armload of jeans and dumps them into a huge box. "I do talk to Rae, and I know she listens, even if she never talks back. I never had a mom. Even though Rae knew her mother for eight years, Camille's moods were petrifying. This shit changes us, forces us to pick a mom because we don't have the one we were given. That's why Rae never let Ginny or me in, even when Ginny tried to mother her."

In the past, before I met Ginny, hearing her name meant nothing. Ginny was just a person orbiting my life. Now speaking of Ginny elicits an odd reaction in my mind and body. "She tried to mother the girl?"

Isis just shakes her head in reply, as if she can't speak because intense emotions are riding her. Busying herself by folding a stack of pretty blouses, Isis forces out, "Camille and Ginny were only eleven months apart, even shared the same grade in school. Identical in looks but opposite in personality. Rae loves Ginny, but won't allow her mother's clone to raise her.

Dev and Ren found comfort in the similarities while it terrified Rae and West."

"Well, shit," slips out before I can stop it. Isis looks at me sideways, shocked that I just cursed.

After witnessing Auggie's breakdowns throughout the day, I'd thought it ridiculous. I kept placing myself in a similar situation with my parents. The only difference, my parents are still alive, and I'm a forty-three-year-old woman. Isis didn't have a mother from day one, with Auggie losing John when he was a small boy. Rae, the mother she was given tortured her emotionally during the formative years of her life. There is no comparison. No amount of putting yourself into their position will ever garner how these tortured souls must feel on a day when it brings all the pain to light.

I voice a fear I've had since Byron mentioned Audra, and Sage had a bitter reaction to the news. "The kids don't resent Clover, do they?"

Kicking a box marked **Rae & V's room** out into the hallway, Isis shouts, "R-O-R-Y! Truck!" Emotionally stunted herself, Isis looks close to shutting down on me. "Rae respects Clover, and she chose Clover as her mother. Raven actually gets excited and chatty around her new mom. Truth be told, there is no history with Clover– nothing that haunts our family. So it's easy for the kids to love Clover, where it is hard for them to do the same with Ginny or me."

"Makes sense," I mutter to myself. Not wanting to prolong this chore, I get to work. As I box up an endless assortment of junk, I marvel over how a girl of sixteen can amass such a collection of clothing, shoes, bags, jewelry, DVDs, books and magazines, old toys, stuffed animals… it's never-ending.

When the last box is packed and kicked out into the hallway for Rory to tote off to Auggie's pickup truck, Isis and I just stand in the middle of an empty room.

So quiet, I can barely hear her, the hitch in her voice so subtle, I wonder if I imagined it, Isis whispers, "The only thing I know about my mother is that she wanted me to have this bedroom." Isis's coal-black eyes slide to the side to meet my shocked gaze. Isis never opens up. The aunt and niece have more in common than a curvy body shape, and eye and hair color.

"Dad never spoke of my mom. It was too painful for him. Penelope Mason was the love of John Mason's life, and he went a bit nuts himself after she died. Dad said he didn't blame me, but how could he not."

"Isis," I cry out, reaching for her hand. As quick as a snake, Isis sidesteps my touch.

"So, everything I know of my mom I heard from Malcolm. He didn't know much either, 'cuz he was just a little guy when she died. My brother told me my mom loved me, couldn't wait to meet me and raise her little girl. She spent a lot of time fixing my bedroom for my arrival: wallpapering, painting, picking out the furniture. Mom wanted everything perfect for me, and I was brought home to this room motherless."

Walking across the room to the corner, Isis kneels down on the carpeting. I can't see what she's doing, but a tearing sound draws my attention. Raising to her feet, "I think I'll keep this," she presents a swatch of floral wallpaper. "I look just like my dad: hair, eyes, and my larger size for a woman. I don't even have a picture of my mother. Malcolm says our faces are hers, though. So we'll see her every time we look in the mirror. But I like this better." Isis tucks the piece of wallpaper into her back pocket.

When I met Isis four years ago, I felt a kindred spirit in the younger woman. We share the same emotional fortitude. As Isis prepares to leave her childhood behind, leave her mother behind, we share a similar reaction. Both of us are silently crying, and neither of us acknowledges it.

Sad, lost, and suddenly angry, "I know you met Ginny over a week ago, and since you didn't say a word about it, I assume it went badly."

Sputtering, I'm over-emotional and it causes me to speak in a way I never do. "I fucked up. I don't know how I fucked up, but I just know I did. I only wanted to sit down and share a meal with Ginny, get to know her a little bit. It was different than the times before, and I recognized it. I fucked up."

Pointing at me, "And you'll fix it," Isis threatens– her voice is as icy as her nickname. "I was the one who made sure the two of you never met. I was going to bring you together *after* you had a woman or two and got used to the idea of being a lesbian."

"What?" I breathe.

"I knew you'd fuck up, and that was unacceptable. This is Ginny we're talking about, not some twat looking for a quick lay. I knew you'd hurt her, so I kept you from meeting Ginny face-to-face."

Suddenly angry myself, I lash out. "I'm not some sixteen-year-old indecisive bitch who will hurt her first girlfriend. You know me, Isis. If I hurt Ginny, it won't be on purpose."

"That wasn't a chance I was willing to take." Pointing at me with an angry finger again, "You're going to fix this tonight. I'm throwing the newlyweds a welcome home/reception/house warming party. You're going to fix this shit with Ginny. I know you hurt her feelings since no one has said a word about your meeting."

I'm surprised at the venom in Isis's voice. I've heard her speak to countless people over the past four years like this, but never me. "I'll fix it. I want to fix it. I've been wracking my brain on a way."

"Try harder," Isis demands. "As I said, motherless girls choose their new mothers, and they often become bitter and resentful. Malcolm married Camille, thinking to give me a mother. But I wanted Malcolm as my brother, not my father. John Mason will forever be my father. I wanted crazy-assed Camille to be my sister-in-law. I wanted their children to be my nephews and niece. I didn't want them as my siblings. Ginny kept taking me and treating me like a daughter, only to toss my ass back every time Malcolm came home."

"I… I… what?" I stutter out.

"Ginny told me over and over again how I belonged with Malcolm. I kept screaming how he was my brother, not my father. But she never listened. Ginny kept returning me like I was a lost kitten who strayed too far from home. Ginny may have not wanted me as her daughter, but that doesn't mean I don't see her as my mom." Striding out into the hallway, Isis leans back into the doorway, and threatens, "Best friend or not, if you hurt my mother, I'll kill you."

CHAPTER SIX

Opal Fischer

I haven't fussed over what I looked like in years. I decided on a sundress and sandals– the type of outfit I haven't worn since I was a teenager. I've gotten so used to grabbing a pair of slacks and a blouse, knowing they match, that I forgot clothing was an expression of your personality. Clearing out Raven's room today taught me that. It took me a while, but I finally figured out why Rae refuses to wear those beautiful clothes her aunts buy her. I hated my clothing as a kid because I had no choice in the matter. Rae adores those worn-out jeans for two reasons: her dad bought them and she picked them out for herself.

Standing in front of my floor-length mirror, I try to fluff my hair up so it's not as masculine. But it just ends up looking messy. I reach for my comb and the canister of mousse to smooth it back down to my skull, but a small hand stops me.

"Sage, what are you doing?" I eye my son suspiciously.

There is a reason I placed a cap on the amount of articles in my son's wardrobe. He's a clothes horse. Our happy medium is that there is no monetary limit on Sage's meager wardrobe, a fact he uses to his benefit. Clad in a crisp, short-sleeved button down, with a designer t-shirt beneath, and a pair of pressed board shorts, the kid looks like a fashion advertisement. Even leather his sandals are the height of fashion.

Stealing my comb and mousse, "Don't smooth your hair back– you're not at work." Sage reaches up to muss up my hair even more. Smiling brightly, "Much better."

"I look like a rooster," I grumble to my son's reflection. "It's messy."

"Exactly. It's not stuffy, and I bet stuffy Opal Fischer scared Ginny Jamison off. Show her you can relax." Tugging on my cap-sleeve, "And you even wore a dress to impress her. You look pretty, Mom."

"I know why I'm dressed up, but why are you?" My eyes sweep my kid from sandals to perfectly sculpted hairstyle. Between Sage's clothing ensemble, his '*my hair naturally falls this way*', and the smile that pops dimples, I get suspicious. "I wasn't even aware you were going, yet here you are, dressed like you're going on a date."

"I just want to spend some time with my friends," Sage says innocently enough. I keep staring at his reflection in the mirror, using my mother powers until he cracks. "I haven't seen Rae since summer vacation started. I also hear Ozzy is living with the Masons."

Skeptical, "I wasn't aware you were friends with either of those kids. To my knowledge, your only friend is Desiree."

"I shared gym class with them, and Rae and I had English together, too!" Sage defends himself, face stained pink from a tattletale blush.

"And that makes you friends?" I prompt, trying to get to the bottom of Sage's newfound community spirit. The kid usually holes himself up at the No-Name with Desiree.

"It's Fairport. If they aren't your bully, they're your buddy. Survival of the fittest rules apply." Grabbing my hand, not letting me respond, "C'mon. We don't wanna be late."

***

"Holy Virgin Mary, mother of God," Sage squeaks out as we exit my car.

Coming to a stand-still next to my son on the sidewalk, we gaze at the spectacle of an entire town spread out between several lawns. "How come when you say that, it takes on an entirely different connotation than when your grandmother uses the same phrase?"

Snickering, the little punk. "Exactly," is all he says.

Clutching Malcolm and Clover's gift to my chest, I wonder if it was appropriate to bring a gift in the first place. It wasn't mentioned, so I just did what my mother would have expected of me. Sage's vibrating energy draws my attention. The kid looks like his skin is quivering with excitement.

"Run along and find your *friends*," I prompt Sage, but he's gone, disappearing into the crowd before I get more than three words out. "Holy Virgin Mary, mother of God," I whisper beneath my breath, meaning it in exactly the same way as Sage. "Fuck."

The crowd is spread out like an ocean wave, impossible to discern who is whom in the waning evening light. Being tall myself, I use my height to locate Malcolm towering over all those who surround him.

Protectively clutching his soon-to-be bride to his chest, Malcolm chats easily with the townsfolk. He looks strung-out, though. "Welcome home, Mal," I say in greeting as I weave my way toward him. "How's our Officer Devon faring?"

Without releasing Clover, Malcolm leans forward to place a soft kiss to my cheek, lips lingering too long for friendly acquaintances. Awkward for me. Second nature for Malcolm. We've passionlessly kissed many times, and until recently, it was always on the lips. But never with his bride pressed between us, that's for sure.

Malcolm, without missing a beat, "Devon's doing better. Not great, but better."

"It's all we can hope for," Clover adds in, refusing to be ignored. Her territory-reclaiming tone makes me smile brightly. Good, their possessiveness is mutual.

"I didn't know the procedure, so I brought you a gift." I hand the wrapped box to Clover, thinking she will like my peace-offering best. "Just a little something I made up for you guys."

Surprise and delight light in Clover's eyes. Malcolm holds the box for Clover to tear into it. At his wife's ecstatic display, Malcolm rumbles the happiest sound I've ever heard him release. "You made all this?" Malcolm asks. His surprised reaction causes me to blush.

"It's nothing much," I say with a shrug, commenting on more than a dozen different scented homemade soaps. "I put in all of my concoctions. Just let me know which scents you prefer, and when you run out, I will replenish them."

"Wow, Opal," Malcolm draws out while fingering the homemade labels on the bars of soap. "Who would have thought our Opal was crafty," he teases me.

Blushing so hard my face stings. "It's nothing," I murmur.

"Thank you," Clover gushes while sniffing at the ginger and lemon grass bar of soap. "Mmm… this is fresh. I don't know if we should bathe with them, or just put them in a dish to scent the air."

Happy and thankful they like my gift, I reassure Clover, "I have an unlimited supply, so use 'em up."

Genuinely pleased, Clover says, "We will. Thank you."

I lean out of the way and start walking backward before Malcolm can lean forward and kiss me again. Affectionate in the extreme, sometimes Malcolm forgets we're in public and kisses me like he does when we're in private. I doubt the new Mrs. Mason wants her husband's lips on mine, even if it's not with a romantic or sexual connotation.

Breaking free from the crowd surrounding the soon-to-be newlyweds, I take a deep breath of air and release it in a gush. A sharp, shrill shriek spills from my throat when someone whispers, "That wasn't awkward," near my ear.

Laughing evilly, tickling my earlobe with the vibration, Rob curls his arm around my waist. "Never in my wildest imaginings did I think you could release such a sound."

"You scared the shit out of me," I gasp breathlessly.

"Naughty, Opal. Opal said a naughty word," Rob taunts in a sing-song voice. "Remember how hard you laughed when I made you beg for orgasms using dirty words?" Pulling away from me to stand so we're face-to-face, Rob's laughter is as infectious as an incurable disease.

"Keep your voice down," I warn in a trembling whisper. "I'm not embarrassed. But out of respect for Isis, don't spread that bit of knowledge."

The teasing lilt disappears from Rob's voice in an instant. "Isis was glad I was with you instead of a steady stream of skanks." Noticing my narrowed glare, "Isis's words, not mine. After being with you, I stopped my vengeance fucking. It wasn't worth it. I wanted to be a good influence on you, so you wouldn't go down my destructive path."

"You stopped?" I ask, surprised. Since Isis froze Auggie and Rob out of her bed and body, the guys have been fornicating a wide swath through Fairport and its surrounding towns as punishment. I believe it was more of a self-punishment than anything.

"Since I've been with you…" Rob tabulates his sexual partners in his head. "I've been with Beth twice." Rolling his eyes. "Auggie ruined all the fun in that. Since then, it's just been Auggie giving me blowjobs and only letting me give him a hand in return. Auggie's a total nutcase when it comes to sex. So being with you was a nice vacation from the lunacy. Oh, and I've been enjoying my licking duties."

"Licking duties?" I squeak out, intense heat infusing my flesh all of a sudden.

Rob's mouth twists up at the corners like he's thinking dirty, happy thoughts: big brown eyes heavily lidded, lips parted, and tanned skin flushing. "Oh, you'd like those duties," Rob purrs from deep within his chest. Said in a way that creates an image of Ginny spread out before me with my mouth feasting between her rounded thighs.

"Right now, my dysfunctional partners are ruining our lives, so I've had to adapt. Isis is a taker, hence my licking duties. Auggie is a giver, and I happily give and take. Without me, we'd be so frustrated, we'd be killing one another."

"I'm sorry," I try to sympathize.

"Not what I wanted to talk about," Rob abruptly changes the subject. Leaning into me, he makes a '*tsk-tsk*' sound near my ear. "You better put your twink on a leash before he gets his adorable behind arrested."

"What?" I half-shout, but Rob just keeps talking over me.

"Sage will be seventeen next month. Even though he looks like he's twelve, he's got enough hormones running through him to fuel ten boys his age. The kid reminds me of me. Sage is a peacock acting like a cat in heat."

I try to reason out what Rob is saying, but it's as if he's speaking in a foreign tongue. "I'm lost. Come again?"

"Look over there," Rob orders, tugging me to face all the kids. They are fanned out in a semi-circle near the side of the house. Unlike usual, Sage is behaving himself, hanging onto every word Weston says. West animatedly acts out something for Seth's benefit. Usually quiet Raven shouts '*LIZARD!*' Razzing her brother, Weston jumps two feet off the ground.

While I watch the kids interact, Rob continues to speak. "Weston is my nephew, for all intents and purposes, since my sister is marrying his dad and I've been with his aunt since I was five years old. I used to change Weston's shitty diapers, so I get some say in his life, I believe. I know West looks like a grown man, and no one knows he's gay since he doesn't advertise, but Sage better be careful of Dad. Malcolm doesn't fuck around when it comes to underage."

Still reeling from the fact that Weston Mason is gay, I just gape at the mammoth kid. All the while, Rob continues to school me on the perils of underage sexual predators. "West says he's not interested in your son, but he hasn't hit that hormone surge where everybody looks promising. I was only twelve when it hit, and it took Auggie until he was fourteen to catch up with me. A horny West will seek out Sage, and since both kids will be thinking with their dicks..."

"I don't see the issue with that," I mutter, confused as to why Rob is going on about this. "If it's mutual, and they are safe, there isn't a better kid I could pick out for my son."

"Wrong," Rob growls. "I will talk to both kids separately so they understand the gravity of the situation. Chief Mason is a real bastard when it comes to the law. Let's just say we all had our calendars marked with Isis's sixteenth birthday for different reasons. I was personally acquainted with having Malcolm's gun pointed at my crotch. He will not give two flips if it's mutual."

"Malcolm?" I draw out as a question. "The man who is a big teddy bear, pointed his gun at you?"

"Repeatedly… at my dick. Sometimes pressing the muzzle of the barrel against my jeans. The one time he caught me going down on Isis in the living room, he pulled the trigger. I pissed my pants, not knowing the gun was unloaded. I earned the nickname *Pissy Pants Robin* because of it."

"Holy Virgin Mary, mother of God," I mutter, shocked.

"So, hear me out. Looks can be deceiving. My nephew is only fourteen, and he cannot consent until he turns sixteen, no matter how much he may want it. Since Weston won't hit sixteen until well after Sage is eighteen, your son is fucked."

"What?" I huff out, heart beating out of control in my chest. "Malcolm wouldn't dare."

Stressing firmly, "He *would*. He *will*. I can guarantee it. It would *only* be statutory rape– and I say only because there is a period of time where West will still be fifteen to Sage's eighteen, where it will be a lot worse. I'm talking a sign in your front yard, informing the town of your residence, not being within so many feet of a school or playground sort of worse. Sexual predator. Got it?"

"Jesus Christ," I hiss, meaning it like my son usually means it. In a rush to save my child from a horrific fate, I seek out the blasphemer in question.

CHAPTER SEVEN

Ginny Jamison

Parties are only fun if you have someone to share in the insanity. I'm not too proud to admit how entertaining it is to make fun of the other party-goers. My usual partner in crime is the reluctant hostess, who obviously wants to go hide out in her tent with her man. Wandering around from group to group, I've handed out my business card to a few people looking to buy and sell property, and listened in to a lot of gossip. One bit of juicy chatter was about the reclusive Opal with an angelic boy in tow– the boy who's always hanging out at the No-Name.

I'm confused as to how I feel about this bit of information. Part of me wants to leave, because the dominant part of me wants to hunt the woman down and give her a piece of my mind– after I kiss her first.

The decision is taken out of my hands, because my quest to find nourishment puts me in Opal's direct line of sight. Wearing my comfy clothes– a baggy sack dress –the kind that isn't flattering in the least, I want to duck and hide before Opal spots me. Just as I'm weaving to the right, Opal hesitantly raises her hand, waving me over to join her and her son at the refreshment table.

"Hi," I mutter shyly, feeling uncertain and self-conscious. My heart starts pounding out of my chest at the way Opal is dressed. Wearing a flowing dress, with her hair mussed up in exactly the same way I fantasized about– thoroughly fucked is the best way to describe the sexy, reckless style.

"Hi," Opal responds, just as shyly. "I…" she stumbles over her words, eyes cutting toward her son, as if she wants to say something but can't in his presence. "Ginny, this is my son."

I learned a lot about the angelic creature known as Sage from the gossip mongers. Dressed like he just stepped out of one of those magazine ads, where the kids look trendy but slightly sexy in an androgynously creepy sort of way, Sage knows he looks good. Turning on the charm, his hand flexes like he wants to shake my hand, but custom demands I initiate. This proves my suspicions on the Fischers being a well-bred family.

Presenting my hand, "It's nice to meet you, Sage. I'm Ginny Jamison."

"Don't," Opal warns, eyes narrowing at her son. Confused as all hell by Opal's reaction, I shake the boy's hand as he chuckles evilly underneath his breath.

"It's very nice to meet you, Ms. Jamison," Sage says this in a manner that piques my curiosity. This kid is a naughty brat. I can tell.

"Don't you dare," Opal warns again, but this time her hand raises in a '*I'm gonna smack you silly*' gesture.

"I'm Sage Fischer, and I'm…" the kid pauses for dramatic effect, causing his mother to gasp. "A liberal," he admits gravely while hanging his head. As if he just said, "*I have cancer.*"

"What the fuck?" Opal breathes out, and then her hand flies up to cover her mouth like she never swears. "Why say that? I thought you were going to do that '*I'm gay*' spiel?"

Turning to his mother while wearing an evil grin, "I'm a liberal is what I say at parties now. Aren't we at a party?" Sage gazes around at the hundred-plus guests milling around the yards. "After I met all of Grandfather's asshole friends and co-conspirators, the '*I'm gay*' introduction failed to get a rise out of 'em. Last weekend, I created a new intro they found far worse. Now they look at Grandfather like he brought Satan's spawn to their parties."

"You didn't," Opal mouths, looking faintly ill.

Proud, Sage says without shame, "I did. Isn't it fantastic?"

Poor Opal is mortified. "You're going to give your grandfather a heart attack. As his oldest grandchild– a grandson no less –you have a responsibility to behave as such, Sage."

"Kid," I say to stop the shit-storm from brewing. "You're my new party companion. I bet the two of us could gossip about these assholes like nobody's business."

"Really?" Sage sings, getting excited. The kid is adorable in a demented sort of way. "I knew I'd like you, Ginny. Maybe you'll loosen Mom up a bit."

"Don't encourage him," Opal warns. "Sage will only amp up his '*fabulousness*'." Turning to her son, "Go find your friends, and behave."

"Really?" Sage responds, suddenly looking feral. "Because I might not be able to keep my dick in my pants, since you and Rob think I'm destined to live the life of a sexual predator." The angry young man stalks off. When he gets halfway across the lawn, Sage flips his mother the bird without missing a step.

"Whoa…" I murmur, impressed. Opal is intimidating on a good day. What will she be like when she's pissed off? "What did I just interrupt between the two of you?" Then I think better of what I just said, "None of my business. I apologize."

Sighing heavily like she's unaccustomed to being challenged by anyone, Opal turns to me. "Actually, it *is* your business. Rob brought it to my attention that Sage has his first crush."

"Aaawww," I drawl out. "That's so sweet. Whoever it is, is a lucky kid. Sage seems like he'd be entertaining, to say the least."

"Your nephew," Opal spews bluntly. "Sweet. Special. Unrequited at this point, thank God. But my kid is head-over-heels for Weston. So Rob brushed me up on the legal statutes of the age of sexual consent versus the age of majority."

Confused, I look to where Sage is entertaining no less than ten kids with his antics, Weston included. "So?"

"He might not look it, but Sage will be seventeen in July, going into his senior year. That's the why of it. I was told by Rob, from his first-hand experience, how Malcolm doesn't dick around when it comes to the law."

"Oh, fuck," I breathe out. "Poor kid. Weston looks and acts older than he is, but he's only going to be a freshman. My nephew is barely fourteen."

Opal leans against the refreshment table, looking emotionally strung-out. "Sage and I have this dominance contest on a daily basis. Sage is cute, and funny, and entertaining, and intelligent, and he looks more innocent and younger than he is. My son and I get along for the most part, but he gets upset if he thinks I don't trust his judgment. I *do* trust Sage infallibly. What I don't trust is his hormones, or when Weston's finally kick in."

"Word of advice?" I make it a question, not wanting Opal to think I'm butting in.

"Please," Opal nearly begs, and the sound sparks off an ear-gasm. Speaking of runaway hormones, my mind has this formidable woman begging for something else entirely.

"If something happens between those two kids, hide it– cover it up, and pray Malcolm doesn't find out until your son is off at college, and then don't let Sage come back until Weston is of age."

"Good point," Opal says with a smile. "Right now, I'm torn between being a good mother and a good citizen to someone else's child. It would solve it all if Weston continued to be ambivalent toward Sage. But the mother in me, the woman who knows what it's like, wants her son to get what he wants."

"I can understand that," I mumble, knowing how I feel about my nephews and niece, but knowing it comes nowhere near how Opal must feel about her son.

"Enough about everyone else for the rest of the evening," Opal declares. A zing of trepidation fires throughout my body, forcing disappointment to flow in my veins.

"Well, I'm…" I stammer out. "I guess I'll be seeing ya around." I turn to leave, but Opal's hand on my bare arm stops me in my tracks. My eyes widened with surprise as I stare down at the long, tapered fingers braceleting my forearm in a firm, restraining grip.

"That's not what I meant," Opal says softly near my ear. "I seem to lose all finesse around you, Ginny." With a sigh, Opal releases my arm and steps backward. "I want to apologize for last weekend. I wasn't myself. I was thrown by seeing you sitting there and knowing Malcolm set me up. Plus, something went down just before I met you, and I was feeling raw. Do you understand?"

"I think so," I reply hesitantly, not truly understanding what Opal is saying.

Opal reaches out as if she longs to touch me, and I want to say, "*Please, it's been forever since someone truly wanted to touch me.*" But I don't say anything. I simply step closer to Opal, hoping she can take a hint.

A small smile twists the corners of Opal's lips, and then she touches me. The warmth of her hand seeping into the small of my back is as much of a surprise as it is welcome.

The instant I saw Opal at the No-Name Diner, I knew I was done for. I'm not gushing about love at first sight, or insta-love, or even instant lust. Opal gained my curiosity– intrigued me – made me want to get to know her on a deeper level than some quickie in a club's bathroom stall. After too many failed, bitter romances, I've had a steady diet of sex without intimacy. My sexual habits remind me of my nutritional habits– unhealthy and devoid of nutrients.

Guiding me toward the refreshment table, Opal reaches for a paper plate. Handing me the plate, "I want to apologize for my behavior. As I said, I wasn't myself. I don't know how I insulted you. I just know I did."

Opal grabs her own plate, all the while her other hand never leaves the small of my back. Fingers flexing for an instant, her touch suddenly falls away, leaving me feeling disconnected. "Mmm…" she purrs. "This looks good. I'm starving."

As Opal leans forward to scoop up some fruit salad, her arm brushes the side of my breast. It seems innocent, and my breasts are large enough that they get in the way, accidentally bumping into everything.

"Are you cold?" Opal asks me as I stand as still as my shiver will allow. "I want us to do a repeat. I want to sit down with you and share a meal while we chat. No pressure of it being a date, okay? I just want to get to know you."

Instead of verbally agreeing, I just follow Opal's lead. I scoop a small portion of all the healthy stuff onto my plate, fearing Opal will think I'm a big, fat pig. I'll try to remind myself to take dainty bites as I eat, so I won't sicken Opal by the sight of the huge woman shoveling in food. I've been subjected to hundreds of vocal comments, and Lord knows what my dinner companions were thinking at the time.

"Are you sure you want to eat a piece of cake? Aren't you on a diet?"

"You can't possibly be that hungry. Why don't you only eat half, and save the rest for another meal."

"Bulking up for the apocalypse? I bet you could survive two months without eating."

"Coke? Don't you mean Diet Coke, Sweetie? I'll bring you a Diet Coke instead."

"There's almost as much food spilling onto your chest than what's going into your mouth. Are you saving it for later?"

My mood deflates as insecurities and a self-defeatist attitude assault me. With my hookups, I didn't care. The women approached me, so I knew they were attracted to what I had to offer. But this feels different, more important– fragile.

Leading me to a picnic table, I sit opposite of Opal. I pretend to eat as if I eat like this every day– slowly taking small bites of the various fruits and vegetables I'd placed sparingly on my plate. I'm so engrossed with my act, that I don't realize Opal is chuckling, until a hotdog overflowing with brown spicy mustard is placed on my plate.

"How about some phallic-shaped meat?" Opal says wryly, grinning at me from across the table. "I noticed you liked this type of mustard at the No-Name Diner. Ginny," she sighs my name like she enjoys the sound of it rolling off her tongue. "Don't pretend with me. It defeats the purpose of getting to know one another if you're faking it."

"I just... I..." I just keep stammering like an idiot, unsure how to explain what my malfunction is.

"First thing you need to learn about me, I'm blunt. Which my son inherited from his mother," she says with a humorless laugh. "Second thing you need to learn about me, I'm blunt to the point that I unwittingly insult my companions. I spend my days around patients and doctors, where my bluntness is a virtue. My only female friend is Isis, and you know how caustic she can be. Don't play games or be subtle with me," Opal warns.

Still suffering from a massive case of insecurity, I bite into my hotdog and watch Opal eat.

"I can tell you enjoy food," Opal says after she wipes her mouth on a napkin, and there is no censure in her voice. "There is no sense in hiding it from me, or anyone else for that matter. So just own it."

"You must be disgusted with me," I mumble, tears pricking at my eyes. It matters how people see me, no matter how much I may lie to myself. But I can't diet anymore– I just can't. I truly believe I'm at my natural body size, and to get larger or smaller wouldn't be my authentic self... and I'd be even more miserable than I already am.

A handful of chips appears in my line of sight, dropping them onto my crudité. "Another truth, since I can tell you're not able to talk yet. I spent the day with Isis, who offered up a plethora of information on you, Ginny."

"No!" I cry out. I want the earth to open up and swallow me whole. "Isis doesn't like me much." Understatement, that.

"I was under a very different impression, seeing as how Isis threatened to kill me if I hurt you." Opal's voice turns soft, intimate.

Surprised, my eyes flick up to connect with Opal's. "Really? She said that?" I've missed Isis every single day since she stopped talking to me eleven years ago. Isis begged me to keep her, but Malcolm wouldn't allow her to stay. Since that day, Isis isn't outwardly snotty to me, but she doesn't speak to me, either. We just share the same space and acknowledge the other's presence.

Thoughtfully nodding while chewing on a spoonful of potato salad, Opal politely waits until she's done swallowing before answering me. "Don't be self-conscious around me, Ginny. There is no point. I can physically see you sitting before me. Obviously you're voluptuous, which is impossible if you're sustained by a diet of raw vegetables," Opal says wryly as she eyes my crudité. "I was blessed with a fast metabolism, so no one would ever guess I am the unhealthiest eater on the planet."

"Bullshit," I challenge, interest piquing to the point that I don't realize I'm helping myself to the cubed cheese off Opal's plate until she pushes it in my direction. "Sorry," I mumble, feeling shame-faced.

Nonplussed over my reaction, Opal reaches over to grab my plate, and then dumps its contents on top of hers. "We'll share the wealth," she says to take the sting of my blush from my cheeks.

Opal changes the subject so fast, it's dizzying. "Sage's preposterous behavior is a direct result of my upbringing. My son is sticking it to my father in defense of his mother. It's sweet, misguided, and highly disrespectful. It annoys me to no end, yet it secretly pleases me. As you've no doubt surmised, I came from money– a lot of it."

"I came to that conclusion," I mutter, refusing to explain that was the reason I bailed at the No-Name. As the fat daughter of a cop and a housewife, I felt inferior to Opal's classy mien.

"Appearance is everything with the affluent. You have to maintain your status or you could lose it all. You'll note when I mention my past, I'll call the hospital where I worked *my* hospital. Since I was a child, my father has been the Chief of Staff, and now my ex-husband is the Chief of Surgery. There is a lot of politics involved if you wish to maintain your position of power."

"Oh, no." I cover my mouth as what Sage said comes rushing back in.

"I see you recognize my plight. Since I was a child, I knew my behavior would have a direct impact on my father's career.

No matter how good of a doctor Dr. Rick may be, he had to be an even better politician to keep the position. The way I dress, the way I talk, the job I hold, and even who I married, are all a direct result of my upbringing."

"And your son is against everything your father and his father stands for?" I prompt, assuming this is where the conversation is headed.

"Exactly. In order for me to truly be myself, I had to get away from them– move away –and I haven't been back since. Mostly, my need to stay away was born out of guilt and fear. Naturally, Sage resents my freedom right now. Until Sage graduates from high school, he is bound by his father's and my custody agreement. When Sage goes to his father's every weekend, Byron totes him around like an engaging show-piece. Sage is lashing out nicely, doing what I never had the balls to do when I was his age. Hell, I'm forty-three, and my balls still haven't dropped in regards to my parents. My son is my hero."

"I'm a liberal," I mock Sage, all the while snorting with amusement.

"Speaking of liberal– I feel liberated with my newfound joy in swearing," Opal says with a grin. "My son doesn't give a fuck if his behavior impacts his father or grandfather's career. Sage believes his behavior should only influence how people see *him*. Do I agree with him? Yes and no. There is a difference between familial and individual responsibility. Right now, Sage is spitting on our family just to be a dick."

Spying one of Clover's cupcakes on our community plate, I reach for it without shame. "Who can blame the kid?" I say a heartbeat before sinking my teeth into the divine treat. Purring, "God, that's good."

"I don't blame Sage– I applaud him." Leaning forward, Opal takes a bite out of my cupcake while I'm still holding it. Wide-eyed, I stare at Opal as she chews with her eyes closed. "I can see why Malcolm is marrying this woman."

"Clover used to be my dream girl," I admit, all the while staring at Opal's lips as her tongue laps up all the frosting. Another hormone-induced vision assaults my mind, involving that same tongue but a different set of pink lips. "I'm rethinking that now, though," I murmur dreamily.

"When I was a girl, I was subjected to the same incredibly boring parties as Sage. Only I wanted to chat science and politics with the men, not hear gossip with the ladies. I'd sit around the dining room table, watching all the woman pretend to eat while they drank too much in order to suffer through the evening. I promised myself I'd wear the mix-and-match expensive threads, suffer through the all-girls school filled with painful temptation, and do as my father bid in all things. But the one thing I refused to do was pretend to eat."

So involved in our conversation, I hadn't realized we had chaperones: Isis, Rob, and Auggie are sitting at the opposite end of the table, not even bothering to hide their eavesdropping. They watch us like we're a television show on HBO, and their popcorn is dozens of delicious cupcakes.

Opal is the one who drew my attention to them, as I finally figured out where her endless supply of treats is coming from. Reaching over, Opal plucks two more cupcakes from the tray Auggie is guarding like a hungry pig at a trough. Peeling the paper back from the bottom of the cupcake, Opal presses it to my lips, offering me more than a taste.

"Every kid rebels in some way. My kid just so happens to introduce himself as "*I'm Sage Fischer, and I'm gay.*' With the new codicil of '*I'm a liberal*'. I'm prim and proper, but everyone can see I'm over six foot tall– there is no hiding it any more than you can hide how much you weigh. I could not survive on the meager amount those heiresses ate. So I rebelled by eating like a full-grown man, and it infuriated my father to no end."

Thinking through Opal's moral, I find a glass of sweet tea to my right– no doubt Isis passed out the beverages as Auggie stole the tray of cupcakes. "So… what you ordered at the diner was your normal portion?"

Laughing while taking a fourth cupcake, Opal peels the paper back and pops the whole thing into her mouth. "That was me being prim and proper," she says with a wink. "Nurses are the unhealthiest lot you'll find. We range from morbidly obese to chain-smokers. We don't practice what we preach, because we know how short life truly is. My point," Opal stares me down unflinchingly, "Enjoy life while you can. Fuck liberal or conservative. I live in moderation."

CHAPTER EIGHT

Ginny Jamison

I've always been a girly-girl. My mom loved playing with Camille's and my hair, painting our nails, and doing facials. Mom loved bargain hunting, which inevitably created my obsession with shopping. I was the little girl with the pink room, pink ribbons in her hair, and would shriek at the sight of bugs and dirt. I was a momma's girl who loved baby dolls, tea parties, and Barbie.

For a few years, it was just Clover and me in college, and we kept up with the tradition of thrift store bargain hunting and do-it-yourself spa treatments. When we came back to Fairport, I lost my Clover time because she became a wife and mother. Shortly after, I lost my mother, and even when my sister was still alive, she was checked out of life.

In a need to connect with another human being like my mother taught me, I looked to Isis, showing her how to shop and primp. Isis allowed me to treat her within reason, but had no issue pushing me off. After Devon and Kieren, I was thrilled to have another girl in my family. But Raven has built a veritable brick wall around her person, refusing to let in the woman who looks so very much like her dead mother.

I hate stereotypes: Dyke. Butch. Lipstick lesbian. I'm just Ginny, but I've had many girlfriends who weren't good with me being *just Ginny*. From past experience, I learned those stereotypes are actually classifications, because everything needs a balance. I've dated girls who are just like me, and it was boring, and we spent a lot of time fighting over the bathroom. I've dated girls who were very masculine, who made me feel like shit because I loved all things pretty and soft and refused to exercise, enjoy the great outdoors, or play sports. Sarah was the closest match I found, almost a perfect balance… but that ended badly.

It's been years since I engaged in the joys of girly-girl with other women. A part of me is insanely giddy to be invited to the impromptu primp session. Clover's wedding is untraditional, to say the least.

Clustered in an office just off the Courthouse's atrium, Clover's entourage primps like nobody's business. Essie bustles from girl to girl, checking for a stray hair out of place or smudged makeup. Rae's doing that '*back the fuck off*' death glare that is ten times more intense than the average teenaged girl. Willow is issuing a death glare of her own– one that is screaming '*bring it, bitch. I dare you,*' every time Essie gets too near. The bride and her purple-shaded daughter are primping each other like monkeys searching for fleas.

It's pure chaos, with the cloying scent of hairspray and perfume wafting in the air, the chatter of excited women filling our ears, and the energy of many lives on the cusp of change. It's messy, loud… and absolutely perfect.

"May I?" I ask a silently brooding Isis. Without waiting for permission, I run a brush through her raven tresses. Isis allows me this small amount of affection without saying a word. We may not have had a meaningful conversation in over a decade, but I can still read her writing on the wall.

Isis is very upset. The position of daughter was torn from her when she lost her mother at birth. For a tenuous amount of time, Isis herself was going to be a mother, only to tragically lose the dream. The only thing she had left was the role of sister. Today was Isis's turn to play the sister in the wedding, only to have it stolen from her.

By me.

'*It wasn't my choice to make*', I long to tell Isis. But even if it had been my choice, I wouldn't have relinquished my post, even to her. I understand Clover's reason for choosing me to stand witness, and someday Isis will as well.

I know I'm welcome to brush Isis's hair, because she doesn't scream at me, launch heavy objects at my skull, or get up and run away. All of which I've experienced many a time during her teen years. Isis doesn't speak to me, either. But it's a vast improvement on our previous violent, silent conversations.

Relaxed, swaying slightly with the movement of the brush through her hair, Isis watches Essie's buddying belly with naked longing. My biological clock may be ticking away, softly saying I'm aging, so I better find a life. But Isis's clock is screaming to swallow her fear and finally accept the life she's always had.

Either brave or stupid, Essie steps in front of Isis while wielding a tube of mascara. "Everybody assumes your eyelashes are fake," Essie murmurs in appreciation to Isis.

"You know what they say about assumptions," Isis says without missing a beat, and she's actually wearing a smile.

"Ass," Willow snarls– her horrible acting skills crumble to pieces under the strain of her ex-best friend giving attention to another female. The gossip whore in me loves the strife, while the rest of me is sad over how everyone can't just get over their shit and hug it out.

As the last Jamison standing, I know all too well how life is too short to dwell on the past.

Essie, a woman proficient in Willow's mercurial moods, presses Willow's buttons to get a rise out of her. "I hope my baby has your skin, Isis. It's flawless, just like Devon's."

As if the topic is permission, Isis's palm finds its way to rest on Essie's baby bump. "It's a boy," Isis declares as if she's a seer. "What are you going to name him?"

"Now's the chance to stake your claim on your future children's names, Isis," I prompt. Eyes flicking over to Clover to make sure she's listening, "We all know your brother is like a jacked-up rabbit on Viagra. You better take the names before he puts a bun in Clover's oven. We have plenty of witnesses."

Blushing, unsettled and unsure, Isis stumbles over her words. "I… it's no big deal. Essie, your son deserves whatever name you give him, same with Malcolm and Clover's future kids."

Knowing Isis better than anyone in this room, my hand clasps her shoulder, pressing her into the chair before she can bolt like a spooked horse. "Isis calls dibs on Penelope," I declare. "We all heard it– let it be known."

Slowly turning to look at me over her shoulder, Isis is the epitome of shocked senseless: blue eyes as dark as coal, nearly popping from their sockets, mouth parted, and face flushed. "You remembered?" Isis breathes as if she's surprised I remembered something she told me when she was no more than ten years old.

"Remember the woman holding up the wall, over there?" I gaze at Opal for the first time since we said our hellos when I entered the room. Opal winks at me, lending me the strength to comfort Isis with the truth. "Opal was able to pump you for information on me all day yesterday. Well, that information flows both ways, baby girl. I remember everything you've ever said– no matter how big or small, it was all important to me."

Everyone in the room is staring at me like I have snakes slithering out of my eye sockets. I step away from Isis, knowing we both need the space before she gets emotional– not a pleasant sight to behold. It involves a lot of snot and violently thrown objects.

"Future Masons…" I muse, trying to get the women to at least blink. Their staring is making me uncomfortable. "Isis has dibs on Penelope. I have a feeling Auggie and Malcolm are going to have to have a death-match over the name John. But since I will never procreate, any of my sister's children can use their mother's name or my parents' names for their children. I would be honored."

Sensing my discomfort, Clover makes a funny, "I would be honored if none of my children, born of my body or otherwise, would name their children after me, or any other nature name for that matter. Let's break that ridiculous Prynne tradition."

"Ah, shucks!" Willow feigns disappointment. "Violet had her heart set on Poison Ivy."

"Shit yeah…" Violet drawls out. "Big sis ain't lying. I was gonna name my daughter Ivy."

Can of hairspray in hand, poised at the ready to spray Violet's hair, Clover mutters dubiously, "Seriously?"

Giggling, stealing the hairspray from her mother's hand, Violet nods her head. "Yes, I was being serious."

"I call dibs on Basil!" Willow jests. "In ode to Robin's horrid middle name."

Opal's sharp bark of laughter has all our heads turning in her direction. "Rob's middle name is Basil?" Her chuckles turn into girlish giggles. "Priceless. My kid's name is Sage, for fuck's sake. It's my maiden name, though. My father forced me to name him Sage."

"Is Opal possessed?" Isis breathes, watching her stoic friend swear with ease– and giggle.

Finally joining the conversation, Rae says from her post of sitting on the floor cross-legged, "Sage is awesome." Sullen mood changing to naughty. "Don't worry about naming your kid Ivy, Violet, unless it's a fur-baby."

Violet laughs, sticks her tongue out, and laughs some more. "Oh, I'm gonna have a Poison Ivy, even if it's a boy." Violet smirks at me, so I know the dig is going to cut deep. "Gin, don't worry about Rae stealing the family names. She's been drawing hearts all over her notebooks with the word *Zephyr*. Rae's gonna name her kids Oliver Junior… all twenty of 'em."

Pointing an angry finger in Violet's direction, "Shut it!" Rae demands. "Not true. Not a word of it."

Violet mouths, "*L. I. A. R.*"

"Fuck me," Clover sighs. "How long until all of my children graduate? Not long enough, I reckon."

"You're marrying Malcolm," Opal reminds Clover. "So it's a good bet that answer is always going to be eighteen years from the last time you had sex, until the day you go through menopause, just saying."

A horrified chorus erupts from Willow, Violet, and Raven. *"Eww!" "Gross!" "That right there is the best birth control on the planet." "I'm never having kids now." "The vision of our parents having sex is burned into my retinas." "Kill me!" "Seriously, best birth control ever."*

I find my way toward Opal as the kids razz Clover over her wedding night with Malcolm, and Isis starts lobbing baby names at Essie. "Way to start a riot, Ginny."

Blushing, "I even impress myself sometimes," I say self-deprecatingly.

Bumping her elbow into my arm, Opal leans down to whisper into my ear. "You always impress me."

Face flaming from a mix of embarrassment and arousal, I try to think sad, miserable thoughts to cool myself down. I've been in an odd state of bliss since last night. Opal and I stayed at the party until well after two a.m., eating cupcakes and chatting. We talked about things of importance and things of little consequence, all the while Sage laid on the top of the picnic table and snored.

Feeling like a teenager again, I woke up to my cellphone ringing. Opal. We chatted for a few minutes while I laid in bed, and we hung up only because we knew we'd be seeing each other for the wedding.

I have no idea what the future holds, but I've learned to live in the here and now. People come and go in our lives, and some day we will have the misfortune of being the one to go.

Opal understands this part of me– the part that wants to grip onto life with both hands, refusing to relinquish the stranglehold. I've lost too many people to ever pause and look back. As a nurse, Opal sees more loss in the hospital on a daily basis than most people do in their lifetime. I can't imagine having to give an endless stream of condolences. It was why Opal said nurses are unhealthy. Life is too fragile not to live it. You only get one go around.

I have no idea what the future holds, but I can wait to find out when I get there. I've already lived through the past, and I don't want to suffer through a rerun. All I know, right now, I like the balance Opal adds to my present.

"Your dress is lovely," Opal whispers heatedly near my ear, removing all my insecurities in an instant. I love the way Opal looks at me, like I'm a prize she's lucky enough to have won. No compliment will ever be as strong as the one shining from Opal's eyes.

Giggling like a besotted fool, "I don't know how you do it, but you make even the most conservative clothing look classy-sexy." Going beyond any of the flirting we've done so far, "I love how you never wear a bra."

Gasping, Opal turns her face away, acting as if no one has ever spoken to her in such a manner. Face flushed, eyes bugging out, I realize maybe no one ever has. A pity I will soon remedy.

"The first thing I noticed about you, when you walked into the diner, was how your nipples were beaded against your blouse– teasing the ever-lovin' fuck out of me. I went from hungry for food to hungry for you. You're my new diet plan, Mrs. Fischer."

Leaning heavily into my arm, Opal breathes into my ear, "Ginny. Oh. My. God. You have to stop before I implode." Blue eyes peeking at me from beneath the fringe of her lashes, something naughty flashes in their depths. Whispering like it's a secret, "The first thing I noticed about you was how badly I wanted to get lost in the valley of your breasts. So soft and sweet."

A fake coughing sound draws my attention. Clover is standing near us, hand covering her mouth in a mockery of a cough. "I need my maid of honor."

"Pre-wedding jitters?" I ask without missing a beat, but my face is as flaming red as Clover's. No doubt she caught the last of what Opal was saying.

"I'll leave you ladies to it," Opal graciously says to make her exit. "I believe I have a duty to preform myself. Isis is going to have a tantrum. I can sense it."

"If my brother finds his way in here, we'll have two screaming toddlers on our hands," Clover says as a joke, but she's being serious.

"I can handle Robin Prynne, even on a bad day," Opal murmurs more to herself than to us as she crosses the room to join Isis.

"Damn, girl," Clover draws out, barely holding her giggle at bay. "We so have to talk." Looking indecisive, like she's sworn to secrecy but wants to tell me anyway, "Damn."

"Damn?" I imitate Clover teasingly. "As in, damn?"

"Damn, as in, I have to go get married when I want details. Illicit and graphically explicit details."

"Got a thesaurus hidden in your sundress?" I joke. But then I admit the truth. "I have nothing to tell."

Laughing, looking blissed out, "Yet," Clover stresses. "Soon–" Whatever else she was about to say is cut off by Robin Prynne's arrival, which means it's time for the wedding… and Isis and Rob's temper tantrum for not being in the wedding party.

Will the wayward children ever grow up?

CHAPTER NINE

Opal Fischer

Conquering Auggie's favorite piece of furniture just for the fun of it, Ginny, Sage, and I sit on the antique sofa in the Spook House's living room. We're surrounded by the entirety of the Mason, Prynne, and Webster clans and their counterparts. Clan is the most apt description. We Sages and Fischers, we tend to stick together but not truly like one another. These clans are different. Even at odds, Willow and Essie seem to try their damnedest to stay mad at one another, catching themselves smiling and chatting on accident. The girl looked like she wanted to punch herself in the face when she inadvertently reached over to rub Essie's belly.

The blissed out newlyweds are across the street with all the doors and windows locked and their phones shut off. The residents of the home dubbed '*The Pink Taco Hut*' were ejected and told not to return until the following weekend. Another astute observation, these clans like to name their homes and freely share them with each other. The Spook House is filled to max-capacity with the refugees from The Pink Taco Hut and the *Shithole*, the Mason kids' new home that hasn't went through escrow yet.

"I miss Clover already," Ren whines while eyeing his plate of party leftovers. "You didn't poison it, did you?"

"You'll eat what I serve, or you'll starve," Rob barks at Ren, and then he smirks evilly. "Now, would I do that to you?"

"Yes!" comes from a dozen voices in unison.

Jumping up from her seat on the floor, Violet imitates a police officer, "Freeze!" Eyes flicking around the room to make sure we're all paying attention, "Everybody check your purses. Uncle Rob likes to steal your eye drops. Can you spell diarrhea?"

"Can you?" Seth taunts his twin sister, and then pops a dinner roll into his mouth.

"I don't steal eye drops. I steal EOS lip balm," Rob grumbles, blushing as hot as Hades. "It's for personal use."

"Is it because you dream of a supple sucker– oh, my bad. I mean pucker... or is it because you have chapped lips from kissing so many body parts?" Rory razzes Rob, and receives the middle finger in reply.

"Listen up, bitches," Rob calls out, gesturing with a slotted spoon mid-scoop of potato salad. "Clover taught my ass to cook, and I've been feeding myself since I could reach the stove. If you don't like it, your ass can hit the road. Got it?"

Eyeing her hamburger dubiously, poking at its bun, "We have nowhere else to go," Rae pouts.

Proving he doesn't buy Rae's manipulations after a lifetime of dealing with Isis, Rob sets the potato salad on the coffee table, and then mocks Rae. "We have nowhere else to go," Rob whimpers pitifully. Hands beneath his chin, he pulls off a Puss 'n Boots expression. "No home to call our own."

"You're mean," Rae whines, looking hurt.

"Toughen up, baby Vixen," Rob says in a syrupy sweet voice. "Eat, don't eat. Starve, whatever. But your ass isn't leaving this house until your daddy is..." searching for a PG-13 rated word... "Satisfied. Tonight we're having a sleepover with games and junk food. Tomorrow's breakfast is waffles, lunch is up to you to make for yourself, and supper is Taco Night with all the fixings. I'm Uncle Rob, and I let everybody do as they please. So you've got it made here, Raven."

"I'll stay here with you, Rae," Isis offers.

Not answering, Rae takes a big bite of her hamburger.

Auggie steps from the shadows, striding right up to Isis, and fiercely whispers something into her ear, which turns into a heated discussion none of us can hear– no matter how hard we strain to listen.

I turn to Ginny, who is avidly filing away everyone's reactions. I learn she loves juicy gossip when she leans into Sage and starts whispering. The two of them are peas in a pod. I'm happy they get along so well. But I feel left out since I'm not much for gossip. After years upon years of high society parties where gossip is a specialized skill used in order to survive your peers, I can barely suffer through it. Maybe Ginny would fit in with my family after all.

"How thrilling can the wedding night be after going at it like two crazed rabbits for the past month?" I ask Ginny to gain some attention. "My wedding night wasn't that exciting, and it was our first time together– my first time, period."

Smirking at me like she has a naughty secret, Ginny starts to say something, but then thinks the better of it when Sage leans in to listen. "Clearly, you've been doing it wrong," Ginny settles on, causing Sage to snicker.

"Did you know my dad is sixty-four years old, Ginny? I'm guessing he's been doing it wrong, since he always picks girls who wouldn't know the difference."

"Says Mr. Experienced," I taunt my kid.

"Your voice sounds sarcastic, yet your words speak truth," Sage dishes right back to me. "I bet I've kissed more boys than you have," he says slyly while looking as innocent as an angel.

"I should hope so," Ginny mutters, laughing, while Sage and I engage in an intense staring contest around her. We both know I've only kissed two guys sexually, Byron and Rob– Ginny doesn't know that –which means Sage has been naughty at least three times.

"Who?" I barely breathe, the threat of punishment thick in my voice.

Heavily lidded eyes and an arrogant expression are all my son gives me in reply. College can't come fast enough. Sage is my punishment for how I treated my parents. The last year of Sage's high school education is going to be a test of my sanity.

"Definitely not kissing me!" Rae chirps as she comes to stand in front of the sofa, hamburger clutched in her hand. "Aunt Ginny?" The girl takes a big bite of her burger, staring at us intently.

Reaching forward, Ginny brushes some crumbs off Raven's filthy t-shirt. "Whatcha need, Hun?"

"Dad said I'm to listen to you when he's not around. So I thought I'd ask you instead of Aunt Isis. Is it okay if I ask Opal if Sage can come to the sleepover?"

Sage's eyes look everywhere but at me, straying toward the ceiling. I glare at the side of my son's face as he tries and fails to pull off feigned innocence. Ginny, catching onto the plan, laughs outright at the idiots. "Well played, Raven. Well played," Ginny drawls in appreciation.

"What?" Raven's better at the innocent routine than Sage, whose lips are now curled up into a grin, even though he's still refusing to look at me.

A ruckus draws our attention. "Get off my back, ya boney bitch!" Ozzy shouts as Violet takes him to the floor.

Breathless, sitting on Ozzy's thighs while pinning his arms to the small of his back, "So that's how I brought the perp down," Violet says enthusiastically. "He was bucking around like a bronc at a rodeo."

"Get your knee off me. You're bruising my ass! You psycho bitc–" Ozzy protest, and Violet silences him with a firm hand tugging at his mop of curls, wrenching his head backward.

Eyes glazed as if high, Violet controls a snarling boy by yanking his hair. "See, Ozzy was struggling exactly the same as he is now." Winded, she laughs out, "He ought to learn a new trick, I suppose."

"I'll show you a new trick," Ozzy warns, but he's getting nowhere fast.

"Great form, V," Ren praises, while patting her on the back to let Ozzy rise. "I have an idea. Let's scrimmage in the yard." Hopping to his feet, "C'mon! To the yard!"

"Me first!" Willow shouts, running headlong toward Ren, only to hop onto his back. "I call dibs on my sister. Carry me, Stud. I gotta conserve my energy."

"Are they joking?" Flabbergasted, I turn to Ginny, only to find her laughing with Raven. "This is not normal."

"Who ever said we were normal?" Rae replies, and for the first time in a long time, she's glowing with life. "You can't beat the shit out of strangers," she says like I'm the odd one.

"You aren't supposed to beat anyone," I mumble to myself.

Standing in the middle of the Spook House's living room with Willow clinging to his back like a spider monkey, Ren claps his hands to gain our attention. "Okay, I'll referee. Here's the standings: Spanky versus Princess. West versus Ozzy. Aunt Isis versus Rob. Seth versus Rae."

"Me!" Sage calls out, jumping from the sofa like his ass is on fire. "Let me take on Seth." Turning to me with an eager light in his eyes, "Please, Mom?" he begs. "I promise to behave. I'll stick with Rae tonight. Let me stay. P-l-e-a-s-e."

No is on the tip of my tongue, and then Ginny rocks my world. Whispering in my ear so no one can overhear, "Let Sage stay. Rob will watch him like a hawk. Sage will never get this opportunity again. Let him be a kid. Trust me."

"I don't know," I grumble in indecision.

"This is just to occupy the kids so the adults can play bedroom sports, you get that, right?" Ginny breathes into my ear. "Let Sage stay, and you and I can go back to my place and sit in the hot tub and drink wine. I promise I'm not a heathen, my classy lady."

Everyone is staring at me, a 'c'mon, say yes,' glowing from their eyes. How can I say no to that? "Okay, but you have to behave," I warn.

"Yay!" all the kids yell in unison.

"Okay, we have a change. Seth versus Sage– winner takes on Rae. Spanky versus Violet. Isis versus Rob. Weston versus Ozzy. The winners of each round will take on each other until we crown the ultimate winner."

Auggie's booming voice fills the air, "I've got Rory, and the winner of our match will take on the lot of you."

Laughing, Rory calls back, "Better make Beth and Essie our medics, then! Let's go!"

"To the yard!" Willow shouts, kicking Ren's side to get him moving.

Stunned speechless, thoughtless, I watch the Spook House empty of its occupants in a rush of taunt wielding human beings. An older couple comes out of nowhere to follow the kids out to the yard. "My family uses their wits versus their fists. Dad didn't need to spank us when he could just humiliate us."

The living room is empty save for us. "Oh, this is so much more satisfying," Ginny says from beside me on the sofa. "It's the perfect way to settle any disputes and release all of your frustrations."

"I know Malcolm is from the school of thought– fight it out. But Clover is going to have a conniption."

Laughing so hard the sofa vibrates, Ginny turns to me with tears of happiness filling her eyes. "Who do you think taught Weeping Willow and Violent Violet to fight? The older couple who just skipped through here were Clover and Rob's parents– Dave and Mary. Anybody who created Rob had to be blood-thirsty."

At a loss, "Do we go watch?"

Full, pink lips curving into a devastating smirk, Ginny whispers a single word that intrigues me. "Nope."

"Nope?" I murmur, eyes never leaving Ginny's lips.

The Spook House is empty, silent– filled with possibility. A sense of intimacy descends on Ginny and me, as we sit on Auggie's favorite sofa, which reminds me of the empty Playroom overhead. A spark of lust fires up my spine, fueled by the knowledge that I may be getting what I want but never had the opportunity to receive.

Ginny gazes at me with hazel eyes that hold a depth of hidden knowledge that I've yet to learn or experience.

Suddenly shy, the unfamiliar feeling propels me to be brazen. "Have you ever visited the upper floor of this building?"

Silently laughing, "Nope," is all Ginny says.

"Nope?" I mimic, reaching out to run a fingertip along Ginny's pouty bottom lip. Her resulting shiver elicits the same reaction within me. "Hmm… would you like to?"

"Nope," is Ginny's instantaneous reply. Rejection and disappointment roll me over, taking me down. Heart stuttering, I prepare to leave, but Ginny's bright smile stops me before I can even move. "I designed my own playground– a playground with an occupancy of two. Care to visit it?"

My fingers find their way from Ginny's curved mouth to the back of her neck, where they weave in her silky, sandy locks. Heart pounding out of my chest, I take the leap of a lifetime. "Hmm… Sage is otherwise engaged in bloodsport. I seem to be free until morning."

Wanton.

I release the wanton creature my parents tried so very hard to smother. Leaning toward Ginny, I finally realize what had been holding me back from taking the life I was meant to lead. I've always accepted my attraction to the female sex, but never acted upon it.

The sin wasn't in the wanting. It was in the taking.

Oh, how I've always wanted. Longed. Hungered. Starved.

Moving to Fairport was not my liberation, it was my way of going into hiding. I hid from myself, more so than from my parents. My family knows what I am, and they accept it as long as I don't act upon it. Looking into my father's eyes and seeing the silent accusation glaring back at me was too much to handle. Running away, I could play pretend. Everyone in Fairport knows what I am, and they've tried to be helpful by thrusting temptation in my path– a temptation I threw back into their faces.

Other than our political affiliations and our views on a public versus private declaration of sexual orientation, I thought Sage and myself were one in the same. I was wrong. Not only does my son know what he wants, he takes it for himself because he knows he deserves it– he knows it's not a sin to want or to take.

Yet again, Sage is my hero.

I've finally found something that has a greater pull than my fear.

"Take me to your lair," I murmur as I lean into Ginny. Brushing my lips against hers, barely touching her skin, "Teach me to be who I truly am."

With a startled, throaty sound I will cherish for the rest of my life, Ginny bridges the gap between our mouths to fuse her lips to mine. Fingers weaving tighter in Ginny's hair, I pull her as close as possible. Turned sideways on the sofa, I press my breasts against her arm, luxuriating in the sensation of my nipples caressing her skin.

Shaking, my hands move to cup Ginny's face in my palms. Mouths opening on a gasp, I slide my tongue past Ginny's lips, slipping inside her soft, wet warmth. Tongue eager to meet mine, Ginny playfully coaxes me to kiss her harder. Her taste is sweet, intoxicating, just as a girl should be.

Stunned, I experience my first kiss with someone I truly want.

Surreal.

Control snapping, I roll Ginny beneath me on the sofa, straddling her lap. Her face in my hands, her mouth attached to mine, her tongue dueling with mine, her breath sweetly panting into my mouth, all doubt of what I want, of who I am, vanishes from one heartbeat to the next.

Nipping my bottom lip with her teeth, Ginny releases an embarrassed giggle– no doubt embarrassed for me since I'm acting like a teenager lost to their hormones. Wrapping her hair around my palm, with a firm yank, I give Ginny something to laugh about.

"You smell so sweet," I purr against her throat as my lips attack the sleek column of her neck. "I want the scent of my soap on your skin."

Meeting my challenge head-on, Ginny swivels on the sofa, rubbing her pillowy breasts against my tightly budded nipples. "No fair," I whimper, lips seeking her mouth.

"OH! MY! GOD! MY RETINAS!" Willow shrieks, causing my head to whip up. I meet her startled gaze, neither of us daring to blink. "What's up with that sofa? Is it laced with Ecstasy or some other lust-inducing drug? That sofa sees more action than a whore's cunt. Seriously, I take naps on that thing."

Groaning, I slide off Ginny's lap. "I love my privacy," I state boldly to both Ginny and Willow. Turning to the girl, "I'm sure you appreciate privacy, Willow. I'm sure we can call ourselves even after the memories I have about you, right? Memories I'd love to burn from my brain, too."

"Oh, right you are," Willow mutters, looking like she's going to piss her pants. "I saw nothing. Nothing." With a zip of her lips gesture, Willow silently promises never to speak of this.

"Somebody hurt?" Ginny asks, looking thoroughly amused.

"Nope," Willow bounces on her heels, ponytail bopping on her head. "We need water and sweat towels. So far, Violet's kicked everyone's ass. Even gave Ren a run for his money."

"Seriously?" Ginny and I say in unison.

"Seriously. I didn't nickname her Violent Violet for nothing. We've broken bones before," Willow says in a voice laced with immense pride. "Violet handed me my ass out there. When I left, Rory was taking her on, unable to catch her sneaky behind. It was too cute... Later," Willow chirps, skipping out of the room toward the kitchen.

"About that privacy..." Ginny throatily purrs. "Let's get some."

CHAPTER TEN

Ginny Jamison

Since I can't keep my eyes off of Opal, it's easy to recognize how I've rendered the woman speechless. Mouth slightly ajar, she does a complete three-sixty in my living room, taking everything in.

Nervous, I busy myself. "Wine?" I ask as I walk toward my ultra-modern kitchen. "It's the good stuff you're used to. None of that swill Malcolm plies Clover with."

Offering Opal the chance to get acclimated to my home, I take the time to allow the chilled bottle of wine to breathe while I prepare a tray of various cheeses, fruit spreads, and water crackers. I add two wine glasses and linen napkins to the tray.

"Proof that I'm not a heathen," I tease as I walk through the living room and out to my oasis– my patio.

I marvel to myself over how uptight Opal is, and how unraveled she became when our mouths were pressed together. The contradiction is thrilling. I want to see if I can make her come undone again.

I continue to ignore the fact that Opal is immobile in my living room. I flick the switch on the hot tub, getting the bubbles roaring, and then make my way to the stereo system. I select something low, gravelly, and erotic for our listening pleasure.

Sensing my eyes on her, Opal sighs, "I don't know what to say other than wow." Fingertips skating over the surfaces of my home, Opal looks dumbfounded. "It's not so much your belongings, or their expensive quality, it's that it's just so you. I don't know you, not really. But everywhere my eyes touch, I recognize it as you."

Leaning my hip against the arm of my sofa, I gaze around at my home as if seeing at it for the first time with fresh eyes. While tastefully done, everything is expensive. After growing up with just enough money to fill my belly, put a roof over my head, and thrift shop clothing on my ass, I've went the opposite direction as an adult. I have no children and no debts, so I can afford the very best I can provide myself.

"It is me," I admit without shame. "I've meticulously chosen every single item in this house, right down to the doorknobs. It's my fifth home, and the one I'll live in forever. I've upgraded to the point that I'd never be able to sell it. But that's not why I stay. It's just me," I say with a shrug.

Softly smiling to herself, Opal walks over my wall of pictures, ranging from before I was born to this year. It's all that's left of the Jamison family, with a tenuous thread weaving through the Mason children.

Studying the images, Opal says absentmindedly, "I have no attachment to my home. I moved into it, that's it. My son picked out the few personalized touches. When I lived with my parents, I understood it was my father's home. It wasn't a place to live– it was a place to show off. My mother feels just the same about the house she lives in– my father's house."

"How depressing," I grumble. "I'm not materialistic per se. I just feel that my home and my clothing are my versions of self-expression. My body isn't a living hanger, but the clothing I wear shows who I am on the inside as a person, as does my home. This is cozy, soft and pretty, and expensive."

Opal gazes at me from over her shoulder, lips curved with pleasure. "So very you," she says softly. Turning back to my framed pictures, "What was your mother's name?"

"Maeve Price, and still to this day, I can't say her name without my voice wavering. Hearing some kid shout the word Mom just about brings me to my knees," I admit for the very first time.

"Your mother was a beautiful woman, just as her daughters. Lovely," Opal compliments while running her finger along the picture frames. "So much history on this wall. Not unlike the wall in my father's study. Your father's name?"

Out of reflex, his name rolls of my tongue. "Barry Jamison. Dad was a big ol' teddy bear. All-around good guy. He loved to eat as much as I do. John– Malcolm's dad –used to tease my dad over failing his physicals."

"I want memories like the one that put such a beautiful smile on your face," Opal muses, looking at me but not entirely seeing me. "My mother's name was Gayle Wilkes," Opal volunteers. "Now she's Mrs. Richard Sage. Not Mom. Not Gayle. Not Mrs.

Sage. She is only known as Mrs. Richard Sage. Ironically, everyone calls my father Rick. Dr. Rick by his colleagues."

"What do you call him?" I prompt, knowing she wants to tell me for some reason.

"Dr. Rick." Opal tries to pretend it doesn't bother her, but she fails miserably. "Watching everyone while they got ready for Clover's wedding today, and then later at the Spook House, it was so chaotic. But they all love each other, know one another on a deeper level– truly get each other. Sometimes organized is just… sterile… and messy actually means well-loved."

"I'm sorry," I blurt out. "We were dirt-poor, white-trash without a pot to piss in. My dad was a lousy cop– a pushover. My mom had a mental illness. But we were well-loved."

"It's obvious," Opal breathes, eyes flicking back to my pictures. "How come you didn't have children? Well, aside from the not wanting a penis near you, that is," she stammers out, embarrassed that she asked such a private question.

"No one has ever asked me that before," I realize for the first time. "Straight or gay, I never would've had a child. The mental illness that weaves through our family is genetic. My mother had bouts that were torture to witness. Mom tried to hide it, and usually she succeeded. If Mom were alive today as an example versus the nightmare my sister left behind, I might have changed my stance on having children. But my sister was more imbalanced– the illness was harsher –fatal. I thank God every single day that it passed me over. But there were no guarantees with my children, with Camille's children."

"Are Malcolm's children okay?" Opal's voice breaks with terror.

My eyes close from the oppressive weight of the truth. "No, Devon's not just in drug treatment. His doctors have him a drug regimen for bipolar disorder, and are watching him closely. So far so good with Kieren. Rae's moody, but that's usual teenaged girl bullshit. Weston's too young to tell, but the outlook is positive."

"Oh, Ginny. No," Opal's voice is barely a flutter of sound. "I'm so sorry about Devon. I didn't realize."

"It's not an easy diagnosis, and the doctors couldn't begin until after Devon was detoxed. Malcolm brought that news back with him from Arizona, but we all suspected Dev was ill for a while now. We'll deal just fine." I admit, feeling hopeful. "They have made great strides with mental health in the past decade."

"Devon will get through it. After hearing all about John Mason, that man's grandchild will persevere."

I chuckle at that. "Sick of the '*John Mason*' speak, are ya?" Sobering up, "So now Devon is going to be a father, passing on our defunct genetics onto another generation. My mother was too ignorant to realize the severity of her illness, and then passed it to her daughters. My sister wouldn't have gave two shits either way. But I couldn't in good conscience bear children to satisfy my natural urge to procreate, only to force them to live a life filled with misery. It's both selfless and selfish thinking on my part. I wouldn't want to be in Malcolm's shoes right now. It's hard enough as the aunt."

"This is a big debate amongst my father's colleagues. I've met mothers like that. Ones who were given a fifty/fifty chance of their child carrying a genetic disease. One case in particular was gender specific. The sons would be born handicapped to the point of being bedridden, with the daughters being a carrier. People looked at me as a monster when I voiced my opinion against it. I'm not speaking of children already conceived or born, as if being handicapped isn't a good life. I'm speaking of those created to satisfy the mother's need to carry her own child, essentially sentencing their children or their children's children to live a life of disability."

"Exactly," I breathe, relieved Opal understands. "It was my choice to make, and I chose not to have children. With that saying, Camille's life, her children's lives, are precious. So I will never, ever voice these private thoughts with Malcolm or his children. Devon was a wakeup call– one we will all heed from now on."

"I'm sorry," Opal murmurs, eyes settling upon the last picture we took as a complete family. I was twenty-one and home from college for Spring Break, Camille was twenty-two and pregnant with Raven, our parents were almost forty. The children were hard-pressed to sit still: a fourteen-year-old Isis yanking on a six-year-old Devon's arm, all the while she was trying to hold a squirming and kicking toddler Kieren. Malcolm, not much older than Devon is today, with his head tossed back, laughing at the chaos his boys were creating. I loved this image more than any of the formal, well-behaved ones, because it was real, not staged for all eternity. A little over six months later, Camilla was committed, Malcolm was undercover, and my parents were dead, leaving me to fuse this family together the best I could.

"I need mass quantities of wine," I whimper as I turn to leave my living room and head out the French doors to the patio. A silent Opal follows me as I'd hoped. I stride over to the table where I'd placed the tray, and begin pouring each of us a glass of wine.

"Ginny," Opal says hesitantly, trying to earn my attention. When my eyes flick in her direction, she continues, "I'm… speechless."

Doing my damnedest to forget my dead and gone family, I gaze around my patio area, trying to see it as Opal is seeing it for the first time. A six-person hot tub, an outdoor kitchen, and a table and chairs. Past the patio, my fenced-in, well-landscaped yard is filled with an in-ground pool and lounge chairs.

"I grew up in a six-room house, and the only pool we had was made of six-inch-deep plastic my mom bought at a yard sale for fifty cents. I didn't own a pair of jeans that weren't new-to-me until after I became a realtor. Some would say, I'm over-compensating. Some would say, I don't deserve this when others go without. All the money my parents left when they died, all the equity I received when I sold their home, I gave to their grandchildren."

"I'm not judging," Opal tries to say, but I cut her off.

Rolling my eyes up to meet hers, "But I simply say, I fucking earned it." I hand Opal a glass of wine and retreat a few steps. I take a sip, appreciating the quality, the bouquet, the smoothness of the liquid sliding down my throat to warm my belly.

"I envy you," Opal declares. "I envy your ability to know what you want and take it. I was raised to only want what my father wanted me to have, and to only take what he gave me. He didn't even trust my medical abilities when I joined him at the hospital. My professors wanted me to further my education and become a doctor, but my father said no. The only reason I married Byron is because he saw past the fact that I had ovaries instead of testicles."

"Dr. Rick's loss," I say with complete sincerity. "Did you want to become a doctor?"

"Not really," she whispers. "But I would've been good at it. Dr. Rick wanted a son to follow in his footsteps, but he created several politicians instead. I was the only one who walked in Dr.

Rick's footsteps." Eyeing the bubbling water with unadulterated lust, "May I?" Opal gestures to the hot tub, and I nod in assent. "I don't have a bathing suit," she murmurs to herself as she toes off her sandals and begins to step out of her sundress. "Hope you don't mind."

"I envy *you*," I stress, as I watch in awe as Opal strips completely nude before my very eyes. My gaze devours the six feet of pale perfection that has never been kissed by the sun. Tall and lithe, with high, palm-sized breasts, Opal is shaped like a runner.

Smirking while blushing faintly, "I have no body shame," Opal says as she slips into the bubbling water. She moans in a way that turns off all my thought that isn't centered on her. "Ahhhhh… I'm in heaven." The tips of her light hair darken as bubbles splash up and soak into the strands. It's even hotter than her mussed up hairstyle from last night. "Are you getting in?"

"Uh…" I hesitate, scared to allow Opal to see me in a bathing suit.

"Join me," Opal beckons, simultaneously looking inviting and lonely. "I have no body shame because I'm a medical professional. I see dozens of patients on a daily basis. My father examined my mother, myself, and my siblings, and when I was older, I assisted him… Then the Playroom with its twenty-one to death's door naughty Playroomers."

Worry slams into me, a worry stronger than my fear over my chub. What if Opal only sees me as another naked body, like those in her hospital? I want her to see me as a sexual being, even though I know I'm not built perfectly.

Wanting more, I find my inner courage to ask Opal outright instead of wavering in self-doubt. "I know you won't find me attractive, but I fear you'll only see me as you see your patients, telling me to lose weight and asking about my cholesterol level and blood pressure rate."

A deep chuckle warms my ears and causes a blush to bloom on my cheeks. Opal takes great joy in my fear, laughing deeply from her taut belly. "Do you try to sell your family and friends homes? Don't you turn off the realtor in yourself when you're interacting outside of sales?"

"Well," I draw out, and then begin laughing uncomfortably. "Until recently with Malcolm and Ren, that would be a yes." I eye my very large, black bathing suit with trepidation. Even tailored to be formfitting and to drape in the most flattering ways, it still doesn't hide the fact that I'm a size twenty with a large belly and jiggly thighs, and an even larger pair of breasts. I wish I was built like Opal, where I'd have no body shame, and no one would gaze at me with disgust over my gluttony.

Staring at me like she knows the direction of my thoughts, Opal continues the conversation as if we aren't having another one entirely inside our minds. "Unless someone needs assistance, I'm volunteering, or I'm wearing a pair of scrubs, I turn that part of me off." Humor fading, voice twisting into something more intimate, "Trust me when I say, I will only see you as all woman."

"I…" I hesitate as I reach for my bathing suit where it lies on the table. "Okay," I mumble when my fingers come in contact with the Lycra. "I'll be right out in a few minutes," I say in a rush, in a hurry to flee.

"Ginny?" Opal calls out after me, stopping me just as I enter my living room. "No bullshit between us if we're going to do this." Voice lowering, becoming husky, "I'm naked, and I want you to join me."

CHAPTER ELEVEN

Opal Fischer

I truly didn't think Ginny would come back to join me. For many long minutes, she stood in her living room, debating on whether or not to don her bathing suit. I worried she wouldn't join me either way, clad in too much fabric or naked as the day she was born. I was happy with either way, even if she decided to hide her body from me.

I lean my head back against the edge of the hot tub, luxuriating in the warm, bubbling water. I've been in a few spas in hotels, and heard women gloating about owning hot tubs both in their bathrooms and in their indoor pool areas while suffering through Father's parties. But we didn't own one growing up, and I never thought to purchase one for myself. I'm rethinking my stance on exorbitant spending, just as long as it enriches my everyday life.

I feel extremely enriched at the moment, as I rest in a hot tub while sipping high quality Riesling.

Sheepish, skittish, Ginny peers through the French doors. I pay her no mind, allowing her the time to sheer up her courage. With a deep breath, she comes back out to the patio, bathing suit in hand instead of covering her creamy skin.

"Close your eyes while I get in," Ginny warns, sounding grave.

Smirking, I allow a bit of Sage's deviousness to fill my eyes– the deviousness he inherited from his mother. Slowly my eyes shut, not planning on staying that way for longer than a few seconds. Speaking of my father, listening to Ginny speak of her family, I promised myself there was no sin in the taking any longer.

The sin is in regret– regretting all you didn't do when you had the chance. Life it too short to live miserably by not taking risks because of fear of the unknown and the judgment of others.

My eyelids take a risk when I hear the whoosh of fabric landing on the tile floor. Peeking like a naughty child, I avidly watch as Ginny unhooks her bra, unleashing her mammoth pink-tipped breasts. Being on the smaller size of a B-Cup myself, I have no idea what size Ginny's breasts are, but I instinctively know they bypassed DDD several sizes ago.

Mouth gaping, eyes bulging, thighs clenching against the insane rush of lust that flashes within me, I openly stare at Ginny's breasts as they jiggle and sway as she steps out of her lacy panties. Sensing my attention, Ginny quickly slides into the tub, but it doesn't hide my newest obsession since they float, plumping them up even more.

"You peeked," Ginny whines. "No fair."

Swallowing thickly, my eyes never rise past Ginny's chest-level. "I never said I'd close my eyes, now did I?" I tease in a sluggish lust-drugged voice.

"Stop looking at me like that," Ginny demands, but I can hear the pleasure in her voice. "You saw my belly and thighs."

"Actually, I didn't," I answer honestly. "I was fascinated– too busy fantasizing about burying my face between your gorgeous, soft breasts… and don't act like a modest virgin. I've heard the gossip."

"I'm not being modest," Ginny protests, patting her hand on the surface of the water, splashing the both of us while making her tits jiggle even more. "I think you're blind!"

"I think that if I wanted to touch a women who looked exactly like myself, I'd masturbate," I say with blunt wryness. "Since I don't have soft, sweet smelling curves, I tend to notice those who do." I voice the truth I've always tried to ignore. "If I had a type, she would be you. My eyes always rove toward curvaceous women. Even my faux-lover Bethany Essex isn't a dainty thing. My mother is stick-thin with misery in her eyes. Lord knows, I'm only thin because of genetics and a fast metabolism. You look soft, comforting– like home."

It's Ginny's turn to gape up at me. The fear in her hazel eyes is replaced with intense longing and barely veiled lust. "What's it like being with a man?"

I volley back, "What's it like being with a woman?"

Instant surprise crosses her features. "You've never been with a woman? Ever?" Shifting in the hot tub, Ginny reaches for her wine glass, completely forgetting that she's now flashing all that perfectly fleshy skin above her belly button.

If I don't buy a hot tub in the near future, I hope Ginny doesn't revoke my privileges, because the combination of bubbling hot water, smooth wine, and Ginny's naked breasts is pure decadence.

I answer her question with total honesty. "Until I kissed you this evening, I'd never touched another woman prior. I never gave into temptation, knowing I'd never be able to go back to the life I was living."

A soft, surprised laugh rolls from Ginny's throat. "I was maybe ten years old when I figured out I liked girls. I didn't come out until I was in college, fearing my parents would put a stop to my slumber parties." Laughing, looking amused by her past behavior. "As for those rumors you've heard, they're most likely true. I was shameless. All the girls around my age came to me to teach them how to be touched and like it. I created a generation of women who made sure the boys in their lives gave them orgasms, and their boyfriends appreciated it."

"I don't know how this works without the standard of virginity," I fumble over my words, feeling inadequate when it comes to lesbian sex. "How old were you when you lost your virginity?"

"Ah," Ginny purrs, getting clued in. "Twelve," she answers without a hint of ignominy. "I've never been penetrated with anything but a finger or a tongue, and a wide variety of toys. No male flesh, for sure. I've never even seen an aroused guy, let alone touched one. But that doesn't make me a virgin. Sex is sex, whether it's with a man or a woman. It's called oral *sex* for a reason."

"I'd often wondered that," I muse to myself. "Wondered if lesbians considered themselves virgins because they've never met the societal and religious standards of sex."

"It's a cop-out to say otherwise," Ginny says quickly. "When I was a teen, I considered myself a virgin. I was with a bunch of straight girls, going down on them, getting them off… I loved every minute of it. But it wasn't until I had my first long-term lover that I realized I was being juvenile by protesting my virgin status while my face was buried in my lover's pussy. If I was as worldly as I believed, then I was being a child by claiming virginity."

"I was twenty-four when I lost my virginity, so I can relate to why you'd hold onto that label. My parents and my priest tied a female's virginity to her pureness of faith– total religious propaganda, since losing my virginity on my wedding night was something that was required of me. So explain how it would damn me to Hell two minutes prior to the '*I dos*' versus doing my wifely, Christian duty afterward. Yet the man is never preached to about saving his first penetration for his wife. I was Byron's first wife, and he was no virgin at forty-five."

"Today, virginity isn't about purity. It's more about using shame to control women," Ginny breaks into my diatribe. "Most often, the women are worse than the men when it comes to the shaming part, making it easier for the men who are fucking the women to control them. But, before, I believe it was put into place to guarantee genetic bloodlines when there was no DNA testing. If a girl is banging a bunch of guys out of wedlock, who's the daddy?"

"Ah," I grunt out in appreciation. "A woman after my own heart. Way to get me hot and bothered by discussing religion and medical technological advancements," I tease.

Ginny smiles at me faintly, as if she's worried that what she will say next will upset me. "I don't practice any form of organized religion. I just know right from wrong, and live by my own set of rules."

Surprised by Ginny's admission, I ask, "Are you worried I'll take issue with that because I still consider myself Catholic? Because I don't care. If you ever want to have a theology versus science debate, pull up a chair at the Sage family dinner table. My son, more often than not, comes home hoarse from shouting."

Smiling faintly, "I was worried, actually. My lack of faith isn't about my lesbianism, and the virginity thing was just because I was confused. But after hearing a bunch of girls I'd given more than twenty orgasms to, by having my tongue spear their cunts and asses, tell their boyfriends they were virgins, I decided they were lying to themselves along with everyone else."

"We all lie to ourselves," I muse.

"But we shouldn't," Ginny scolds me. "I was born this way, and I can't do a damned thing about it, nor will I ever apologize for it. I'm not a label: woman, lesbian, fat, blonde, tall, white, virgin or whore. I'm Virginia Jamison– deal with it."

It's my turn to laugh uncomfortably. "I've only found one other person I could talk to like this– Isis. The total acceptance of oneself, and anyone else be damned. So refreshing," I murmur in awe. "Never in a million years would I have said the two of you held a similar belief system."

I needn't have worried about offending Ginny. A glow of pride fills her face. "I can take a lot of credit for that. I was going through one of my first bitter break-ups when Isis was discovering Rob and Auggie. Back then, I was the one she came to for advice." Sounding wistful. "Back when Isis still spoke to me, that is. Plus, you will find my nephew has a similar stance, more so even. He's Weston Mason– deal with it."

I shudder, even with the heat of the hot tub. "Heaven help us when Sage finally catches Weston's eye. *I'm gay* Sage and *take me as I am* Weston."

"Whoa…" Ginny drawls out, contemplating the ramifications. Changing the subject back to her original question, "What's it like being penetrated by a man?"

"Odd conversational transition, but I can see where two guys together would make you think of that subject."

I shift in the tub, reaching for my wine glass, only to discover it's empty. Without shame, I rise from the water to cross over to the table, all the while feeling Ginny's eyes devouring me. The sensation of her eyes following the rivulets of water sluicing down my thighs warms me more so than any gaze before. Somehow knowing it's Ginny staring at me with barely veiled lust, makes it more intense than any of the attention I've received at the Playroom.

I refill my glass, and then walk back over to Ginny to refill hers as well. As I lean over, her fingertips trail a bead of water sliding down the back of my thigh. A jolt of pure energy shocks me to my core. I whisper to myself, "You're so soft."

Climbing back into the hot tub, I decide to explain my past liaisons to Ginny, knowing I'm explaining it to myself at the same time. Settling back against the side of the tub, I want to sit closer to Ginny. But, at the same time, I want to see her facial expressions as I speak my piece.

"It's all I've ever known. My ex-husband is more than twenty years older than me. By the time we'd married, he'd already sowed his wild oats, so to speak. Byron's more cerebral than physical, so we didn't even kiss before our wedding night."

"He knew," Ginny breathes so softly I have to read her lips over the whirling noise of the tub.

"Byron sensed I was a lesbian," I agree emphatically. "We held hands, hugged, and kissed on the cheek and the forehead. Our wedding night was slow, painless, and filled with adoration. It wasn't about lust or passion– and I didn't know there could be such heat at the time, so I didn't know I was missing it."

"Someone showed you that?" Ginny sounds shocked and extremely curious.

"Yeah," I admit hesitantly, refusing to say Rob's name, knowing that revelation would turn Ginny off quicker than anything. "Byron wanted a child, but not as badly as my father wanted a grandchild. We were lucky to have a son early on in our marriage. I had a tubal ligation since we were thankful for Sage, knowing he was enough for us. So sex became an intimacy we shared twice a month on a scheduled day. Our lives revolved around the hospital and our family. Sex wasn't a priority. But when Sage came out of the closet, I realized I was young compared to my husband, and the feelings of longing and regret inundated me."

"Oh, Opal," Ginny cries out, reaching over to brush my hair off my forehead in an act of comfort. "Even when I was down on myself after horrible breakups, I still sought out physical attention. I can't imagine."

Ginny's sympathy makes me feel warm inside, so the need to reassure her overpowers me. "It might've not been passionate, but Byron and I did have love. I used my fantasies when I masturbated to satisfy my natural urges. But the sex between us was lovely. Byron never failed to satisfy me. But a few months ago, another man showed me just how much was lacking in my marital bed."

"You're bi, then?" Ginny squeaks out, recoiling from me.

"NO!" I shout, fearing I'm scaring her away. It's the main reason I will never release Rob's name. "With Byron, I'd never even had oral sex before, giving or receiving. All sex was in the biblical sense. When I found out Byron had a live-in girlfriend, it hurt. So I sought out attention, thinking to punish Byron but more so myself. It ended up being the best experience of my life– rewarding and educational."

Voice tight, "Do you still want to be with him?"

"Yes and no," I admit honestly. "I would enjoy his attentions again. It was passionate and intense. I find him attractive because he's my friend. I found the sex incredible because he's *that* damned good at it. I have a connection with him, and I enjoy being connected to him during sex. I may be a lesbian, but that doesn't mean I don't enjoy penetration."

An odd expression crosses Ginny's face. Not offended or sickened, more like she's curious and wondering if she's missing something. The light in her eyes scares me. In no doubt, it's the same look I had in my eyes when I asked Rob to fuck me. Ginny said the rumors were true, the rumors that worried me since I am as inexperienced as she is experienced. Those rumors mean Ginny's curiosity will get her into major trouble fast.

Ginny says the words I feared most, "I want to be penetrated." She's almost pouting– plump lips pursed with her hazel eyes glazed over with want.

"Hmm…" I purr, trying to divert Ginny's curiosity with my own. Raising all ten of my fingers, while licking my bottom lip, "I can do that for you, Ginny."

Pink mouth dropping open in shock, Ginny's hazel eyes bug out of her head. I watch her throat work as she swallows convulsively, trying to form words since my gesture rendered her speechless.

"If afterward, you are still curious, allow me to help you with this, Ginny," I beg, fearing Ginny going off to a skeevy club and being taken in a bathroom stall by some slimy douchebag with a disease. "You know my Playroom status, and I've known these people and their desires for over four years. Promise me," I demand.

"I promise," Ginny says, taking me seriously. "But only if you use those fingers on me tonight," her voice drips with lust. "It's fair. I really, really like you. I think you and I could be close friends, and wait and see if we could be more. You've only been with men, and I've only been with women. I want us to be equals. So promise you'll let me explore if we decide to have a relationship."

"I promise." When I make a vow, I keep it. Even though Byron and I are divorced in the eyes of the government, we will always be married in my soul and in the eyes of the church. My being a lesbian will never break that bond. Nor will my bond with Byron ever lessen whatever bond I may build with Ginny. Voice thick with need, I rasp out, "Now… I want to taste you."

"Do you want me to taste you first?" Ginny offers eagerly, eye glowing brightly with lust.

I just shake my head no as I slice across the bubbling water, with Ginny as my destination.

Warm water caresses my body like a lover's kiss as I make my way toward Ginny. Her eyes never leave mine, as if frightened a blink will render me a mirage. I'm scared myself, shaking so badly the water would be wavering if it wasn't for the hot tub jets. I want to make excuses and apologies for my lack of carnal knowledge. For once, my shame involves not knowing what I should instinctively know as a lesbian.

I don't know how to do this… how to please Ginny.

I may not know how, but I want to so badly it's a physical ache.

As with all things, I stop thinking and let my natural instincts control my actions. I want to kiss Ginny's pouty pink lips, and as if she knows my secret thoughts, the tip of her tongue sneaks out to wet her bottom lip in anticipation.

Where to begin?

Nowhere?

Everywhere?

With a kiss?

Yes, with a kiss. Never breaking eye contact, neither of us says a word as I lean in to capture Ginny's mouth with a hesitant kiss. Water separates us like an unbridgeable expanse with the exception of our mouths pressed softly together. I sigh in relief, the sensation of longing finally being fed.

Ginny's fingertips trail along my cheek– the gentle caress causes my eyes to flutter shut in pure bliss. "You're so soft," flows into her mouth from mine. "Creamy. All I've ever known is a male's touch. My ex-husband's hands are calloused, as are the men who've touched me in the Playroom. With the exception of *him. He* is very soft, but nowhere nearly as delicate as you."

"I'm cushiony," Ginny sputters self-deprecatingly against my lips, causing me to snort.

"Don't change on my account," I breathe huskily, and then I finally draw us together.

Finally.

"Christ," I utter as a benediction. Ginny may be an atheist, but I was born a Christian as surely as I was born a lesbian. God made me this way, and I finally take in the bounty He offered. Surely there is no sin in something as pure and pleasurable as the sensation of Ginny's pillowy breasts pressed softly against my chest.

Nervous, shaking, I draw closer, sliding down until the buds of Ginny's nipples rub against mine– the water making it more slippery than the rub of friction. We moan in unison– mine deep, hers throaty and thready. We move together: sliding, rocking, writhing, causing waves in the tub to splash over the edge to dampen the tile floor. We keep ourselves apart, except for our resting lips and our stroking nipples. My hands ache to touch Ginny, to squeeze, to caress– to impale. Our flowing movement is glorious, erotic– the hottest sensation I've ever experienced. Our nipples not only greet and become acquainted, they move straight into fornicating.

Ingenuousness forgotten, instinct takes over as my mouth seeks Ginny's again in a searing kiss like none other I've ever experienced before. Her mouth parts on a gasp when my palm seeks out her breast. Using her exclamation to my advantage, I thrust my tongue into her mouth for our very first penetration.

I've always denied myself, because there is power in the denial. Unearthing my self-control made me feel invincible, even as it made me feel lonely with long-forgotten desire. Now I find power in unleashing my desire for Ginny, in realizing she is exactly what I've been waiting for, why I never gave in until tonight. She may not believe in fate or faith, but I do. We were placed in this moment for a reason, and I will take His lesson as His acceptance in my sexual wants and needs.

"I'm in heaven," spills from my lips as I manipulate Ginny's left breast with my palm and fingertips. Overflowing my hand, I've never felt anything so feminine in my entire life. With the rhythmic squeeze of my fingertips, my eyes become heavily lidded with intense lust. My new obsession with Ginny's breasts rages into an inextinguishable fire– I'll never get enough of her flesh. She wiggles against me, using her body to communicate her desires.

I may love the press of our mouths together, but I let off for Ginny's comfort– panting wildly, barely catching her breath, unable to kiss me back. Eager, impatient for more of Ginny, my hands slip beneath her armpits and lift. Following direction, Ginny rises to sit on the edge of the hot tub without so much as a word of protest– her earlier bashfulness completely forgotten by the force of my yearning.

Half in, half out of the hot tub, Ginny allows me to feast on her, to take my fill before she touches me back. We are both working on instinct. Whereas she is experienced with women, she isn't experienced with me. Yet Ginny somehow knows her touch would be my undoing.

Kneeling in the tub, with a goofy grin plastered on my face and my eyes held wide in wonder, I palm both of her breasts, squeezing and squishing, watching them jiggly and warble from my manipulations. Ginny's giggle makes me pause. My eyes flick up to hers, worried I'm making her uncomfortable. But she's only laughing at my enthusiasm, with obvious delight etched across her features.

"You're in trouble," I warn. "I'm going to rest my head," I roughly palm her right breast, "Right here, while we sleep tonight."

Plucking Ginny's nipples in utter fascination, I slowly lean in to take a tightly beaded bud into my mouth. Ginny shivers and moans as my tongue lightly flicks her nipple, causing a shiver of my own to run up my spine. Then she releases an ear-piercing scream when I sharply bite–blunt teeth clamping hard on her flesh. Apologetic, I give her a soft lap of my tongue as I pull away, but her fingertips twist into the damp strands of my hair, pressing me tightly to her breast.

"More," Ginny moans, pressing me harder to her nipple. "Gimme more." She roughly rasps, "Harder."

Groaning, I almost orgasm when my teeth compress her nipple, nearly meeting through her aroused flesh. The sensation of my teeth and the sound of my ecstasy is the catalyst that finally snaps Ginny's control. Hands fisting my hair, she rubs my cheeks, my lips, my forehead, even my teeth against her breasts.

Ginny, knowing exactly what kind of reaction her touch would elicit, slides a rounded, smooth thigh between mine, caressing the flesh only a man had ever touched before– even my doctors were men.

"Ginny!" I shriek in a high-pitched feminine tone. I come undone, frantically orgasming from the smooth slide of her soft thigh caressing my slit. Her knee grazing my clit is the final touch that pushes me over the edge. Moaning in utter disbelief, I feast at Ginny's breasts: teeth gnawing, lips sucking and kissing, tongue lapping.

An eternity later, I come back down, mystified to discover my fingers impaling Ginny's flesh. Instinct was driving the bus as I climaxed, making sure Ginny was right there with me. Eyes drooping in a lust-induced stupor, Ginny slouches against the side of the hot tub, coming back down from the throes of passion.

Unsure where I want to touch, where I want to look, what I want to taste… Ginny is a veritable smorgasbord of pure, unbridled sex, and tonight, she's all mine for the taking.

Shaking, but more so from restraint than from nerves, I slowly slip my fingers from Ginny's spasming flesh. A whimper is torn from my throat at the sight of her cream coating my fingertips– I did that. I made Ginny orgasm. I put that satisfied uplift to her lips, the glazed look in her eye, and the flush on her breasts.

Limp, sprawled, Ginny no longer has a single insecurity when it comes to me. She is confident that I want her in all ways. Flaunting her curves, there isn't an inch of skin that isn't on display.

I did that to Ginny. I made her comfortable, secure– replete. I did that.

Nuzzling her soft, rounded thigh with the side of my cheek, I luxuriate in how smooth and creamy Ginny's skin is. It's intoxicating. Shuddering with waves of aftershocks, I touch her gently, not wanting to over-sensitize her. My soft brushes turn into a peppering of kisses.

Nudging her thighs apart with my chin, I catch a whiff of her sweet scent, and it renders me immobile. I simply stare between her legs for long minutes, marveling over how Ginny trusts me this much, over how this is truly happening. Pink and puffy from arousal, a bead of moisture trickles enticingly from the entrance hidden by her swollen lips. Ginny is beautiful between her thighs, turning me ravenous. Suddenly thirsty, I crave her taste, fantasizing about lapping at that rivulet, causing more cream to pool from her entrance to satisfy my new-found thirst.

"As you can see," Ginny's voice draws me from my inner musings, "I'm a natural blonde," she teases, trailing a giggle.

Playing along to abate the heavy emotions inundating me, "Hmm… I can't be sure. Ms. Jamison, I think I must examine you further. You may have dyed your pubic hair."

"Oh, Nurse Fischer," Ginny draws out in a purr-like tone, "By all means, conduct your examination. But a word of advice, I believe the only method that will determine whether or not I'm a true blonde…"

"Is with my tongue–" "–is with your tongue," we say in unison, and neither of us laughs afterward.

Overwrought with conflicting emotions, my fingers gently bracelet Ginny's ankle, drawing her shapely leg out of the water. I reverently kiss her knee in thanks for the epic orgasm it provided me, causing Ginny to gasp in shock. My tongue sneaks out to lick a smooth line from her inner knee to the inside of her thigh– a hairsbreadth from her blonde-flecked nether lips.

Heart beating in my throat, nostrils singing in glee at the exquisite scent of Ginny's cream, I take a deep breath and throw all my worries out with my '*reluctant-lesbian*' status. I'm no longer reluctant. I'm positively fervent in my desire to conquer Virginia Jamison's pussy– conquer it and make it mine.

Spread out before me like an offering, Ginny's heels are resting on the edge of the tub, her toes curled in anticipation, her thighs spread wide, opening her body to my avid gaze. The scientist rears her inquisitive head, but it's sexier than usual. Tentatively reaching forward, even though a few minutes ago my fingers were thrust deeply inside her clenching chasm, I gently part Ginny's lips with my fingertips, opening her to my gaze… and then I stare in awe at her highly aroused pussy.

I did that, too.

My fingertip flicks out to stroke over Ginny's tightly budded clit– almost purple with want, peeking at me from beneath its hood. She grunts in reaction, nearly toppling over the side of the tub. I smirk to myself, feeling naughty and smug. I flick it again, distracting her while I lean in to lick a long, wet line from anus to clitoris.

Panting wildly, toes curled tighter than before, Ginny grips the edge of the tub with her fingertips, nails desperately trying to find purchase. Deeply inhaling Ginny's addictive scent, I marvel in wonder over how quickly your life can change– how you can lose everything in a second… or gain everything in a chance meeting, if only you have the balls to overcome your fears and take it.

Life's too short, so I take the offering openly and willingly– eagerly even.

"Opal," Ginny gasps my name as my tongue circles and laps her soft folds, eliciting shivers of bliss from both of us. A fierce hunger propels me to dive into Ginny's hot and willing pussy, tongue spearing her entrance. Legs quivering near my ears, my palms grip her thighs, nails biting into her supple skin, to hold her open for ravishment.

Moaning in time with Ginny, I penetrate her body with my tongue. Not only is Ginny soft and fragrant, she's hotter than the Sun, nearly scalding the tip of my tongue. Whispering my name, spearing me forward with her vocal encouragement, I feast at the welling pool between her thighs, and I love every single second of it.

"Opal...Opal... Opal," falls from Ginny's parted lips, chanting as her fingertips twist in my damp hair, tugging at the strands. Clenching my face in the vise-like grip of her thighs, Ginny rides my face, twisting her hips, grinding her pussy against my lips– saturating my cheeks, my lips, inside my mouth, even my forehead, with her cream.

Close to suffocating, and glorifying in it, I manage to purse my lips around her swollen clit. Remembering her violent reaction to my sharp kiss, I wrap my front teeth around the hard nub and bite.

Bucking, screaming, nearly toppling off the edge of the hot tub and taking me with her, Ginny rides out her orgasm on my face, forcing me to struggle to keep us both afloat. It's the most sexual moment of my entire life– a moment that took over forty-three years to occur.

I can now proudly label myself a lesbian, and mean it in every sense of the word.

"Holy shit!" Ginny whispers fervently, completely out of breath. Her hazel eyes are glazed over with shock. Her face is rosy and beaded with sweat from exertion. Her thighs are dimpled with fingertip bruises from my efforts to keep us both in the hot tub. Reaching forward, Ginny abruptly kisses my lips, sucking her taste from my tongue. "Girl, get on the fucking chaise lounge. I'm not done with you yet."

"Educate me, Ms. Jamison," I say like an apt pupil, trying to sound teasing, but it comes out as how I truly meant it. I'm eager to learn all Ginny wishes to teach me, and then some.

I get out of the hot tub on shaky legs, drained of most my energy from the warm water and the thrilling excitement of my first lesbian experience. I reach over and drain the contents of my wine glass, only to catch Ginny doing the exact same thing. I wipe the remnants of wine clinging to my lips with the back of my hand.

Ginny and I share a potent look. Neither of us wishing to remove Ginny's taste from our mouths. We're just that parched from our endeavors, and that is almost as satisfying as the orgasm itself.

Swaying, and it's not as a flirty enticement for Ginny, I climb up on to the circular, padded chaise lounge. "You have your own veritable paradise back here," I praise. Uncertain what to do next, I simply lie down on the cushion and wait.

Wanton, my legs part on their own, offering Ginny a taste of me in return. Bright eyes laser in on my movements, staring in undeniable want at my slightly parted nether lips.

Mouth curving up into a smirk, "You're not a natural blonde, Mrs. Fischer," Ginny teases.

"I'm not a young woman anymore, Ms. Jamison," I volley back lightly, not offended in the least. "My hair turned white from its natural light brown when I was in my late twenties."

Eyes bugging out, "W-O-W," Ginny drawls out.

"I like this better, though," I admit as I ruffle up my short, white locks. "I wouldn't recognize myself with hair the color of my son's. But I have a feeling Sage will continue on with the Sage family tradition of premature white, not gray, hair. I proudly wear it as badge of honor of a life well-lived."

"It suits you," Ginny says sluggishly, still avidly staring between my thighs. "Light brown or white, either will suit that gorgeous pussy of yours."

Ginny sways toward me, and she is definitely flirting with me, trying to entice me with the fluidity of her movements: the jounce of her breasts, the swish of her hips, and the anticipatory smile on her lips. This is a woman who knows how to work her body to her advantage.

Breathless, fear slams into me out of nowhere. Giving pleasure is one thing– the ability to lie back and take it is another. Even when submitting to a man, I was still in control. Ginny makes me feel anything but controlled, and it's terrifying in a thrilling sort of way.

The loss of control makes me feel alive.

"After six years of servicing the majority of Fairport High's straight girl population, I'm much more selfish than I used to be. After being a giver, and having it never be enough to keep my ex-girlfriends' interests, I take first before I give." Standing over me, smiling while cocking an eyebrow, "Fair's fair. Ginny: 2. Opal: 1. Let's make it an even three, shall we?"

"Holy Hannah," I breathe out, not knowing if I have two orgasms in me to give to Ginny. "I'll try, but no promises."

Reaching down, Ginny twists her fingertips in my hair, wrenching my head back roughly. I gasp in shock, never having anyone touch me in such a ruthless manner before– my pussy spasms with ecstasy before my brain catches on that I secretly love it.

Leaning down with a feral smile on her lips, Ginny whispers against my mouth, "The man you refuse to name, the one who you said knows how to fuck? Well, I'm a woman who has a great wealth of knowledge when it comes to forcing reluctant climaxes out of women. You don't have to give it to me, 'cuz I'm just gonna take it."

"Control? What control?" I mutter beneath my breath as Ginny slinks to the edge of the circular chaise. I jump when her fingers touch the sole of my foot, fingernail scratching me from heel to toe. All I can do is shiver with anticipation and try to regulate my breathing.

"Fair's fair," Ginny breathes against my knee, and then she tenderly kisses it.

On the precipice of climax, body flexing involuntarily as Ginny licks a path from the back of my knee, stopping just before she makes contact with my nether lips. "Oh, shit!" Lust causes me to become fluent in profanity. "You're... you're going to do to me exactly what I did to you."

Hazel eyes rolling up to connect with mine, I can barely make out Ginny's devious grin down the length of my body. Winking at me, Ginny lowers her face, with my light brown fuzz-covered mound hiding her wicked smile. "Girl, you better ride my face as hard and fast as I rode yours," she cautions, and then she descends, tilting my world view on its axis.

The last thing I hear for many minutes as I unravel while screaming Ginny's name, as I ride her mouth, lips, tongue, teeth, and chin like a wanton creature, "Opal: two."

Unable to blink, all I can do is stare up at the star-speckled night sky in wonder. Unable to stop quivering with aftershocks, all I can do is endure as Ginny laughs smugly. "You doing okay?" she prompts for the tenth time since I stopped writhing.

"Er... ungh... um..." I utter complete and total nonsense. My ability to form coherent sentences vanished the moment

Ginny's tongue penetrated my pussy and demanded the most intense orgasm of my entire existence.

"Word of advice to whoever the hell that dude is, nobody will ever eat pussy as good as a lesbian. I crave cunt more than I crave cake, and we all know who my BFF is– the cake baker from Heaven."

Unbidden, a manic laugh is torn from my chest. "Cake baker," I snicker. If only Ginny knew who *he* was, she'd laugh with me, and then probably slap my face in disgust.

"And as a self-admitted fat girl, I really, *really* love cake," Ginny sounds jealous of Rob.

"You do know he's not your competition, right?" Rolling to my side, I face Ginny instead of staring off into outer space. I reach out to caress her cheek, so she realizes what I'm about to say is important. "You do realize that if you get a crazy notion of *"fair's fair"* and you want to be penetrated by a guy, *he*'s the only one I trust, right?"

"Yeah," Ginny says hesitantly, clearly still colored green with jealousy.

"And I'm never telling you *his* identity– no matter what. It has nothing to do with you, or me, or him, and that's all I have to say on that subject," I warn– case closed.

Eyes narrowing, a purr of pure possessiveness rumbles from Ginny's chest, causing sparks of joy to light in my body. "I said three, remember?"

"Holy fuck!" I shriek, already rung dry.

Still reeling with possessive jealousy, "I may not have a dick to impale you with, but there are still things I can do that he can't. This is one of them," Ginny warns as she rolls over on top of me, twining our legs.

"*He*'s not your competition," I reiterate, truly meaning it, trying to reassure Ginny. My hands softly flow down her back in a soothing massage as she lies on top of me.

"I know that," Ginny responds like she means it, too. "I'm just showing you the grass is greener, sweeter, and more passionate on the lesbian side of the fence."

Framing my face with her palms, Ginny kisses me with fiery desire and utter determination. In a move I will never perfect, even if I try for the rest of my days, Ginny connects us like perfect puzzle pieces by positioning me where she wants me: mouths, lips, and tongues entangled in a passion-filled kiss, breasts pressed together tightly in intoxicated bliss, pelvises perfectly aligned.

Ginny reaches down between us with her fingertips, opening up my nether lips, and then she presses our sexes together, and slowly grinds. I thought I was tapped out, but I was wrong. The sensation of Ginny's clit rubbing against mine, sliding in a combination of our slick cream, thrusts me over the edge.

Lost to Virginia Jamison, "Three," is the last word I utter until morning, then in which I say, "Four… five… and six."

CHAPTER TWELVE

Ginny Jamison
The No-Name Diner Do-Over.

Sipping on sweet tea and gazing at one another from across the diner booth, Opal and I try this first date business again. It's the afternoon after eighteen hours of straight sex, sleep, and constant talk. I've never felt so connected to another human being so quickly before, and it scares me senseless.

I've known *of* Opal Fischer for over four years, yet I've only known her for a little over a week. But you can learn a lot about a person during difficult, high-stress situations: a chance meeting, an impromptu pre-wedding reception, a wedding, an after-wedding party, and a night of intense sex and even more intense conversation. The fact that we're both blowing off work to spend a few more hours together is telling.

"It's my quest in life to make sure you visit all the businesses on Main Street by the end of the month. So today, after we're finished with lunch, you're visiting Macomb's Thrift Shoppe for a pair of *new-to-me* jeans, and then I'm going to show off Jamison Reality."

"Tis a shame I didn't go through you when I bought my house," Opal says with a slight frown marring her beautiful features. The woman can look downright stark when she's lost in thought, but I know how brightly she shines when in the throes of passion.

"My faith-filled friend," I tease with a wink, "That was not meant to be. We were meant to meet when we did, how we did, and in the time in our lives when we did. I was living with a woman, contemplating a long life with her when you moved to town. If we'd met when we did, you weren't ready and I was in a committed relationship."

"I'm glad Sarah was a cunt," Opal fiercely bites out, sounding just as possessive as I am when I think of '*He who shall remain nameless*.' My eyes continually search out the other patrons of the No-Name, looking for this mystery man. It's all I've thought of since Opal told me of her recent past. I'm a gossip hound, and I can't leave a secret alone, even if it's to my detriment.

Laughing humorlessly, "I'm glad I didn't spend more years of my life with that vicious, gold-digging bitch. But the pain of my own stupidity sure did hurt while I was going through it." Sighing, I change the subject to more pleasant manners. "Well, I guess since I blew off work on Monday and most of today, I better communicate with my clients tomorrow."

"Me too," Opal agrees. "Since I usually work at the hospital on the weekends, I have Monday and Tuesday off anyway. But I always volunteer at dispatch in my downtime. Nina is probably missing my expertise right about now. She gets flustered on medical calls. I better stop in there at some point this afternoon."

"Ooooohhhh…" I draw out, "Since I'm going to show you my office, can I see the dispatch center? Pretty please?" I bat my eyelashes and flash a shit-eating grin.

"Only if you clean your plate," Opal teases just as Marta delivers our huge bounty of fried food: curly fries, mozzarella sticks, jalapeno poppers, and breaded mushrooms. "And, for added adventure, you have to try all the sauces at the No-Name. If I will forego my ketchup, you'll forego your spicy brown mustard."

Laughing, nodding my head sure, my attention is drawn by the bell dinging over the front door. A loud, raucous crowd files into the diner. "Fuck me–"

"Anytime," Opal cuts me off, grinning, not noticing the newest arrivals yet.

"Fuck me," I repeat, "Can't we get away from them for more than a few hours?"

"Huh?" Turning around to face the door, Opal catches sight of them at the same time she finally hears their chaotic song. "Well, I'm glad to see my son is still alive, but I planned on not having to see him until early evening." Sighing, Opal slumps back against the booth, and then grabs a handful of fries, which disappear into her awaiting mouth.

"I'm not cooking!" Rob shouts, "And I'm not paying either, you ungrateful bastards!"

"You promised waffles," my niece huffs, glaring at Robin Prynne with pure malice. "You promised Taco Night, too!"

"It ain't nighttime yet!" Rob argues like a teenaged girl. "And you promised to stop being a sulking bitch, Raven. But that ain't happening anytime soon, either," Rob volleys back. "If you recall, I said lunch was up to you to get for yourself. I fed you pancakes– not my fault the waffle iron shit the bed."

"I'm buying– order whatever," Auggie's voice booms out as their party takes over the entire No-Name Diner: Auggie, Rob, Isis, Willow, Ren, Essie, Raven, Weston, Violet, Ozzy, Seth, and Sage. I sink back into the booth, hoping they don't spot us and ruin our first date. Auggie points at the girl squeezing on Seth, "Blame Willow on the broken waffle maker."

Shoving Seth to their sister, "I was making a Panini with it!" Willow grumbles, face blazing with embarrassment. "So sue me, will ya?"

"Was the Panini any good, is the real question," Ren asks to stop the impending girl-fight between his girlfriend and his baby sister.

"Ham and cheese," Violet purrs while rubbing her tummy, sounding famished. "It was yummy. Mom would be proud."

"It was damned good," Rob agrees, finally calming down. "The waffle iron put tasty, little squares on the bread."

"I'll have to buy the Spook House and Shithole some waffle irons and Panini presses," I muse to myself. My compulsive buying obsession pings with pleasure every time I buy people things they want and need.

Opal just gazes at me, silently laughing, as if she can already read my thoughts after our tryst. Ignoring my family and friends, I reach forward to grab a mozzarella stick. "How long before they see us?" I muse. "Because I don't feel like playing referee for Raven. Let Isis field whatever shit the girl is stirring."

"Why's Rae being so snotty to Rob, anyway?" Opal asks a very good question.

"Girl power," I mumble, deciding I need to set my niece straight. "Raven is angry at Isis, Auggie, *and* Rob. But she was raised with Auggie as her uncle, so she can't be mad at him, and she can't be mad at Isis. So she's taking out her frustrations on Rob. She just wants them to be happy, but she's blaming where no blame is due."

"Isis is the one who needs to fix all this shit," Opal practically growls, and I find her vehemence off-putting since she is Isis's only girlfriend. "Rob is doing his damnedest to fix the situation, and Auggie and Isis are only making it more difficult."

Opal's words are undoubtedly true, yet they draw my eye to the man in question. I eye Robin Prynne, truly looking at him for the first time: average height, slim-build, brown eyes and hair. He is the epitome of average. Then when Rob speaks or smiles, you're caught in his web of manipulation, and buy whatever shit he is selling. Robin Prynne can be highly intoxicating when he tries to win your affections. The emotions behind Opal's sentiments force me to contemplate whether or not Rob is her mystery man. With a shake of my head, I toss the idea off.

No. Fucking. Way.

"M-O-M!" is a high-pitched shriek from a boyish voice. In the blink of an eye, Sage moves from Rae's side and is at the edge of our booth. "Nice afternoon glow you're both wearing," the kid teases, blue eyes shining with deviousness.

"Nice glow you're wearing," Opal growls, hand lashing out to grab Sage's wrist to abruptly tug him onto her booth bench. A seething whisper into his ear, "What have you been up to, son?"

"Not a damned thing like you have, Mom." Sage's face twist up as if insulted. "I'm happy for you and Ginny. But don't think I'm being bad because you are."

"I don't think," Opal whispers. "I recognize that gleam in your eye, is what I know."

Rapidly firing off, voice loud and shrill, "I stayed with Rob last night. He wouldn't let me out of his sight. For Christ's sake, he shoved his bed up against the door so I couldn't leave, and then he tossed an air mattress on the floor for me to sleep on. I'm not a sexual predator," Sage whines, sounding hurt.

"I didn't say it would be unwelcome," Opal stresses. "I'm just watching out for your future while your little head is ignoring the common sense of your big head."

Deeply chuckling, proving the kid uses a high-pitched voice on purpose, Sage grins up at his mother. "The gleam in my eye is from observing all the other idiots make their lives more miserable. I don't even have to rile 'em up to get 'em going. They do it all to themselves."

I reach across the table, taking Sage's hand in mine, "You're a boy after my own heart," I sing teasingly, yet I'm being completely serious. "Spill the juiciest shit."

Smiling proudly like a Cheshire cat, Sage takes my breath away. The kid is going to incinerate the hearts of all the men in his life. "Rae is being a bitch because Ozzy sees her as his sister, which is why Rae is buddying up to me. Rae's baby bro doesn't see me like I want him to see me, or so she thinks. So to Rae, we're kindred spirits."

"Ah," I sigh. "I can understand that." Leaning across the table, I whisper, "Rob's guard dog routine was because he was more afraid that Weston feelings for you weren't unrequited, and he was protecting both of you from yourselves."

Laughing, pointing at his rosy cheeks, Sage purrs, "Hence the glow… and hence why no one gives two shits if Ozzy's alone with Raven, while Rob literally slept in front of his bedroom door to keep West and me apart. Rae can throw herself at Ozzy all she wants, but he won't bite, and anyone with a brain assumes Weston's going to give in to me eventually."

"Poor girl," Opal murmurs. "Smart Rob."

Intuition lighting up, I hate the sound of Rob's name on Opal's tongue. "What else, kid? Don't hold out on me."

"Violet is Weston's new BFF, which created an epic screaming match between the twins last night. Seth was saying some pretty crude, woman-hating shit. Willow had to step in and tear them off each other. Then, to everyone's surprise, Willow smacked Seth across the mouth."

"You're shitting me," I grunt out. "Willow was just hugging on him."

"Yeah, 'cuz she feels guilty," Sage is more perceptive than most seventeen-year-olds. Leaning over the table, almost crawling into my booth bench, he breathes a secret. "Isis stayed in Auggie's room last night, leaving all the girls to have a nail-painting sleepover in the living room, with Seth, Weston, and Ozzy camping out in the yard with Ren's supervision."

Just when I thought Opal was against gossip, she leans across the table, until all three of our heads are bent together as we fiercely whisper to one another. "Isis stayed with Auggie?" Opal mumbles, sounding awed. "For real?"

"What color nail polish?" I ask, causing both Sage and Opal to gape at me in utter disbelief. Chuckling, "I'm just fucking with ya, kid. Did they… ya know?" I trail off.

"Purple," Sage answers my phony question without answering the real one. Opal grabs her son's chin, swiveling him to face her. Their resemblance is astonishing as they engage in a silent staring contest.

First to break, "Did they? Was Rob okay? What did you guys talk about?" Opal interrogates Sage, suddenly sounding exactly like her son.

With narrowed eyes, I glare at the side of Opal's face as she battles Sage, trying to discern the reason for her sudden interest.

Turning to me as if she can read my thoughts, "I've been riding their tumultuous relationship for the past four years, rooting for their happiness. Like everyone else in their lives, I want them *all* to be happy– no one left as the odd man out. We're talking twenty-four years of history, Ginny. It matters if Auggie and Isis were together while Rob was left babysitting my son."

My heart breaks, and then instantly heals because Opal genuinely cares for my family. All the while, I feel guilty over gossiping over their pain. I close my eyes as I nod my apology at Opal. She reaches out, as if feeling what I'm feeling, and takes my hand in hers. I swear she whispers, "Not your competition."

I give Opal's fingers a squeeze, and then focus all my attention on Sage, silently begging him for answers.

"Alright. Alright. Alright," Sage laughs out. "Rob and I had gay talk. I only know three guys who actually like guys, and one of 'em is my *prey*," he taunts. "And no one in their right mind would approach Augustus Kline for advice. He scares the shit out of me. If I ask, Rob answers with brutal honesty. Rest assured, Mom, I'm never having sex," Sage says with a shudder. "No, we didn't talk about Rob or his problems. But he's as big of a gossip whore as we are."

Our heads turn in unison. The three of us stare at the corner table in the No-Name, where Auggie, Isis, and Rob are sharing a meal. As if feeling our attention, they all look back at us with similar expressions of, "*What the fuck?*"

Feeling like a teenaged girl, I giggle uncomfortably over being caught red-handed. In a hushed whisper, "Spill the rest, kid," I order.

Looking baffled and curious, "If I knew, that would have been the first thing out of my mouth when I sat down. Hell, if I know. You tell me, do they look all blissed out like you guys?"

We scrutinize them again– getting caught again. Auggie looks nonplussed. Rob looks amused. Most confusing, Isis waves at us, and she's smiling at me like she used to when she was a girl. I smile back and wave, simultaneously feeling guilty and elated.

"No," Opal says with one-hundred-percent certainty. "They talked all night. I know that look, too. It's a, *"We stayed up all night long talking, and I've never felt more connected to you,"* kind of look." Opal squeezes my hand, informing me she sees the same thing gazing out of my eyes in her direction. We stayed up all night talking, kissing, touching, orgasming, sleeping– simply connecting on a baser level. That's the look Isis is giving both men.

"Did you sleep last night?" I ask Sage.

"Yeah, why?" he grunts out, thoroughly confused.

"I sold Auggie that house." It's my turn to be one-hundred-percent certain. "A hidden door connects Rob and Auggie's bedrooms. Rob was only in his bedroom while you were awake. I can guarantee it."

"Well, shit!" Sage is upset over being out-foxed by Rob. "That explains why Rob asked me to shove his bed in front of the door. When I couldn't budge it, Rob looked pleased with himself– the rat-bastard was testing me."

Opal and I share a good laugh over that, gaining the attention of the corner table. Rob tips an imaginary hat at Sage, like he knows what we're whispering about.

"My favorite auntie," Raven says cheerfully as she slides into the booth next to me.

"You only have two," I remind my niece. "It's not that difficult of a decision. I have a 50/50 shot of either being the best or worst aunt."

I wrap my arm around her shoulders, tugging her into a hug. I squeeze Raven a few times, shocked she isn't pulling away. With Malcolm honeymooning with Clover at the Pink Taco Hut, Rae is probably missing her father's affections.

"Can I stay with you until Mom and Dad are finished making another Mason?" Rae asks, sounding hopeful. The lilt of her voice wavers, turning insecure. I'm not sure if it's because she's testing out the sound of calling Clover Mom, or if she's worried I'll deny her.

I look to Opal, wondering if she and I had plans for the evening– *hoping* we had plans for the evening. "It's summer vacation," Opal says, tugging her son underneath her arm in exactly the same way I'm holding Raven. "I'm sure Rae's new buddy wouldn't mind if she visited us this evening, would he?"

"I'm game," Sage sounds excited. "But are you okay with it?" he asks his mother. "Ya know?"

Smiling over at me, "Sometimes all you need is a simple conversation to bond with someone. Never forget that, children," Opal cautions.

"How about you guys visit us tonight," I prompt, knowing Raven does better in an environment she's acclimated to. She's not much of a joiner. "And I will cook us dinner."

"Hot tub!" Rae shouts loud enough to alert all the patrons of the No-Name. Opal and I cringe for the same reason— we christened that hot tub last night.

"Hot tub?" Sage shrieks. "You're holding out on me, Ginny. No fair."

"Mmm… fried, salty goodness," Rae purrs, fingertips itching to grab a mushroom. "You finished eating that?"

Laughing, "Actually, I haven't been very hungry for the past week," which earns me an eyebrow raise from Opal.

She responds with something innocuous yet salacious, "I know something you love to eat more than cake. I could go for some of that right about now." Pushing the plates to the kids, "I'm not hungry for fried food anymore, either. Ginny's going to show me her office. We'll be back in twenty minutes."

Sliding out of the bench seat, taking Raven with me, "Better make it thirty." I tuck my niece back into the booth, and she immediately starts shoveling mushrooms into her mouth like a starving fiend. "We'll grab your shit from the Spook House. You can stay with me until your parents are satisfied."

"Mmm… hmm," Rae grumbles from around of mouthful of battered vegetables.

"We'll be here," Sage replies for both of them. His table manners are just as impeccable as his mother's— very tidy, and very thorough. "Don't pay," he stops me from tossing a couple bills on the table. "Auggie's buying."

"Hurry," I tug on Opal's hand, and she immediately weaves her fingers through mine. "I'm starving."

"Me too," Opal says breathlessly as she tows me from the No-Name, neither of us noticing the gawking natives. "Let's eat at the same time. Twice."

"Three times," I ante up.

CHAPTER THIRTEEN

Opal Fischer

"You doing okay?" I rasp to Rob over the phone. He and Isis have been on my mind all day as I toured Main Street's shops with Ginny, Rae, and Sage. I use a quick layover at my house to call Rob while Sage showers up before dinner. "What happened between the three of you last night?"

Perpetually amused, "What happened between you and Ginny last night?"

"I'm a real woman now," I tease, softly chuckling to myself. "I didn't think it was possible to have more than twenty orgasms in less than twenty-four hours. I'm making up for lost time."

A sharp whistle stings my ears. "Well, I'm be damned. Opal's a full-fledged carpet muncher."

"Quit being vulgar," I chastise. "And quit changing the subject." I pause to listen for the telltale signs of Sage's shower trickling. The boy is the biggest gossip monger on the planet. I also don't trust him not to trick me. Creeping toward his room, I make sure he's actually in the shower.

"Carpet? It's what you ate for lunch, isn't it? We all saw you and Ginny hightail it to her office for a serving of afternoon delight. Did you get any hair in your teeth?" Rob turns devious when he's uncomfortable. Thank goodness I realize this, or I might get angry.

"Are you jealous, Robin? Or did you have some carpet for a midnight snack? Or was it a cocktail straw you were slurping?"

"Auggie? Cocktail straw?" Rob releases an evil snigger. "Ginny's rubbing off on you in a very bad way, Nurse Fischer... and I love it," Rob purrs. "I don't suck cock," he reveals, surprising me. "Auggie says whores suck, not get sucked. Too bad. So sad. For me, that is. But alas, I have no hair in my teeth, and not because Isis waxes. We talked all night about the past."

"Are you alright?"

"Not really," he sighs.

I lean against Sage's doorframe, listening to him sing poorly in the shower. "Do you want to talk about it?"

"No," Rob grumbles. "If I did, you wouldn't have to pester me to talk, now would you?"

"I'm calling Isis as soon as I hang up on you. You know that, right?"

"Ah, Opal loves me more than Isis," Rob sounds incredibly touched by the fact. "I'm glad somebody loves me more for once," he voices the root of the problem.

"You're scared they love each other more than you?" I prompt.

"Shut your goddamned mouth," Rob snarls because I hit a sore nerve. "Is your kid singing in the shower? Is that... It's Raining Men?"

"Nice," I praise Rob's ability to change the subject. I let it go. If he wants to talk about it, he knows where to find me. "It's Man-eater, actually. You just missed Sage's rendition of Womanizer."

"All gay men love Britney. What is up with that?" Rob ponders.

"How should I know? You're closer to a gay man than I am."

"True. Too true. But I don't care for Britney Spears. I'm more acoustic and indie rock."

"I pegged you as the type with your artistic ability, and Auggie as liking classic rock."

"Aug is also indie rock, mixed with nineties grunge– reliving his youth, I believe," Rob's tone drips with reminiscence. "Let me know when Sage starts belting out Liza Monelli," he snarks.

"I'm just happy Sage's fabulousness doesn't extend to The Golden Girls and Broadway Musicals. He can listen to all the Pop music he wants. I won't lie– every time he puts on a Katy Perry music video, I have to pause what I'm doing and watch. The kid loves hardcore rap, too."

"Who doesn't love Katy Perry? Even straight girls stare at her amazing tits... Wait a cocksucking minute. Did you just say rap? Oh. My. God... that I have to see. Little boy fashion plate/future democratic senator listens to rap." Rob's laughter is loud and lasting, hurting my ear.

"Sage is already accepted to Berkeley, actually. He wants to be an English teacher– no politics in his future."

"Thank fuck," Rob sighs in relief. "Sage reminds me of Stewie from Family Guy. He'd ruin the world if in a position of power. Better that he stays a child predator."

"Better hope my son keeps his penis away from your nephew, or he won't be allowed within three hundred yards of a school. Hard to teach from the opposite side of the street." I laugh at my own lame joke.

"There's always an English Professor. Colleges love to employ criminals to teach our impressionable youth."

"I'm calling Isis now," I say in parting, knowing Rob could keep this banter up for days on end, just so we won't have to talk about anything serious.

Cellphone in hand, fingertip scrolling my contacts, a piercing glare draws my attention. My eyes slowly light on my son, who had overheard the last bit of my conversation with Rob. "Sage… I… I'm sorry," I stammer out.

Standing before me with a towel wrapped around his slim hips, dripping water all over the carpeting, my son has never looked so introspective in his entire life. "I really like Weston Mason," Sage finally admits. "But I won't touch him, even if he asks me to."

"Why?" I breathe, scared shitless to witness this side of my son. He's not joking, or being sarcastic, or taunting someone, or being loving and kind. Right now, my little boy is standing before me as a grown man.

Sage cocks his head to the side, as if deciding how much to say to me. "I lied," he blurts out bluntly. "I have talked to Weston about being gay– I have since the day I met him. He was a little kid then, not even ten yet. I've watched him grow and grow and grow before my eyes. I want Weston," Sage growls. "I even love him, and that's why I'm leaving him alone."

Speechless, I just stare at my son, as he stares back at me in challenge.

"You and Rob can joke about it all you want. I don't find it funny, but I can see why you would. Weston doesn't like me the way I am, and I'm not willing to change for him."

Now *that* makes my tongue move. "What?"

"I'm not Weston's type," Sage admits, sounding pained. "As if any of us actually has a type. He's four-fucking-teen years old. He's a baby that looks like a grown-assed man. I'm not going to ruin either of our futures. I'll wait until Weston comes to me."

Eyes bugging out of my skull, "What if that's soon?" My voice wavers with fear. "Soon means child molestation charges."

"Mom?" Sage shakes his head sadly. He walks away from me, toward his closet. Without a hint of modesty, he drops his towel, showing me he's still small like a boy but starting to fill out into a man. I watch in fascination as he meticulously dresses in a pair of khaki shorts and a pressed lavender button down.

Turning back to me, Sage is buckling the watch his grandfather bought him for his sixteenth birthday. "Do you honestly believe I didn't Google the laws over and over again for the past four years? Do you think I haven't calculated when I could pounce and get into the least amount of trouble."

"What did you decide?" comes roughly from my suddenly dry throat.

Pausing with his hand on his cologne bottle, "It's not worth the risk," Sage whispers, breaking my heart. "If Weston decides his '*type*' has changed before winter break of my junior year at Berkeley, it's going to kill me to say no."

"But you will?" I prompt.

"I won't be coming home once I leave for that exact reason– *no* holidays at home," Sage stresses. "Because if we're alone, and West wants me, I'll give him what he wants," Sage harshly rasps out. Leaning forward, he quickly arranges his wet hair with his fingertips. "So, I hope you have a lot of frequent flier miles saved up to visit my ass in California, because I'm gonna need my mommy."

Tugging my hurting son into my arms, I hold him tightly. "Nothing will keep me away," I promise. "I'll help you through this," I add another promise.

"I'll need you the instant Weston realizes he wants me back. I'll need you to be my conscience. I'm a bad person, because I want that to happen before I graduate. But if I were a good person, I'd hope West never figures out he wants me back, and lives a happy life."

Squeezing him tighter, "I'm a bad person, too, son. A very bad person," I murmur, knowing full and well if Sage and Weston messed up, I'd take their secret to the grave.

"Ya know how my introductions embarrass you, Mom," Sage says as he leans forward to ring Ginny's doorbell. "Well, it's embarrassing how you bring soap every freakin' where we go."

Eyeing my son, I smirk like I know a secret. "You've been kissing on someone," I remind the brat. "I'm sure he appreciated how good you smelled."

"Speaking of which," Sage flashes me a brazen look, "I need some more sandalwood."

The door opening saves my son from whatever reply was on the tip of my tongue. "HI!" Ginny chirps, looking fresh-faced and wide-eyed. "I'm so glad you could make it. Come in," she opens the door further, ushering us into her home.

"Thanks for having us," I murmur. Unsure of the protocol, I lean into Ginny to kiss her cheek, but she quickly turns her face to steal a real kiss. "Well, hello there," I purr against her slightly parted lips. Just before I pull away, I lick the tip of her tongue with mine, causing her to shudder.

Sage is frozen, blocking the doorway. Thinking our public display of affection freaked him out, I go to mollify him. Only my son isn't upset with me– he's in thrall. If it wasn't for his shocked reaction, I'd swear it was a setup.

Sitting on the sofa, watching television, are Malcolm's youngest children: Raven *and* Weston. After ten heartbeats of staring, Sage swaggers across the living room, and squeezes in between the siblings. Weston gives Sage a '*what's up*' chin nod like he's disinterested, while Rae curls around Sage's arm and cuddles up.

"Umm… did they suddenly multiply?" Nervousness puts a waver in my voice.

"They are Masons," is Ginny's reply. But I have no idea what that means. "When I went to pick up Rae's bag, Weston was sitting on the steps waiting for us, with his bag packed too. The twins were fighting harder than ever, and he didn't like being put in the middle."

"More slapping?" I ask as I skirt my way around the outer wall of the living room so I don't walk in front of the television on my way to the kitchen.

"That's the problem," Ginny sighs deeply. "Everyone was at work. Even Ozzy was working with Dave and Rob at Prynne Renovations. That left the three of them alone, with the twins fighting over Weston. They're adjusting to becoming a blended family, and they're drawing battle lines for family voting. As in all things, Weston is–"

"Switzerland," I finish for Ginny.

"Exactly. Clover will beat it out of 'em." If I hadn't seen it firsthand, I'd think Ginny was teasing. But the annual Blended Family skirmish just kicked off its inaugural event.

"Maybe Javi will take off his shirt for us," Sage's voice floats over to me. I catch him nudging West in the side. I notice the kid never shoved over, making more space on the sofa. He's not cuddling with Sage like Rae is, but he's blushing beet-red.

"Hope so," Weston mouths, blushing harder.

"Oh, c'mon!" Rae shouts animatedly at the television. "This is the first episode all season long where Javi isn't walking around in his skivvies! Show us some skin, bitch!"

"Oh, Lord," I sigh. "They're addicted to that idiotic show, too."

"Does Devon crave meth? Heroin? Pot? Booze?" is Ginny's odd way of saying the Masons have addictive personalities, with the youngest addicted to reality television.

Using the children's obsessive distraction to my advantage, I hook a finger under Ginny's sundress strap, and tug her closer to me. "This will sound cheesy," I admit while wearing a goofy grin. "But I've missed you."

Hazel eyes glittering with happiness, Ginny backs up further into the kitchen, allowing me to push her up against the countertop. I gaze down at Ginny with heavily hooded eyes, remembering every single touch we've ever shared. Pure lust roils in my veins to the point I'm shaking with hunger.

Leaning in, I lightly sniff Ginny's throat, loving her clean scent. "That tickles," she giggles like a school girl. But her hands do anything but act girlish. Wanton, Ginny wedges her hand between us, cupping my breast in her palm. Shuddering, my knees go weak.

"I brought you a gift," I rasp out roughly. "I'm so new at this. But one thing I do know, women love presents."

"Gimme!" Ginny demands, practically tearing the gift bag out of my hand. Peeking inside, "Oh, yay! I've wanted some ever since you told me about your hobby." Bag still in hand, Ginny gropes my ass, pulling me into her for a searing thank you kiss.

"Get a room!" Sage shouts at us. "Your moaning is interrupting our show, and I don't want to lose my dinner before I even get a chance to eat it."

Embarrassed, I walk into the living room on shaking legs. "I brought you something, too, Raven." At forty-three, I shouldn't be nervous around a teenaged girl. But I am. I hand her a gift bag filled with soap in the scents most girls enjoy. "Sorry, Weston. I didn't realize you'd be here. What kind of scents do you prefer?"

Channeling her aunt, and behaving just as her stepmother did when I gave Clover a batch of my soaps, Raven has the soap out of the bag in a heartbeat, sniffing each hand-cut bar. "Mmm…" Rae purrs, smiling. "Chocolate. Yummy."

While Raven inhales her gift, I look to the young man who is suddenly quiet. Weston smiles at me, happy to see his sister animated for once. "I'm partial to sandalwood," West says before he can stop himself, not realizing his gaffe because he's too engrossed with his big sister.

Smarter than the average teenager, "Ginny!" Sage shouts, hopping up from the sofa like his ass is on fire, or maybe he has to get away from Weston's great love of sandalwood-scented skin. "Need any help with dinner?"

"Sure. Sounds great," Ginny chirps back, not realizing what's happening.

"Liar, liar. Pants on fire," I sing to Sage as we enter the kitchen.

"No clue what you're talking about, Mom," Sage acts angelic. "What's for dinner?"

"It's *Construct your own Panini Night*," Ginny says with a wide grin, gesturing to the countertop filled with sandwich making fixings.

"Is this like Rob's Taco Night?" Sage pretends I'm not glaring at him with extreme punishment in my eyes.

Blushing, Ginny turns sheepish. "The Spook House is having a Construct your own Panini Night, too. Aren't they?" I ask, thinking Ginny is as predictable as she is beautiful. After we parted ways, I bet it took her less than five minutes to go buy two Panini presses and waffle irons.

"Maybe," she dodges, and moves to hide by pretending to get more ingredients out of the refrigerator.

Catching on, Sage snickers. "And waffles for breakfast, I bet," he reasons.

"Maybe," Ginny's voice echoes from the confines of the fridge.

"I'll help!" Rae scares the shit out of me when she sneaks up behind me. She reminds me of that little, cutie vampire girl from *Hotel Transylvania*. In large groups, the girl remains silent. In a small gathering of family and friends, Rae comes out of her shell.

"Me too!" Weston's deep voice fills the kitchen. Now *him*, I heard coming. "Mom would be happy to know we're cooking with Aunt Ginny."

"I have to be at practice at six a.m. tomorrow morning, Aunt Ginny," West says from across the table, a huge sandwich held between him hands. "I can get myself there. I just wanted you to know in case you wondered why I'm not in my room when you get up."

"Practice already?" Sage's voice cracks– he is way too interested in the interworkings of Weston Mason. I'll give the young kid mad props– West hasn't shown an ounce of mutual attraction. He's just been cordial and responsive to Sage's constant barrage of inquiries.

"Yeah," West drawls out, tanned cheeks always blushing. "Ren graduated when I was finishing up seventh grade. Coach had me train with the team, even back then. I was Ren's replacement, but I couldn't play until I hit freshman year."

"You're going straight into varsity the minute you hit ninth grade?" Sage is beyond impressed.

Beaming with pride, Raven reaches over to chuck Weston underneath the chin. "And my baby bro is starting, too. Gonna be a star, he is."

Smiling, "We all thought Ren would be jealous," Ginny adds.

"He's not," Weston rolls his eyes at his aunt and sister. "Ren trains my ass after he gets home from work every night. He didn't want it as badly as I do. Ren's content with what he's doing."

"You want to go pro?" comes out as barely a squeak. Sage swallows a dozen times, and we all watch his throat work. Hands shaking, he places his Panini on his plate, so we won't notice his involuntary quivering.

Even the tips of Weston's ears are flushed from embarrassment. As the youngest of four in a chaotic family, I bet it's not often he's the sole focus at the dinner table. "I don't know." He makes light of his achievements. "I'm a bit like Ren, except I want to play college ball and get my degree. I'd be content living in Fairport, teaching P.E. and coaching football. I don't have dreams of stardom. It's not for me."

"He could totally do it, though," Rae puts pressure on her brother, and you can see it in the strain at the corner of his eyes.

"Are you going to do it if the opportunity arises?" Sage asks, voice thick, looking like he wants to cry. I go to reach out to my son, but Ginny quickly grabs my hand.

Leaning into me, Ginny whispers, "Let this play out. Either my nephew is a consummate actor or playing hard-to-get. He's not *that* blind to Sage. Who could be? I want to see how this plays out."

"I think you're right," I agree after noticing all the small things we were all too blinded to notice by Sage's unrequited, besotted fool act. "Look how innocent Weston is behaving. I believe he doth protest too much."

Ginny snorts as she pulls away, and we finally notice Rae's knowing glance.

"I'm not going to go out of my way to go pro, but I'd be a dumbass not to take the opportunity. Ya know?"

"It must be hard making adult decisions that affect the rest of your life when you're still a kid," I can sympathize. "On our thirteenth birthdays, Dr. Rick told us what path we were to take after observing our strength and weaknesses during our childhood. Having a scientist for a father was difficult, but it was less stressful to do as Dr. Rick said."

"Did you take, like, tests and stuff?" Rae asks, looking horrified.

"Yeah. Yeah, we did. They were tailored by our gender. I wasn't as proficient in the cooking and cleaning tasks our maid supervised, but I excelled in patient care, with a high aptitude for biology. My father then gave me the boy test, which I scored higher than my two brothers."

"Why not become a doctor?" Ginny asks, even though she already has a good idea.

Sighing, I speak the truth for the first time. "My father took all the tests first, and I scored higher than he did. He couldn't have his daughter outshine him, and he feared if I became a doctor, I'd do better than my brothers."

"It's like a cop family," Rae says, and Weston finishes, "How Grandpa, Dad, and Devon are all cops, and how the entire department keeps pressuring Ren even though he loves being a mechanic."

"Well, you kids come by it naturally. Both of your grandfathers were police officers," Ginny says with a fond smile, most likely remembering John and Barry.

"Ready for the joke…" Sage shakes his head in disgust, thoroughly loathing his grandfather. "Grandfather's second born was a son, and he's a lowlife politician. Next up were two girls– my aunts were forced to be wives by their aptitude tests. Last born was my favorite uncle– Uncle Liam is in Africa, building villages with the Peace Corps. Grandfather never got that doctor son, and the jokes on him for ignoring Mom."

"You're going to be seventeen next month," Rae says to Sage, tugging on his sleeve. "Did you take the test at thirteen? What did it say?"

I huff a laugh at the look of abject horror that crosses my son's delicate features. Biting his lip, Sage refuses to speak the profession my father told him to pursue. So I do it for him, "Blood sucking politician," I say with an evil chuckle. "I assume Dr. Rick's colleagues know of Sage's aptitude, and that's why his "*I'm a liberal*," shuts their mouths right quick."

Releasing a giggle just as evil as my earlier one, Sage and I sound exactly alike. "I scared the ever-loving fuck out of 'em because they thought I'd be running against their children in the future. Since I'm so pretty," Sage says without arrogance, "And charismatic, and I actually give a shit about tolerance, gay rights, and equality, I'd murder their sons at the polls."

"You would, too," Rae says while nodding her head like a faithful follower. "I'd vote for you."

"I got them off my ass by finally choosing a university and a major. It helped that I'm moving across the country, and never coming back," Sage says with vehemence, finally earning a reaction from Weston.

West croaks out "Never?" showing he's more than interested in Sage. I'm not sure what these boys are up to, but I doubt it's went past talking and kissing. Sage wasn't lying when he said he was keeping Weston at arm's length. But I think he was lying about not saying no to Weston already.

"We're in trouble," Ginny breathes in my ear, noticing the same thing I just did. I just close my eyes and nod my agreement. "We're most certainly never telling Malcolm."

"Agreed," we conspire to break the law for the sake of true love.

Weston hasn't woken up sexually yet. Hopefully that isn't for the next thirteen months, when my eighteen-year-old son leaves for college. Even then, Weston will only be fifteen.

"Christ," I hiss, lost in my own thoughts.

Thinking I'm upset about his desertion, Sage reassures me in a way he can reassure Weston too. "Don't worry, Mom. I plan on coming back to New England after I graduate. I'm pissed at Dad right now, but I want to know my baby brother or sister."

Rae spews, "Thank goodness we won't be the only ones with baby sisters and brothers when we're grown. If Mom and Dad have a kid, it will be younger than its niece or nephew. How gross!"

"That will be a battle-of-the-wills," Ginny sounds awed. "Devon and Essie's kid is sure to be as stubborn as a boulder. Lord knows what kind of child Malcolm and Clover could create. Would their kids be cousins? Uncle/aunt and niece/nephew? What a clusterfuck. Wowza. Don't get me started on Kieren and Willow's future kids… that will be some Pennsyltucky shit, right there, with their parents being stepsiblings."

"Ginny, thanks for making me feel so normal," Sage blurts out. "And I'm the gayest person in Fairport."

My cellphone rings, eliciting a chorus of, "No cellphones at the dinner table," from Ginny, Raven, and Weston.

"Sorry, guys," Sage says for me as I reach for my purse. "It's my dad's ringtone."

Looking at my cellphone with disdain and apprehension, I let it ring a few times before I get the nerve up to answer it. With a deep breath, I press answer. "Byron?"

"Where are you?" comes staticy from the other end. "We're at your house, and both you and Sage are missing."

Able to hear his father's bellow, "Better put out an Amber Alert," Sage snarks. "Your seventeen-year-old son is having dinner with his mother. Oh, the humanity," he feigns fainting.

Half laughing, what Byron says next dries up my humor for years to come. "Rick and I are here to see you. Either tell me where you are, or I'll check the GPS in Sage's cellphone."

Knowing everyone could hear my ex-husband, I mouth, "I'm so sorry," just as I hang up.

"It's okay," Ginny says sympathetically, reaching over to hold my hand. "I want to meet your ex-husband and your asshole bigot of a father."

Squeezing Ginny's hand, I feel supported for the first time in my entire life. Someone is on my side. I come first. "Thank you. I appreciate it."

CHAPTER FOURTEEN

Ginny Jamison

Opal and I clean up the kitchen together, triggering a feeling of warmth to bloom in my chest. The kids are back to their paused reality program, chattering with each other and at the television screen, adding to the homey feeling. Even without the children being here, the sense of rightness would still overpower me. Opal looks at home in my kitchen– like she belongs here as much as I do, and I've never experienced this feeling before. Not even when Sarah and I shared a home together did I feel so content.

This house is where I will spend the rest of my days. Several times I invited potential dates over for drinks, only to kick them out after a couple of minutes. It was like they invaded my sanctuary, and it made me feel anxious. But, tonight, here I am, happy to share my space with Opal. It's surreal.

Feeling sedate yet in need of affection, I curl up to Opal's back. She's hand-washing the dishes that didn't fit into the dishwasher. Sighing, Opal presses back into me. "I can leave," she offers for the tenth time. "I shouldn't have had Sage call Byron with our whereabouts. Dr. Rick and Byron are coming here to humiliate me into behaving. I don't know if I have the stomach for you to witness it."

"Opal," I breathe into her ear. I wrap my arms around her chest, pulling her back tautly against my breasts. "How about you stand up to your father this time? Don't do it for Sage, or to impress me. Do it for yourself– for your own happiness."

Laughing without humor, "I'll try." Opal pulls away while drying her hands on a kitchen towel. "They will be here any minute. You should probably shoo West and Rae to their rooms."

Looking out into the living room, I gaze at the kids on the sofa. Dropping all pretense, the boys are holding hands, albeit, hiding their entangled fingers underneath a pillow between them. "What about Sage? I don't dare leave them to their own devices, ya know?"

Sage, having impeccable hearing abilities, looks up and says, "I have to stay."

I expect Opal to argue, but she doesn't. "Okay… Weston?" I call out, even though I know he's just pretending not to be listening. "You want to scoop the leaves out of the pool with the skimmer? Rae can add the chlorine tablets to the floater."

"It sounded like a request, but it was actually a demand," Rae grumbles as she turns off the TV. "I can't wait until I'm an adult."

Flabbergasted, I fist my hands on my hips. "Raven, you love cleaning out the pool. Who you fooling? I don't think acting like a brat is cute, and I'm sure your audience of one agrees."

"I have to stay," Rae's audience says again. Sage explains to Rae and West why they have to give him some space. "Mom needs me, but it's also the rules."

"Rules?" Rae chirps, shocked that no matter how old you are, there will always be rules. "Your mom still has rules?"

Opal snorts next to me, and then walks back into the kitchen. She opens up the refrigerator and pulls a bottle of wine from its depths. Gesturing by toasting me with the bottle, she asks if I wants some, too.

I shake my head no. I don't need to have any liquid courage, because it'll be hard enough when sober to keep my trap shut if Dr. Rick pisses my ass off.

"Rae, your father and I are the exception. We have no parents and we are our own bosses. Even then, I still have rules and laws to follow."

Sage explains the inner-workings of his family. "Grandfather says if you're old enough to wipe your own ass, then you're old enough to hold an adult conversation. No matter what, we are required to attend family meetings. It's torture."

"Ugh," Rae grunts out, deciding she likes being a Mason better. "I'll go clean the pool, I guess."

The gong of the doorbell has me jumping out of my skin. I wait a heartbeat, wondering who should answer the door, and then I realize it's *my* house. Shoulders back, head held high, I swing the door open, not knowing what I'll find on the other side.

Two silver foxes stand on my welcome mat. At first glance, I'd think them twins because of the air of power and affluence emanating from them. Dressed impeccably in three-piece suits, one of the men is wearing a scowl, while the other is smiling politely.

"Welcome," I say cordially, even though I feel anything but. "I'm Virginia Jamison."

Taking the lead, the taller, *younger*, smiling version of the pair steps forward, and shocks the shit out of me. "Richard Sage," flows deeply while he presents his hand to me. "You may call me Dr. Rick."

Blushing for some unknown reason, "Call me Ginny. Please, come in," mumbles bashfully from my mouth as I step to the side. I don't want to like Opal's asshat of a father, but there's a reason he's gotten to where he has in life. Dr. Rick is the total package. A package of what? I don't know just yet.

"Ginny," he tests out for size. Gesturing to the brooding, shorter, older man to his right, "This is my son-in-law, Dr. Byron Fischer. Thank you for welcoming us into your home."

Byron steps over my threshold, scowling and ignoring me on his way by. A man on a mission, he heads straight toward Opal. I swear Dr. Rick breathes, "*Bloody idiot*," underneath his breath as he enters my home. I shut us all in, already wishing I could kick Byron to the curb.

"Why weren't you at home?" Bryon is lighting into Opal, who's draining a wine glass in one swallow. She sidesteps craftily when her ex-husband tries to kiss her on the mouth after insulting her.

"I'm no longer any of your concern," Opal slurs, making me wonder how many glasses of wine she slammed while I was making the introductions. "Dr. Rick," she says brightly, leaving Byron where he stands to embrace her father. "Long time, old man. Looking better than ever, I see."

Smiling, squeezing his daughter tightly, "You don't have to come home to see us, you know? We can meet halfway. Your mother is beside herself, missing you. You were with her every day for thirty-nine years, and then up and disappeared." Dr. Rick holds his daughter at arm's length, and then he fucking winks. "It's not our fault you're not strong enough to deflect our influence."

"Grandfather," Sage chastises, also ignoring his father's seething presence in the room. "We've discussed you pressuring Mom, remember?"

"We've discussed many things, lad. Most of which you ignore," Dr. Rick says pointedly. "Why should I be any different?"

"Point taken." Sage huffs a laugh while moving forward to hug his grandfather.

This handsome, charismatic man is not what I expected. From the way Opal and Sage made Dr. Rick sound, he was old, stuffy, and hate-filled, and without a funny bone in his body. He's teasing his family and being affectionate. But even then, I can tell he's powerful and refuses to heed a no.

"Hello, children. Who do you belong to?" Dr. Rick sets his sights on my family.

The kids are frozen on the sofa, avidly watching Opal's family like they're a reality program brought to life. I decide I better do the introductions since they are speechless. "Dr. Rick, this is my niece, Raven, and my nephew, Weston– Sage's friends."

"Nice to meet you," Raven says sweetly, suddenly a perfect angel. With an, "I have to go clean the pool," she flees outside.

Weston slowly unfolds his large frame from the sofa, doing his damnedest to look intimidating and masculine. In a very deep voice, he says, "I'm Sage's boyfriend," and then he follows his sister outside, leaving us speechless in his wake.

Face almost purple with rage, "You're shitting me, right?" Byron shouts at Sage.

Unaffected by his father's reaction, Sage sits back on the sofa, patting a cushion for his mother to join him. "News to me, but I liked the sounds of it," Sage says to goad his father. "Ginny, sit next to Mom."

"This is…" Byron is at a loss for words as he falls into my recliner.

I settle on the sofa next to Opal, with Sage flanking the other side of her– we present a united front of support for Opal.

Dr. Rick looks highly amused as he slowly lowers himself onto the loveseat. Sage gets his naughtiness from his grandfather. It makes me curious to see what's going on inside Dr. Rick's devious mind.

"Let it be known," Dr. Rick begins. He crosses his legs, and then folder his hands in his lap. "This is Byron's doing. I'm simply here as a mediator, or rather, to mitigate a disaster."

"Come home," Byron begs Opal, looking ready to crawl if he has to. His facial expression can only be describes as crushed. I pity him, not able to imagine how badly it must hurt to love a woman who can't love you back.

"Are you smoking crack?" Sage barks out at his father, making me feel worse for the man. "Are you fucking serious?"

"I second that," Opal says, and then starts laughing manically. "Your girlfriend is knocked up, and I'm no longer your wife. Our son is one year from being a legal adult. I'm trying to date a woman, and I'm happy to report I'm no longer a *reluctant*-lesbian."

Startled, Byron spews, "You're not acting like yourself, Opal. I thought you'd get this stupid notion of being a lesbian out of your system, and then come back to me. But when I found out you'd been fucking a man..." Frustrated and seething, Byron is close to imploding.

I no longer have a sympathetic bone in my body when it comes to Byron Fischer. I'm beginning to see why Opal had a hard time leaving her husband, and once she did, she never went back to visit her family.

"I'm not even going to respond to that," Opal slurs from beside me.

"Are you sure you don't have the wrong villain in your life," I whisper into her ear. "Your dad seems pretty smooth compared to your ex-husband."

Barking a sharp laugh, Dr. Rick leans forward to high-five his grandson. "Oh, don't make the mistake of thinking I'm not an asshole," he says without shame. "I'm controlling in the extreme. But at least I know when to back off."

"Come home," Byron tries again, sounding more hopeless than ever. "I love you, Opal. You're my wife."

"Am I missing something, here?" Opal asks her father, ignoring Byron's sniveling.

"Our boy, he puts on a good front. But he's a fucking mess," Dr. Rick mutters, all the while smiling infectiously. "The psychiatrists at the hospital have a pool going, wagering on when Byron was going to break. Dr. Ernest won, by the looks of it."

Ignoring all of us, Byron stares at Opal with all of his might. In a lulling, coaxing tone, he chants, "Remember how it used to be? We woke together, worked together, raised our son together, and then went to sleep together. I miss that, don't you?"

Opal sighs deeply, as if her patience is being tested to its limits. "We were partners, but it was no different than *working* beside someone– we weren't truly *living* our lives as husband and wife. Neither of us was satisfied. I feel more myself now than ever, and I will *never* go back to living as I had."

Opal gets up from beside me to walk over to her ex-husband. She crouches down and whispers to him, "I love you, Bryon. But I have to love myself more."

Shaking his head like he doesn't get it, "I don't even like Audra," Byron admits.

"Wow, Dad," Sage drawls out. "Audra's carrying your kid, *my* brother or sister, and that's how much respect you show her?"

"Byron, that makes you look even worse," Opal scolds, rolling her eyes. "Really? Marry the girl, raise your child, and move on. Sage is a grown man now, and I'm doing better than ever. I like my life, my job, my friends, and whatever I'm creating with Ginny. You *need* to do that, too."

Trying a new manipulative tactic. "You said you had to love yourself more, but do you love yourself more than God? You're being selfish, Opal," Byron grits out, suddenly furious.

Throwing her hands in the air, Opal lashes out. "Are you fucking serious, you cradle-robbing douchebag?"

"Broadening your vocabulary nicely, I see," Dr. Rick says with a grin. Turning, he levels his sparkling stare on me. "Byron is an atheist. I think that should be said to show the depths he's willing to sink. He only went through the motions when he joined the Catholic Church. Now he's bringing God into it. How Christian of him."

"I'm a man of science," Byron snarls.

Dr. Rick keeps speaking as if Byron didn't interrupt him. "Men of science have a hard time bridging the gap between definitive proof and faith. It's a testament to true genius if you can widen your mind to encompass something you can't see with your eyes."

"I have faith," Byron professes to Opal. "I never had our marriage annulled in the church. We were married before God, the government paperwork means nothing. You will forever be my wife, and Sage is our son."

"And this new kid is what exactly?" Mystified, Sage tries to reason it out. "A bastard?"

"The hell with you," Opal growls as she comes to her feet. "We should record this for you to listen to later. You planned on giving me what? A lesbian intervention? It's *you* who needs help. You need to be responsible and act like a fucking man," Opal hisses in Byron's face. Fed up, she pushes away from him. "I was easy, that's it. You didn't have to work on being a husband after the way I was raised."

"Audra drives me fucking nuts," Byron spews, turning belligerent. "I have to show her how to do every goddamned thing. She doesn't know jack-shit. It's mind-numbing."

"Because she's a pregnant child," Opal screams. Pointing at her father, "This is why I don't come home. Mom is just as bad as Byron. I. Am. A. Lesbian. I don't want to be a man's wife. What is so hard to understand?"

Dr. Rick doesn't even bat an eyelash. "It took your mother and me about fifteen minutes after you moved away before we figured out you were being serious."

"How much more serious does it take? I came out of the closet and you just looked at me like I'd grown a second head." Frustrated, Opal starts pacing the room.

I can feel her misery, but I can't help but see a little girl lashing out at her daddy. Similar to how Rae was treating me earlier. Children, even adult ones, only see what they want to see. Dr. Rick is no saint, and he even confessed to being a controlling asshole, but he seems pretty black and white to me.

"Opal, you were proficient in suffering in silence. Your mother and I could only ask you the same question so many times, and receive an '*I'm fine*' in reply. I'm your father, not your mind reader. I called to clear the air after you got settled in Fairport, but you didn't believe my sincerity. The other four years of your absence is on your head."

"Fine," Opal concedes, sounding petulant. "I can't take seeing *that*," she points at her broken ex-husband, who is clearly dreaming up new forms of manipulation, judging by the calculating light in his eyes.

Leaning back against the loveseat, Dr. Rick stares at Byron with disgust. "If you don't like how Byron is behaving, then tell him, not me."

Head cocking to the side, "What was up with your gay intervention for Sage a few weeks ago, then?" Opal challenges.

Happy expression frosting over, Dr. Rick is wicked pissed. "Intervention? Try asking my grandson what he wanted out of life. Point-by-point, I wanted all the details. No different than I would have behaved toward the rest of our family. I sat Sage down, telling him how his actions have far-reaching consequences on each and every single one of us. He may come to regret purposefully baiting the men he may lead someday."

"I'm not going into politics," Sage mutters hopelessly. "Not on your life, Grandfather."

"So you've said," Dr. Rick states like he doesn't believe Sage. "I've let up on the sexism since competent women have invaded my hospital, and weak men like Byron are tainting the male gene pool. You, my dear," he says to Opal, "Have taught me more than you realize. I may be stubborn, but not as badly as you are."

"Why did you come tonight?" Opal asks, voice breaking.

Saying the fuck with it, I stand up to go over to Opal. I grab her hand, drawing her back to the sofa. "If you're going to have a constructive conversation, you cannot be pacing around asserting your dominance over everyone sitting below you."

Opal flashes me a look like I betrayed her, but I don't let her pull her hand away. In fact, I grab both of her hands, and begin to rub soothing circles into her skin with my thumbs. "Opal," I breathe into her ear. "I'd give anything for two second with my father, just to say goodbye, and yours is sitting right here in the flesh, trying to be here for you. It's up to you to meet him in the middle."

Pretending he didn't hear what I just whispered, "Good point," Dr. Rick asserts. "It was unnerving. For the exact reason you crouched when you tried to connect with Byron, you have to be on a level playing field to be equal. Standing over us, bitching, is counterproductive."

"Why did you come here tonight?" Opal tries again, sounding calmer.

"Your lady is correct," Dr. Rick says, and he's not being disingenuous. The way he's behaving, I doubt he has any issue with Opal's lifestyle. "I'm here for you, specifically to make sure Byron didn't succeed with his asinine plan. We all know how easily he can twist you into a knot."

Eyes cutting toward the brooding man with obvious suspicion, Opal asks, "What exactly did you hope to obtain, Byron?"

"I wanted you to come home," Byron begins, looking eager and hopeful, like he still has a hold over Opal. "I know you don't want to be married to me any longer. But I want you in my everyday life. I thought we could live together, share a bed as we did, work together, and raise our son. The only difference from our previous marriage is I would overlook your proclivities."

"Oh, really?" Opal rolls her eyes, playing along. "So, we play house while I take lovers? What of Audra the baby you share?"

"I don't have to marry Audra to make our child legally mine. The baby will have my name, and I will raise it as such. As for Audra, she and I are through. I'll paying her a stipend."

"Did we go back in time?" I grunt out. The sleeping feminist I keep buried deep inside is snarling and clawing her way to the surface. "You're going to make the mother of your child your mistress? An actual whore? As in, pay her to screw you?"

"You're not hearing him wrong," Sage mutters, sounding as sickened as I do. "Did you miss the part where he said he'd raise *it* while Audra lives elsewhere? He wants Mom to raise his bastard," Sage snarls. "I know goddamned well I'll be the one raising the brat. Mark my words."

Standing abruptly, Opal points at my front door. "I don't live here, but I'm saying it just the same. Get the fuck out, Byron, and don't let the door hit you in the ass on your way out. I'm done. D O N E!" she bellows, shaking everything made of glass in my house.

"Audra doesn't want the baby," Bryon says in a rush. "She's having the child and relinquishing all of her rights. I'm not paying Audra because I'm treating her like a whore. I'm paying her not to abort my child, goddamnit!" Bryon releases a tortured sound from deep within his chest.

"I'm sorry, Byron. I truly am." Opal has tears streaming down her cheeks, and I want to comfort her, but I know the touch wouldn't be welcome. "I love you, but not enough to sacrifice myself to make *your* life easier. Raise the kid you created, hire a nanny, but don't expect me to clean up your mess. Please leave," she whispers, and then more firmly, "Now."

"Jesus Christ!" Sage shouts, coming to his feet. He punches his own thighs with his clenched fists. "What are the odds of you living until you're eighty-two years old?" Rapidly snarling a string of profanities I can't decipher, Sage charges out of the living room and straight out the French doors to the backyard.

"Sit in the car," Dr. Rick orders Bryon. "Don't look at me like that. Your son has every right to be furious with you. When you get your head out of your ass, you'll realize why he's pissed. Maybe then he'll listen to you. But right now, the sniveling is getting tiresome."

Byron just stares at the side of Opal's face, but she refuses to look back at him. However, she does speak. In a tightly controlled tone, Opal says slowly, "It's not flattering when your ex-husband asks you to be with him just so you can raise his mistake."

"Opal, that's not why I was asking you to come home," Byron pleads, voice twisting with desperation.

"Bullshit," Opal says with quiet calmness. "It's even worse when your son realizes the life expectancy of a surgeon is much lower than that of the average population. I suggest you retire and make the most out of your golden years– be with your children," Opal demands, "But leave me out of it."

Knowing this could go on for hours, I take the initiative. "I'm asking politely *this* time. You have exactly five seconds to get your ass out of my house before I call the police." In example, I point at the photo gallery on my wall, showcasing many brothers in blue. "I should also mention. That big bruiser who called your son his boyfriend, he's the Chief of Police's son. So get the fuck out of my sight."

I don't watch Byron leave because I'm too busy determining how Opal is fairing. Dead-eyed, Opal is faraway inside her mind, dealing with the fallout. I want to yank her to me, but our friendship is too new– too tenuous.

Distancing myself, I rise from the sofa. I give the father and daughter space by stepping into the kitchen. I try not to listen in as Dr. Rick says all the right things, and judging by the sincerity in his voice, he means every single word of it.

I've never missed my father more than I do right this second.

I find the half-full bottle of Riesling on the counter next to Opal's glass. I refill it, and then drain it myself, and then repeat until the wine stops flowing. Staring down into the empty bottle is exactly how Dr. Rick finds me.

"Budding alcoholism? Byron will do that to a person," Dr. Rick says wryly. Patting me on the shoulder, squeezing slightly, he tries to reassure me. "You'll be alright."

"It's not me I'm worried about," I mumble, sounding hopeless.

Smiling at me, still in father-mode, "Ah, it was the figurative *you* I meant. As in, you and my daughter. You'll be alright. I can already tell you'll be good for each other."

"Thank you," I breathe, barely a whisper of a sound. "How is she?" I gesture into the living room with my chin.

"Shaken, but Opal will persevere. What she needs right now, more than anything, is to not talk about it, to not dwell on it. Since you and she are so new, I think it's a great idea if you'd spend some more time together, and *not* speak of this."

Suddenly feeling like I did when my own father was alive, I fall into those patterns Opal kept telling me about. I turn into the petulant daughter, asking her father to explain color to the blind. "Yeah, but how do you get over something by *not* talking about it?"

"How do you get over something by beating it to death?" Dr. Rick volleys back. "Instead of growing the problem by overanalyzing it, instead of ignoring it, how about just moving on." He shrugs, and then walks away. "Sage?" Dr. Rick calls out into the backyard. "Tell your grandfather goodbye!"

I walk back into the living room on shaking legs and wobbly knees, unsure how to handle this situation. Instinctively, I show Opal how I feel about her, how I want her to be happy and wound-free, and I do so without uttering a single word. I do, however, make an inappropriate sound or two. Pinning Opal to the sofa cushion, I kiss the living daylights out of her, which is exactly how Dr. Rick finds us.

"Drinking, swearing, intimately entwined on the sofa," Dr. Rick says with a laugh. "Virginia Jamison, I do believe you are a positive influence on my daughter."

"I'll call you," Opal says from beneath me, and then she releases a nervous giggle.

"Evening, ladies," Dr. Rick says in parting.

"Awkward," I groan, rolling to sit on the sofa. "Want to stay and watch a movie? I have soft pretzels–"

"With a gallon of spicy brown mustard, I bet," Opal teases, looking bright-eyed and flushed from our romp on the sofa. But most importantly, she looks relieved that I'm not forcing her to talk about Byron's tantrum.

"Of course," I say with a grin. "And I've got cupcakes and ice cream."

"You sold me on the movie," Sage yells as he enters the living room. "But now I'm in search of those cupcakes."

"I know where Aunt Ginny hides all of the good stuff," Rae says deviously, sneaking past us to raid the kitchen.

"And I know where the movies are," Weston adds, heading straight for the entertainment center. "I want to watch *Bad Grandpa* again. Johnny Knoxville is a trip."

Opal grabs my hand, twining our fingers together. Resting her head on my shoulder, she snuggles down for a long night on the sofa with the kids surrounding us. "Thank you," she murmurs to me, thanking me for many things.

CHAPTER FIFTEEN

Ginny Jamison

"This is so fucked up," I mutter in awe. "I cannot believe I'm going through with this."

"Just lie there on the bed like a good girl." Opal's voice is amused, but there is a thread of worry weaving through it. "Keep your eyes closed while I find something to blind you with."

"Good God, woman," I gasp in terror, hands shielding my face. "Please don't blind me with hot acid or something equally horrific. Go the least painful route, and just tie a scarf around my head."

Opal's snickering is infectious. "I'm looking for a scarf, but your closet is reminiscent of your niece's old bedroom floor."

"Ha-ha!" I mock laugh, but my voice warbles with trepidation. "I'm well organized, I'll have you know. The scarves are on a rack on the back of the closet door."

"Very, very nice," Opal murmurs in appreciation over my finer tastes and exemplary organizational skills.

When I'd answered my door fifteen minutes ago to find Opal on the other side, I was excited, albeit relieved, to see her. That was until she sprang penetrative sex on me like she was asking if I wanted to watch a comedy versus a horror film. I'd laughed. Two seconds later, I realized she was being serious when she said the guy was waiting in her car.

Not that I blame Opal for coming up with a reasonable solution. I've pestered her every single time I've seen her over the course of the last month– sometimes twice per visit. It's highly juvenile on my part, but Opal makes me feel like a green-eyed monster.

Opal is enthusiastic in bed, eager for me to teach her all I know. When we both let go and bypass student/teacher, it's a passionate joining unlike any I've ever experienced with another soul. But in the back of my mind, her mild attraction to a single male nags the ever-loving fuck out of me. Opal says she's just friends with the guy and that she's not lusting over him. She says all it was, was an enlightening learning experience. Ours is a learning experience for her as well, so I get jealous over the thought of her sharing the soft afterglow with this random guy.

I know I'm driving Opal batshit cray-cray with my obsessive interrogation, but I can't get it out of my head.

I'm teaching Opal all I know, but there is still so very much she has experienced that I will never learn. It leaves me feeling empty, ignorant, and helpless, as if she and I aren't on a level playing field.

Opal assures me I won't like it. Not so much the act of penetration, but the inevitable intimacy between the man and me. She said the thought of letting some unknown male touch her, made her physically sick. The only way she was able to do it with Byron and her friend, was because she cared deeply for them, making the ensuing intimacy feel almost normal.

Last night, Opal showed up unannounced, which she tends to do quite often, and it secretly makes me very pleased. But I forgot to close out my web browser, which led to disaster.

Teasing me, Opal asked, "What are shopping for now? Is it for me? I loved the new soap molds you ordered me." Then we both went white as a sheet: me, because I knew what I was shopping around to get, and Opal, because she found the chatroom I was perusing for potential penetrators. "A dick? You're shopping online for some dirty asshole to screw you?"

"Your vocabulary sure is getting colorful, Opal," I teased to evade the oncoming shit-storm: our first fight as a couple.

Even though we've had no such talks of exclusivity, it's a given when you spend every available moment of your free time with someone. Opal and I went from fooling around and sharing meals together, to her having two drawers in my dresser and a half of the vanity in the bathroom. I'm sure giving Sage the spare bedroom to sleep in on nights Opal worked at the hospital, (our way of playing Sage versus Weston keep-away) overruled any talks we hadn't had as of yet.

Disappointment clearly etched across her face, all Opal did was sigh heavily while walking back to my front door– to leave me.

I learned a valuable lesson in that moment. There will be no heated fights between us, and not because we aren't passionate in our endeavors. Opal is all about respect and freewill after the way Dr. Rick suffocated her as a young woman. Opal will not yell and scream about something she feels is my decision to make, with or without her input.

Hand on the doorknob, Opal turned to me, "Don't be stupid, Ginny. We've discussed this at length. It will be a horrible experience for you, and I don't want to see you get hurt. Your usual M.O. is to go to a club and hookup. But a man is not a woman, and some will not stop if you're not having a good time. A guy can give you a disease, but more so, they can impregnate you. When I give you my advice, it's because it's life or death. This is no trivial matter."

"I can't stop thinking about it," I whined, frustration and pain lacing my tone.

"I know," Opal sighed heavily again, clearly I was exhausting her. "Will you give me the peace of mind by allowing me to help you with this? You are precious, Ginny, and if you get hurt, I was threatened with bodily harm. Don't harm me by harming yourself."

"You are impressive with the guilt-trippage, woman," I muttered in awe. "Okay," I breathed, terrified.

"I think it's best if we spent some time apart," Opal said as she left my home.

I didn't expect to see Opal for a long while after last night. Every woman I know, when angry, they tend to stay that way for days on end, or longer. So I spent my evening crying into a carton of ice cream, and then I laid in a bed smelling of my absentee girlfriend and began to sob.

With Opal not yelling at me, with her not making me feel guilty or judged for my stupid behavior, she actually succeeded in teaching me a valuable lesson. I started laughing while crying into her pillow, knowing deep down that the woman employs that nasty trick on her son, as she was taught to do so by Dr. Rick.

Words from conversations' past haunted me last night. *"We Sages don't have to use the threat of physical violence to make someone comply. The mental threat of disappointing those you love is by far more humbling."*

I spent the last twenty-four hours heartsick because I'd disappointed Opal, and I feared I'd lost her for good. But Opal Fischer is no ordinary, angry woman. She didn't leave because she couldn't stand the sight of me. I estimate that our time apart last night was for Opal to make the necessary preparations for this evening. It was not to sit in stew in her pissed-off-ness.

Opal's tactics taught me another valuable lesson: I was falling in love with her, not that I will admit it to her– yet.

"I'm sorry I behaved like a child last night," I apologize to Opal when she comes to the side of the bed. I open my eyes to look at her, noting several scarves clutched in her hands. "Sometimes it's hard to let go of the past. I thought a lot about my earlier relationships, and why they failed. I thought it was *my* weight, but it was *my* issue with *my* weight that tainted it. It was also how I behaved childishly while in a mature relationship."

"Ah," is all Opal says, and it's maddening. But I keep my mouth shut, as an adult would. Because it's not my place to demand that Opal speaks to me when she doesn't want to. Smiling privately, she finally replies. "I see you *did* learn your lesson."

"You were waiting for me to bitch," I gasp out, shocked. "You thought I'd get pissy because you didn't say anything else. You were testing me."

Ever-patient, Opal's lips twist into a self-satisfied smirk. "Maybe."

"I see your point," I grumble. "You've very good at fucking with my head."

"Cerebral fuckage, Sage calls it." Opal's voice is light, but I can tell she's trying to mask her hidden pleasure at being twisted in her intelligence. "My son is far better at it than I am. He'd make an exceptional politician. Thank fuck, he's not going down that path."

Leaning forward, Opal brushes a soft kiss to my lips, barely touching me. Pulling away, she looks down at me with sympathetic eyes. "I'm sorry you were upset last night. I'd apologize for the why of it, but you needed to feel the pain of disappointment to grow as a human being. I'm not trying to be patronizing. It's a situation I've been in too many times to count, so I feel your pain as if it were my own."

"Thank you," I murmur, reaching up to grasp the nape of Opal's neck, drawing her back down to my lips. Kissing her thoroughly, I show her, rather than tell her, how I'm feeling. Pulling away, I mumble, "Thank you is so much better than replying with… *ah*," I complain.

Opal to bark a laugh. "You're welcome," she says wryly while wearing a shit-eating grin. A scarf enters my field of vision, causing my heart to beat into hyper-drive. "Now, close your eyes."

"I cannot believe I'm about to do this," I mumble in awe as the scarf covers half my face.

"You're the one in control," Opal reminds me. "At any point, you can say stop, and it *will* stop. This is for you, and you alone. So if you're not ready, or if you've changed your mind…" Her hands still, no longer tying the scarf behind my head, waiting for my confirmation to either proceed with or to abandon our plans for the evening.

"I need to do this in order to let it go. I know it has nothing to do with being a lesbian, and everything to do with experiencing everything at least once. I mean, how can I know for sure if I've never done it?"

"You're not going to like it," Opal says with complete certainty. "But I think we better find out for sure, before you and I move forward."

"I like that, where you say *you and I* in a sentence together, especially if you add, '*before you and I move forward to greater things.*' Yeah, I like the sounds of that a lot," I murmur dreamily.

"Me, too." Opal releases a naughty giggle, and then everything goes black. With a forceful tug, "Is the scarf too tight? Can you see anything?"

"Ugh! I'm blind!" I pretend to panic, waving my arms about while kicking my feet. "Why can't I see this hottie mystery man, again?"

"Trust me. It's for the best, for all those involved," Opal warns, sounding guilty as all hell.

With the dark emphasizing the gravity of what I'm about to do, I start to fret. My heart beats a rapid tattoo against my rib cage. My lungs are heaving up and down. My skin beads with sweat while I shiver as if freezing. I become hypersensitive to everything around me. I just keep saying on repeat within my mind. *I cannot believe I'm going to do this.*

"Hey, now," I complain, batting at Opal's hands when she tries to unbutton my nightgown. "No."

"Yes," Opal says firmly, grabbing my wrist. "Don't make me bind your hands. I'll do it," she threatens, sounding beyond serious.

"That's what the extra scarves were for," I grumble, getting a clue. "I'll behave. I'd rather have mobility than pride, I guess."

While divesting me of my nightgown with the practiced movements of a veteran nurse, "Pride?" Opal prompts when I don't elaborate.

Lying on my bed, I'm completely naked in more ways than one. Eyes burning, voice thick with tears of shame, "It will be mortifying when the only man who will ever penetrate me, won't be able to get it up because of my big, ugly, fat ass… HEY!" I shout when my thigh is swatted hard. Rubbing the pain away, "Oh, my God. That fucking stings. I thought you said you didn't believe in physical violence."

"That wasn't me," Opal sounds wicked pissed, but it's directed at me, not her slap-happy *friend.*

"He hit me?" I breathlessly gasp, completely aghast. "What the fuck?" Curling into a ball to hide my shame, I stammer, "He's in here already… in the room with us? Shit," I hiss with feeling. "And you let him hit me?"

"I thought you learned a lesson last night, Ginny?" Opal sound disappointed again, causing me to thickly swallow my resulting guilt. "I thought you trusted me."

"I'm sorry," I cry out. To prove that I am apologetic for my ill behavior, I roll onto my back and stretch the length of my body out on the bed, allowing Opal and her friend to see all of me in the flesh.

"Thank you," Opal says softly. "We don't have to do this, Ginny. This is for you, and you can stop it if you'd like."

"Is… is he going to be mean to me?" I ask in a small, scared voice.

A strangled masculine chuckle erupt off to my right– the sound so amused that I can't help but feel silly for asking such a thing.

Opal schools my ass wicked fierce. "He hit you because that was the most idiotic thing I've ever heard, especially coming after you made the revelation about ruining your past relationships because you acted childishly instead of with maturity. If someone didn't like the way you looked, they wouldn't be your lover. If someone didn't like who you were as a person, they wouldn't date you. It is *their* choice to be with you, not yours. That kind of insecurity kills a relationship, because it reeks of a lack of trust on your part."

"I get that now… but I am *fat*," I stress. "There is no hiding it, as you've said so yourself."

"It's as if she doesn't trust me," Opal whispers, and that infectious laughter is filling the room again. "Like I'd bring some douchebag to humiliate her. Unfathomable."

"I'm sorry," I repeat, feeling small and stupid.

A flurry of rapid, hushed whispering erupts, but I can't make out what they're saying. "I don't want you to feel belittled, Ginny." Opal reaches out to caress my cheek in a comforting manner. "I want you to feel empowered. You are the only one here with any say in anything. Own it, or tell him to leave," she demands.

I take a moment to process what Opal just said to me. Is she right? Did I ruin all of my past relationships with my insecurity? Did my girlfriends feel like I didn't trust them, like they couldn't be honest with me? Am I using how I feel about myself to taint how I think they see me?

I do trust Opal. I do believe she finds me sexy and likes what she sees. I do believe she cares about me as a human being. Instead of telling her, though, I decide to prove it.

"I want to do this, so where do we begin?" I hesitate for a second, "We don't just go straight into sex, do we?"

Amused laughter fills my bedroom, and my uncomfortable giggle joins it. "You're precious, Ginny," Opal chuckles out. "My *friend* loves women– too much, in fact. So I think the best place to start is by exploring him."

"What?" I sound confused even to my own ears.

Movement to my right stuns me stupid. My heartbeat is all I can hear– the steady *lub dub… lub dub… lub dub*, eclipsing all other sound. Quivering, I try to stiffen my muscles, but it only makes me shake worse.

"Shh…" Opal soothes, smoothing a hand down the side of my face. "You have no need to be frightened. He won't touch you until you're ready. I thought you might like to touch him, see the evidence of what looking at your shapely body does to him. Shall we?"

I mutter before I can stop myself, "What if I do it wrong?"

Opal's words join the man's amusement, "There is no wrong way. A horny guy is happy, just as long as you're touching his prick."

"Ohhh… wow…" I drawl out when my hand is placed on something hot and hard. I skate my fingertips down his length. "I thought it would feel like an arm or something," I mutter to myself. "But it's warmer, softer than that. It also pulses. Huh? Interesting."

"You sound like a scientist, Gin," Opal says as she sits down next to me on the bed. Softly laughing to herself, she butts me in the shoulder with her forehead. "He wants me to tell you, '*This is sex, not an education.*' But that's not correct, since you're learning him."

Hands I'd recognize anywhere, eagerly cup my breasts, so I don't freak. Opal's fixated with my tits, making me no longer feel self-conscious about the huge bags of fat. Her obsession with my breasts makes me to see them as something desirable– beautiful.

Squishing, manipulating my flesh with her fingertips while making noises in the back of her throat, Opal puts me at ease. She's teasing me, simply trying to put me at ease. She's being silly, and I like this laidback version of Opal.

Opal's playfulness disappears, and it's fervently replaced by toe-curling lust. Tonguing my breasts, she takes me with her. "Yes," I hiss when her warm mouth wets my nipple, and then she bites me– hard. Eyes rolling back into my skull, back arching, I grab the nearest thing as leverage– a stiff length of flesh that gives underneath my death-grip. The man grunts sharply, a hiss of sound forced between his gritted teeth.

"Did I hurt you? Oh, my God. Did I?" I say in a panic, somehow forgetting to release the piece of flesh I'm strangling in my fist. Worried, I start stroking him in earnest, trying to rub the sting away.

"Um… that was him liking it, Gin," Opal rasps huskily against my breast, where she's doing her ladylike version of motor-boating my tits– caressing my skin with her cheeks, lips, chin, and forehead. "He doesn't mind rough. He's just happy you're finally stroking instead of teasing him." Reaching out, she still my frenetic pace by gripping my forearm. "But you better let up a bit, or else he'll be finished before we get to the main event."

"Oh," I mumble, reaching over with both hands. The man moves closer to me, kneeling on the edge of the bed so I have greater access to him. Both of my hands stroke his length in an up and down motion, marveling at how different real flesh feels compared to a toy.

The makers of *CyberSkin* lied– there is a massive difference in texture. A real penis is hot to the touch, heat radiating into your skin for a lovely sensation. They flex and pulse when you do something pleasurable. They're hard, but give beneath your grip.

This dick is slightly curved, and it's so erect it's springy, flopping back to slap his belly when I release it.

Opal's *friend* isn't as big as some of the more challenging dildos I've encountered, but he's larger than the vibrator I use to masturbate. It's odd. A man can't give off intense orgasm-bringing vibrations, but he is *real*– alive. It's the realness that is starting to creep me out. There is a man attached to the quivering piece of flesh my fingers are wrapped around. I want to ask where he falls into the spectrum with other men, size-wise, but I don't want to be rude.

Opal will not be ignored for long. She slides down my body, dragging her beaded nipples across my skin in a tantalizing sensation. Yum, she's the one I want to touch and be touched by, not some man. But if I backed out now, I'd be a coward, living my life in regret… always wanting to know. *What if I'd kept going? What if I actually liked it?*

I lie flatter on the bed, giving Opal greater access while trying to keep contact with the dick. Wiggling, I try not to giggle from her teasing touch. Nipping with her blunt teeth, tongue trailing hot saliva down my body, Opal's lips begin sucking a path to my cunt. Every touch burns me with passion, leaves me breathless and starving for more. My head falls back against my pillow when hers disappears between my parted thighs.

"You're getting to good at that," I moan, trying not to writhe around on my bed. My thigh muscles are tensing and releasing, strained from the need to clench around Opal's face as she feast at my cunt. My toes curl into the sheets, staying me from lifting my hips and grinding wantonly against her lips and chin.

Shuddering in bliss, my fingers are clenching and releasing the piece of flesh between my fingers. I'm in awe that this is truly happening. Opal is going down on me with expert precision while a man watches, while I touch him as he watches. It's as scary as it is thrilling. It adds a level of wickedness that could become addictive if I'm not careful.

Opal groans at the exact moment the cock in my hand begins jerking erratically. Frantically, he wrenches my fingers from his shaft, and then places them on the heavy, squishy weight swinging below. Shuddering against my palm, *Friend* tried to control himself.

I twist a face, which has the guy laughing deeply from his belly and Opal giggling while gasping between my thighs. "You don't like touching his nutsack, do you?" Opal rasps out. "He was about to blow, that's why he shifted your hand. You can touch his dick again."

"They're odd." I roll my eyes beneath the cover of my scarf, thankful they can't see my reaction. Touching his dick is interesting, but I don't like his balls at all. They're covered in wiry hair and alien in texture. Not arousing in the least.

I slide my hand back up to where it's a pleasing smoothness, and the guy moans as a result. Curiosity gets the better of me. "What had you about to come?" I ask the guy, and then I ask Opal, "What had you groaning? I know you love the taste of me, but not *that* much."

Opal pauses her licking and sucking, and sheepishly replies. "His… uh… fingers are busy at the moment." She buries her face against my cunt, and feasts on me as if ravenous. Spearing me with her tongue, tugging on my lips with her front teeth, and then sliding up to suck my clit into her mouth.

Momentarily distracted, I writhe on the mattress, moaning out a distress call. When I come to my senses, I reach down, treading my fingers into Opal's hair, and forcefully yank her from between my thighs. "Come again?"

Instead of answering me, Opal shows me. Weaving her fingers through mine, she draws my hand down between her legs, where a masculine hand is rapidly trusting in and out of her lust-soaked cunt. So aroused, her cream smears on our entwined fingers– a rivulet sliding down my wrist.

Shocked over Opal's reaction, I become breathless. She either loves what this man is doing to her, or it's a combination of what he's doing while she touches me and I touch him. I don't know which one I hope for the most. But I do understand Opal's enthusiastic reaction to finger-fucking after she admitted her past in the Playroom. From the garbled groans she's releasing, she's loving this dude's skills.

I feel uncertain, confused. I'm not sure if it's because I'm witnessing another person touching my girlfriend, or because I'm *not* bothered by another person touching my girlfriend. Either way, the mature part of me erupts. It's Opal's body, and her right to do with it as she chooses. She craves his touch, so I deal with him touching her.

I know Opal respects us as a couple, and she's not doing anything I won't be doing in a few minutes with the same man.

So it's not like I can get pissed about it. It's like, I feel odd because I don't feel like I have a right to be pissed off.

"Why am I not bothered by this?" I mumble in disbelief.

Opal presses our fingers inside her, alongside the length of his finger, until each of us has one finger deeply thrust inside my girlfriend. Gasping breathlessly, Opal explains. "There are several types of people who come to the Playroom. Usually the eager asshole husbands are towing their reluctant wives. The eager becomes the jealous and angry when their wife is touched, and the reluctant becomes the exultant. You thought yourself the jealous sort, only to find out you weren't."

"Makes sense, I guess," I muse.

"*But*," Opal stresses, "You'd have a different reaction if it was another female joining us. I am most certain of this, as would I. I wouldn't like that one bit," the possessive curl to her voice warms me unexpectedly. "I don't even like thinking about it."

Opal's candor gives me the courage to voice my most secret needs. "May I feel him? Inside you…" I trail off, having no words to put my thoughts in order. "I need to know what it's like to have sex with a man, without actually having sex with one. I'm frightened," I admit, voice quivering ever so slightly. I suddenly feel ashamed of myself for having to ask such a thing, but also proud to realize I trust Opal enough not to judge me for it.

Opal pulls our fingers from her body, her cream cooling on my fingertips. She lies down beside me, wrapping her arms around me out of comfort, not lust. "What are you asking? I have to hear the words, Ginny."

The man hesitantly caresses me as well, patting my shoulder in a '*There-there*' sisterly manner. His touch is fleeting, as if he's as reluctant to touch me as I am him.

Their comfort gives me the strength to soldier forth. "I shouldn't ask you this, but could he… could he enter you… and could I feel it?"

"Oh," Opal breathes against the side of my neck. But the man's reaction is more visceral: frozen into stillness, the hand that was hovering over my shoulder is now impaling my flesh with its fingernails. Other than his laughter and a few groans, I haven't heard a peep from him until now. Gasping for breath, the man sounds close to hyperventilating.

"Is he okay?" I ask, concerned. "I mean, you don't have to unless you want to. I just figured since you had in the past that you wouldn't mind," I ramble, embarrassed. "Forget I asked. I'm being stupid again."

"You can't unsee this," Opal reminds me. "If you get upset, it's not reversible. You'll forever remember a man having sex with your girlfriend on the bed we share. You have to be certain before we proceed, and you have be above blaming me if you don't like what you see."

"I get that," I reply quickly. "Being next to you while it happens will be easier for me to deal with than what's playing out in my mind, making me a jealous bitch. So, if you are comfortable with it, I'd like you to try for me–"

Before I can even finish my sentence, Opal is turned onto her back, her arms still slung over me, and the man is forcing his way inside her body. Stunned, I lie still as Opal clings to me. *Friend* goes at my girlfriend like a man making love to a woman he hasn't been with in a very long time. It's not clinical like I thought it would be. He's situation between her thighs, body draped over hers, with his mouth pressed to her ear, grunting words I cannot understand. It's raw yet filled with intense emotions.

"Is he okay?" I ask a shocked Opal, again.

Pumping into Opal in a fluid motion, he finds my hand, and draws it down between their bellies, until I'm touching their joined flesh. A saturated shaft rubs my palm as it flows in and out of Opal's pussy, getting wetter and wetter with every thrust.

Practically purring, the man smothers Opal like a hot, living, breathing blanket, and Opal clutches him to her. This is what she meant by sharing this intimacy with a stranger, how I'd freak out and he might not stop. Opal glorifies in it, and I'm not sure how I feel about it.

Unsure what to do, I just lie in shock as the man's cock flows through my hand, directly into my girlfriend. Shoring up my nerves, I hesitantly ask what's been plaguing me for the past month, "Are you going to be able to give him up, or will he be sharing our bed for as long as we're together?" I'm proud I say this without any censure lacing my voice.

Opal's reaction makes me wonder about her sexuality, or if it's just the man himself, or if it's simply the man's reaction to Opal that has her in such a tizzy. I pray it's the latter. I can imagine how heady it would feel to know you're driving your lover insane. I've experienced the intoxicating sense of power that overcomes you, because I turn Opal into the wanton creature this man has transformed into.

Panting next to me, she tries not to moan with the flex of the man's perfect ass. "He just told me this is his demented version of goodbye." Opal grunts with every word she utters, because now he's pounding into her with such great force that my hand is getting smashed between them. He swivels his hips, grinding my hand into his nutsack on purpose.

I'm secretly pleased that Opal doesn't sound sad over the fact that this is goodbye. She sounds more hopeful, actually. While I'm openly ecstatic that this is their goodbye. This dude has felt like my competition since the very moment Opal and I met, and I'd like him out of my way for good. The only reason I'm not tearing off the balls he keeps mashing into my palm, is because Opal isn't making *my* sounds. That coveted sound only I elicit from her.

I put an end to this fiasco, because the green-eyed monster is rearing its head, and not within me. I can sense the possessiveness wafting from the man, like he had debated making my girlfriend his at some point.

Opal and I have to be equals in all things. "I would like to know how it feels," I decide on the spot. "A man inside me. But I have to be able to look at him first."

Freezing, Opal *and* her friend shout, "NO!" in unison.

"I know who's inside you, Opal," I drawl out. "Like I'd let some asshole inside my girlfriend without knowing who he is, same with inside my own body. What I really want to know is… why?"

"What?" Opal gasps, shocked. "If you know, say his name, and I'll take your scarf off and explain."

Opal thinks I'm bluffing, but I'm not. "Robin Basil Prynne," I say with such certainty that I reach up and remove the scarf myself. I roll over onto my side, and stare at the entwined couple fornicating on my bed beside me. I tug my hand free from between their bodies, and bust out laughing at their gape-mouthed expressions of horror.

It's worse than I expected– how perfect they look together. There isn't a single inch of their bodies not connected somehow. When they froze, Rob was sucking on Opal's neck, his body buried between her thighs. Opal's fingernails are clutching his shoulder and his opposing ass cheek, pressing him further inside her. One of my girlfriend's knees is being leveraged up by Rob's arm curling under it for a deeper position. Both of them are flushed and covered in a sheen of sweat. They look like star-crossed lovers caught in the act. But that's not what has me asking why.

"Why?" I ask Rob. "I'm not jealous or angry." Scrunching my eyebrows up, I admit the truth. "Well, maybe a tiny bit jealous. I can tell you both get off on each other. I also know that I make Opal more insane than she's making you, so I'm not hurt. But why do this with me? Why are you saying goodbye to each other?"

"A mutual party was petrified for you," Rob whispers, looking shell-shocked. "The three of us kept envisioning you going off to a club and getting in way over your head."

"So the little girl I helped raise tossed me her boyfriend?" I ask, thoroughly offended. "That's not at all creepy, or anything."

"It's complicated," Rob mutters, sounding exhausted. "Isis isn't doing well, and I'm trying my damnedest to fix it without going nuts myself. She's pulling an Auggie, thrusting me at Opal, hoping I'll find what I'm looking for so I won't miss what she's not giving me."

"What?" I blurt out.

Looking desperate for me to understand, Rob spews all of his issues in torrent of agony. "Auggie and Isis are both fools. Isis stepped away, hoping Auggie and I would fuse together as a couple, but we didn't. Auggie went to Willow as a way to sacrifice himself, hoping Isis and I would be a couple, but we didn't. Now Isis is being a dumb bitch, trying to hook me up with Opal, knowing we enjoy each other's company on many levels. That's why this is goodbye. I won't be distracted from my true purpose any longer."

Slapping her hand on Rob's ass with a loud *smack*, "Good!" Opal says exuberantly while wearing a huge grin. "It's about time. Willow was not your replacement part, and I will not be Isis's, either."

"I expect both of your help in the near future," Rob warns. "As for why?" he answers me finally. "Why I'm rutting with insanity? I haven't been laid in months, and I'm starving. I refused to be with anyone except for Auggie and Isis, but tonight was an exception. Why in regards to you?" Rob's expression turns soft when he gazes at me. "We all love you, Gin, and we worry about you. We also know you're going to hate it. Let this be a lesson to you. If we do this, it won't last but a minute."

"I don't know," I grumble, sounding defensive. "Opal looks very satisfied with the results of you impaling her with your almighty cock."

Snorting at the sarcasm in my tone, "Yeah, well… Opal and I have a different sort of relationship than you and I do. So at best, it's going to be awkward. At worst, you're going to murder me."

Lying on my side, I watch with avid curiosity as Rob pulls free from Opal's body. My eyes follow his dick, completely engrossed by the piece of flesh I've only shaken hands with. It's ruddy, covered in Opal's cream, and thick with the need to rupture. I cock my head to the side, staring at it inquisitively– fascinated yet unaroused by it.

Opal rolls to her side to curl around me, immediately searching for my lips. "Are you mad at me? I was worried you'd hate me if you ever found out the truth." I hate the quiver in my girlfriend's voice– if the disappointment I felt about myself last night had a tone, this would be it. I tug Opal to me, squeezing her tightly to my breasts.

"I'm not mad, nor am I judging you. Confused. Curious. But not mad." My lips seek hers, fusing us together with a hungry moan. Rob's taste is lingering on Opal's tongue– they must have kissed while he was inside her. It's not a bad flavor, just foreign.

"AH!" Opal shrieks a high-pitched sound I didn't think her capable. Rob is laughing sinisterly, his hand still raised where he'd smacked Opal's ass.

"Bit slap-happy, aren't ya?" I accuse while trying hard not to laugh. "I didn't think Opal could make such a sound."

"Oh, that's not the first time I've torn it from her," Rob mutters arrogantly. "But, sadly, it will be the last." Rolling a condom on his penis, Rob issues me a challenge. "Ready?"

"Are you going to hurt me?" I ask in a small voice as I roll onto my back.

"No," Rob mouths. "Not intentionally anyway. But I don't believe this will take more than fifteen seconds. Thirty at most."

"That good, are ya?" I tease to hide the warble in my voice. I grip my sheets, trying to contain my violent quaking.

Shaking his head to and fro while wearing nothing but a feral grin and a condom-clad erection, "No, I most certainly am not *that* good. I'd bet my life we won't be finishing, is what I'm saying."

Wide-eyed, suddenly feeling threatened, I stare at Rob's jutting hard-on. It's curved and perfectly proportioned, but it's not doing anything for me in the least, especially that alien bag that hangs beneath. I shudder, but Rob takes it for nervousness.

Smirking devilishly, Rob kneels between my legs, touching me nowhere except with the outside of his thighs rubbing against the inside of mine. Fisting that odd protuberance, he leans into me. My breath seizes in my lungs, and Opal reaches out to comfort me.

"I won't hurt you," Rob reassures me. "But you will get this insanity out of your head," he warns, and I squeak and squirm around when he slides into me smoothly. "And you'll learn your lesson."

"Oh, my God. A man's inside me," I grunt out in astonishment.

"About time someone realizes I'm a dude, goddamnit," Rob grits out toward Opal– an underlying resentment surfacing.

I clench up, confused that it's not uncomfortable or painful, but also not the way Rob and Opal looked moments ago, either. All I feel is the smooth, pleasurable slide of his body moving easily inside mine, and I get nothing out of it. It's like getting an exam, and absolutely nothing like the hot, sexual experience I made it out to be in my fantasies– *nightmares*. I close my eyes and stare at the insides of my eyelids, with the background music of Rob taunting '*I told you so*' laughter.

"Are you okay?" Now Opal's asking me the question I kept lobbing at Rob earlier.

Before I can answer, Rob's collapsing all of his weight onto me, covering me with his body while he gives three quick thrusts of his cock. "Okay, everybody out of the pool," I order, shoving at his shoulders and chest to get him off of me. "That's fucking creepy as all hell, Robin," I screech in a prissy tone. "Don't get cuddly. Eww, your alien balls are touching me. Get them off my ass cheek," I shriek.

"Awkward," Rob breathes into my ear, and then he's kissing my forehead. "Now, imagine doing that in a filthy bathroom stall with some creep who wouldn't do this," Rob pulls from my body with a flourish and a shit-eating grin. "They might ignore a no, and that's on you for being stupid."

"Yeah, I get it," I growl, skittering across the bed to cover myself up. "I'm an idiot."

"Not an idiot. You've just been schooled," Rob says with a grin, reaching over to muss up my hair. "Not all men are animals, but you're not always going to find a gracious guy like me, who's willing to stop when you say stop."

I watch with avid fascination as Rob rolls the barely used condom off his still hard cock. It bobs, slapping his belly. How is he still hard after all this awkwardness?

"Are you okay?" I hate the worry in Opal's voice.

Reaching for her, I pull Opal into my arms. I bury my face in the juncture of her neck and shoulder, and breathe in her soapy scent. "I'm good. Happy I did this bullshit with Rob, or else I'd be mortified. What's next?"

"What's next?" Rob and Opal mutter in unison– Opal's frozen beside me and Rob's reaching for his pants.

"This," I gesture to mine and their nakedness. "It seems rather anticlimactic. I'm not suggestion I try *that* again," I stress. "But maybe something since this is your goodbye and all."

"Idea," Rob whispers as he flashes across my bedroom to the light switch. The room goes pitch-black. "Mattress wrestling, where we pretend we have no idea whose fingers are touching us or whose mouth is sucking and licking and biting," he salaciously purrs, suddenly next to me on the bed.

"Eager, much?" Opal taunts, softly chuckling.

"I'm always eager for beaver," Rob says lamely, causing us to laugh at the assmunch. "Everyone thinks I'm gay, and I most certainly am *not*."

CHAPTER SIXTEEN

Opal Fischer

I shriek in surprise as two sets of hands upend me, flopping me onto the mattress. With a bounce, I land on my back, head hitting the pillow. "Looks like you got me to make that sound again, Rob," I utter breathlessly.

Popping up to whisper in my ear, "You know damned well I will find ways to freak your ass out on a regular basis. Be prepared."

"Save some of that enthusiasm for Isis and Auggie," I caution, drawing clear boundary lines.

Rob's love-making stunt earlier was too much to bear. That wasn't about Ginny or me. Rob was a man on a mission, and it freaked me out how real it felt– for him, not me. It was too close to how Byron treated me in our marital bed– slow and lovely. I couldn't stop myself. I fell into the past's destructive patterns, where all I cared about was my partner's happiness, with no regard of my own. It made it worse that Ginny witnessed something she will never be able to erase from her mind.

"I know," Rob rumbles softly into my ear. "I'm a plotter, and plotting is what I've been doing. Tonight is my victory celebration. Isis and Auggie are trapped now– stuck with me for life." Sounding sure and proud of himself, Rob piques my interest, my need to find out the minute details. A creature of curiosity manifests, dragging my inner kicking-and-screaming-and-clawing gossip whore up to the surface.

Ginny crawls over me, trying to get closer so she can eavesdrop. "What? Share the news," she pleads, going as far as to edge right up to Rob's face. "Don't make me beg. Just so ya know, I will, though."

Voice flowing with a soft, intimate lilt, Rob lets us in. Finally. After months of pestering him to open up, he is. "This is my last hurrah. After tonight, I'll never touch anyone besides

Auggie and Isis. Ever. Again. I'm going out with a bang. Doing a favor for my favorite ladies, while saying goodbye to a life I may or may not even miss. The jury's still out on that."

We attack as a unit, rolling Rob beneath us. Ginny pins him to the bed, while I straddle his hips. The bastard wiggles, trying to impale me on his erection. I flick Rob's hands away when he tries to grab my hips to maneuver me into position.

"I'm not trying to fuck you!" I yelp, blushing bright red. "Man, it's getting easier to swear like a Prynne."

"I taught you the very best," Rob rasps throatily. "Now, move just a bit to the left, and we'll both be very, very happy. Ah…" He purrs, rubbing his cock on my slit. "A little bit more… almost."

"Jackass," Ginny snarls. "Tell us the gossip, bitch. Before I tear your alien nutsack off your body." Violently shaking a laughing Rob, Ginny ties to force him to comply.

"Wait!" I call out, grabbing Ginny's wrist before she throttles Rob. "I have a better idea." I lean forward, rubbing my pussy all over Rob's pulsing dick. I ignore the pleasure that flashes up my spine. Resting my lips against his, Rob stills beneath me. "Tell us what we want to know, and we'll help you get it– whatever it may be."

"You have no fucking clue what I've had to do to get where I am right now," he breathlessly pants against my lips. Jerking his head forward, Rob bites my bottom lip, hard, nearly drawing blood. Gasping for breath, Rob confesses his sins. "I gave Isis what she's always wanted but never would admit, all the while traversing around her biggest fear."

"What?" Both Ginny and I whisper as we lean closer into Rob.

Voice filled with arrogance and a thread of something else, "In a few weeks, don't be surprised when you hear about an immaculate conception."

"Holy fuck," I breathe, awed. "That's impressive, even for you. No way, no how."

Thrown for a loop, Ginny fires off rapidly, "How? Why? When? Who?"

Turning wry, "I don't know, Ginny. Who? That's not hard to figure out since Auggie and I can't conceive a child."

I smack Rob upside the head for Ginny, and the idiot gets off on it– cock flexing, on the edge of orgasm. "Dumbass," I growl. "Is the kid yours or Auggie's?"

Turning obstinate, "I'm not telling," he grumps out. "You have no idea how much pussy licking I've had to do as of late, and the other unimaginable feats I've pulled off. I even impressed myself."

"I'll let you lick my pussy if you'll tell us," I try to negotiate.

"Fuck, I'd suck your cock if you'd tell us," Ginny offers, sounding sick to her stomach yet equally nosy.

"Um… no… Eww," Rob drawls out, shuddering. "Suffering through Opal's poor, albeit enthusiastic, attempts at cocksuckage was enough for me. Thanks. I'll stick to getting head from Fairport's resident cocksucker. A guy who loves cock will always give the best head. It's a proven fact."

"What can we do?" I negotiate in a breathy voice.

"Hmm…" Rob pretends to be thinking it through. But the conniving bastard already had this planned out, I'm positive. "I want Ginny to eat your pussy, and then when you're coming, I want fuck you unconscious. Bonus points if Ginny licks up my spendings."

"Oh, God. I'm gonna be sick." Ginny mock-heaves.

"Okay," I rumble my agreement as I slide off Rob's body, twisting my hips on his cock just to torture him. "I'm game. No one eats pussy like a lesbian," I lob back at Rob for insulting our cocksucking skills. "Proven fact," I taunt as I get comfortable on the bed.

Laughing evilly, Ginny rocks my world. "That right there is why I'm falling in love with you. Use that devious mind of yours for good."

"Holy shit," I breathe in utter disbelief, heart hammering wildly in my chest. *Falling in love with you."* "Christ!" I hiss when Ginny buries her face between my thighs and begins her feast. "Proven fact. Lesbians are championship-worthy cunt lickers." I gasp roughly when she does that clit suck/lick/bite maneuver. Fingertips strangling the shit out of Ginny's sheets, I whisper back to her, "This is one of the many reasons I'm falling for you, too."

Robin Prynne

Crawling around the bed, I'm trying to get at an optimum angle. "Wait, what are you doing to make Opal purr like that?" I kick myself in the ass for turning out the lights. "I need to know your witchery."

"It's not witchery," Gin roughly rasps out from her position between Opal's long, lean legs. Gloating to the point that I know the bitch is grinning at me even though I can't see her face, "It's called having an insatiable taste for pussy."

"Show off," I mutter, pushing Gin to the side. "Share with me," I beg, shuffling down the bed to lie on my stomach. Resting cheek-to-cheek with Gin, the musky scent of Opal's pussy filling my nostril, I settling in to get an education. "Technically, I took your virginity. It's the least you could do for me," I manipulate.

"What a fun time that was," flows flippantly. "I'm truly a lesbian, if whatever mojo you're using on my girlfriend fails to impress me."

Offended and hurt, I pretend Gin's words didn't wound deeply. "Yeah, it's called knowing me since I was shitting in my drawers. Opal showed up after I was a grown man with the sexual skills of a well-seasoned whore, that's the difference," I snarl.

"Are you really that good?" Gin asks, sounding surprised.

"Better than you can imagine, sweetling," I taunt. "Of the three of us in this bed, two of us love women like an addiction. Hint: one of them does *not* belong to the pussy in our faces."

Pulling out her badassery, "Prove it," Gin challenges. "Lick my bitch."

Huffing a laugh, I use action instead of words. Groaning in bliss, I dive into Opal, tongue impaling her as swiftly as I would with my cock. A shudder rolls down my spine at her sweet yet musky taste.

Touching Opal all those months ago was a grave mistake.

I hadn't realized Isis was setting me up with Opal until it was too late. The night I found Opal sitting at Rush, drowning her sorrows, I'd been fighting my own demons, and losing the battle miserably.

I've been small and cute my entire life, causing everyone who took one look at me to automatically assume I was gay. Day-in and day-out, everyone questions my sexuality– my masculinity. I can be artistic with dimpled cheeks and still be straight. I am *all* man, and I love women just as much, if not more, as every other straight man on the planet.

I also have the confusing misfortune of falling in love with a man– a devoted worshipfulness which overrides my natural sexual persuasion.

The only person in my life who believes I'm 100% straight, is the very man who reluctantly allows me to touch him because of it. It's an impossible situation when the man in your life won't allow you to fuck him because you're straight, and at the same time, the woman we're both madly in love with won't let us fuck her, either.

Desperate desolation.

The fateful night I found Opal sitting at the bar at Rush, Auggie had denied me, Isis had denied me, three separate men had hit on me, and a woman laughed in my face when I asked her to go into the Playroom with me– she had thought I was gay, too.

That night was a recipe for disaster. Two hurting friends came together, and I've thought of little else since. I felt connected to another human being for the first time since before the pregnancy from hell. I felt like someone understood me. I went to Isis afterward to prove that I was still a man, and words and actions do indeed make me bleed. Instead of being angry, Isis pushed Opal and me together every single chance she got, never backing off until Ginny came into the equation.

Ginny made me fight for what's mine, and I've never fought so hard in my entire life. I could lose everything, or gain what should have been rightfully mine since I was in kindergarten.

The only thing harder to do, is to give up the intimate connection I share with Opal. Especially knowing Auggie and Isis may never willingly give me what I need in return, leaving me to walk through life alone.

I'm terrified.

Abandoning my tongue-fuckage of Opal's drenched pussy, I opt for long licks from her asshole to clit, causing her to wiggle around and weave her fingers into my hair. Opal bucks her hips and sighs my name, but I don't turn her insane like Ginny does. Gripping Opal's thighs, I spread her wider, getting my face right in her heat.

Frustrated, "What were you doing down here, Gin? Ya gotta give me a hint," I beg. "I can get Opal to squeal and tug my hair, but not that throaty purr she elicited when you were going down on her."

Patting my back, Ginny has a smile in her voice. "Lesbian trade secret."

"I promise to use it for good, never evil," I vow, meaning I'll only use the trick on Isis.

"Well, in that case…" Ginny shoves me out of the way a bit. "We've got a deal." She leans into Opal, munching down, and a low moan echoes around the bedroom– the sound I covet. "The trick is to make the woman so aroused, she feels like she'll die if she doesn't get off, and you're the only one who can get her there."

"Most women are difficult to get off, but not Opal," I grumble. "You're a lucky bitch, Gin. I envy the fuck out of you. You ever downgrade, pass me your girlfriend, and I'll cherish her forever."

"I hear a note of jealousy and possessiveness in your voice, Rob. Don't make me cut off your nuts," Gin warns, and I know she's fantasizing about it. The woman really did get freaked out by my hairy balls. "What about Isis?"

"Help me love her the right way," I beg, voice wavering with emotion. "Please."

Ginny wraps an arm around my back, holding me like she understands. "Fair enough, Rob. Fair enough. Now, get Opal primed like you always do, and when you get her on the edge, I'll give you a hint."

"You don't sound like you want to share," I mutter flatly.

"I don't want *you* using *my* trick on *my* girlfriend," Gin stresses. "But since I won't use myself as an example, I'll deal."

"All I know is, if someone doesn't get to fucking licking and sucking, I'm going to draw blood," Opal threatens. An instant later my head is buried in her snatch, with my hair being yanked out by the roots. "You pussy teasers keep bringing me to the brink, and backing the hell off. Not fucking cool!"

Laughing, my face is covered in pussy juice. I wipe my cheek on Opal's thigh and get down to the business at hand. *Bring her to the brink,* Gin said, and the brink is where I'm headed. I'm not pussy-footing around, pun intended. Tongue lapping at her clit, nose bending from the force, fingers thrusting in her sopping wet cunt like I have pistons in my forearms, I make Opal thrash and whimper… but she doesn't go insane.

Whispering in my ear, "Suck all of Opal's clit into your mouth– the whole thing. Flick your tongue in a rhythmic pattern while you continue to suck, and then lightly set your teeth at the base of her clit for added pressure, but no biting. That's the trick."

"How the fuck do you do all that at once," I grumble in awe, knowing it's impossible.

Stuck at the precipice because of my ineptitude, Opal snarls obscenities like she's sworn since birth. I'm losing strands of hair by the dozens, as they snap off in her clenching fingers. Pussy juice and saliva drip down my chin because I can't swallow it fast enough. My jaw aches… and I got nothing.

Gin tugs me off her girlfriend and out of the way. "I'll put Opal out of her misery," she says, but she doesn't sound gloating, more concerned than anything, actually.

"I lost my mojo," I whimper, pouting. I fist my ever-ready cock, and he doesn't seem to care that I can't eat pussy anymore. He flexes eagerly, patiently waiting his turn.

Opal erupts like a lit powder keg filled with feral cats: shrieking a sound I'll never forget, nor one I've ever heard from her before. I'm not proud of the fingernail scratches to my shoulder since I didn't earn them, but they strike like lightning to my balls anyway.

"Rob," Ginny growls at me. "You're up, dumbass. It was your plan, so hop to it."

"Huh?" I grunt. "No sense, I suck."

"I'll explain why Opal didn't make that sound for you afterward." Gin shoves me on top of her girlfriend, and then thwacks me in the ass to get me moving along like I'm a stubborn donkey.

My cock doesn't giving a shit either way. He just knows a woman is in the throes of orgasm against him– his favorite thing in the whole wide world. Easily sliding inside Opal's clenching snatch, I somehow find myself thrusting away without a conscience thought on my part. My dick is going insane, preparing for ejaculation, just because the pussy is contracting like a fist and the woman is screaming my name.

I'm feeling pretty shitty, low on myself, but then Opal reaches up to pull me down to her. She kisses me full on the lips, tongue hunting mine down for some attention. Wrapping her arms and legs around me, Opal grinds into me dirtily, making all these orgasmic sounds I've never heard from her before. This is not the woman *I* fucked senseless a few months ago. This woman is fucking *me* from beneath.

"Gin, you're the one with the mojo," I gasp out breathlessly, floating in a cloud of awe. "Lesbian witchery."

"Opal's *my* girlfriend," Gin reminds me. "I'll always know how to please her better than anyone else," she taunts. "But it works the same way for you, Rob. I know two people who won't be satisfied without you," she mollifies me. "Now, that must be the moves Opal whispers about in the middle of the night. Your ass rolls like you're belly dancing."

Feeling like the man again, I forget about everything but the pleasure Opal is giving me, and the pleasure I'm giving her in return. "Rob," Opal gasps, pulling me back down to her lips, and I go readily.

I curse the connection that snaps us together– the same connection that freaks Opal out. It's not entirely emotional. It's not entirely sexual. It's chemistry mixed with trust. I love Opal, but I'm not *in* love with her. I could live the rest of my life never being inside her again, but I couldn't live without being around her.

Real friendship. The missing intimacy I've strove so hard to gain from those who won't give it to me. But Opal freely give it back, without question.

"I'm going to miss this," I breathe into Opal's ear, slowing my pace. Gin, refusing to be left out, lies down next to us, putting her ear near my mouth so she can overhear. She even wraps her arm around my shoulders so I can't get away.

"Stop using me as a crutch," Opal chastises me, but instead of pushing me away, she draws me closer. "Either connect with Isis and Auggie, or all of Fairport will kill them for you," she threatens. "We can't suffer the fallout anymore."

"Yes, Ma'am," I tease, earning an ass swat from Ginny, who leaves her hand on my ass. "You're imprinting my movements to memory, aren't ya? Lesbian witchery," I chuckle.

"Shut up and fuck," Opal rasps in my ear, wiggling her hips beneath me, grinding upward.

I grit my teeth against the insane need to shoot, balls aching fiercely. I find an intense rhythm, like I have music infused with heavy bass playing out in my mind. I fuck the hell out of Opal while Ginny's hand learns a thing or two about rolling your hips in a wavelike motion.

Grunting and sweating, Opal and I are wrapped around one another, bodies sliding in our combined juices. Opal's nipples etch across my chest, her pussy sucks my cock like a slurping mouth, and her fingernail sting with the sweetest bite of pain.

Refusing to kiss someone else's girlfriend, I suck at Opal's neck while panting in labored puffs. I make up for not being the best Opal's ever had. Ginny can hold the title as the best pussy muncher, because I'll hold top billing as the hottest sex a guy has ever given Opal.

"Fuck," I grunt out sharply, not able to hold out any longer. Shuddering, a pressure builds at the base of my spine, radiating out until I either let go or implode. Balls tightening, my cock jerks to a beat of its own creation.

Profanity-laden Opal erupts, "Don't you fucking dare pull out until I'm done!"

"I'm trying, goddamnit," I grit out, but it twists into a snarl. "Hurry the hell up, woman."

Shuddering violently, Opal fractures. Shouting my name and several other choice words, Opal sets her nails into my shoulders, and another set creates perfect crescents in the flesh of my ass.

99…

98…

97…

96…

I count backward, hating the insanity of having to ride out Opal's orgasm before I can have my own. Some dumb fucker forgot to put on a condom. The same dumb fucker who enjoyed this same raw ride last time and got to cum deep inside. But now, Virginia Jamison is in the equation, rubbing on this well-fucked pussy, and she's a fertile bitch.

85…

84…

"Hurry the fuck up, Opal!" I scream, waiting for her fingernails to disengage or I risk losing a pound of flesh.

Wrenching away at the last instant, I fling myself off of Opal, rolling to the side of the bed. Hand stroking rapidly, I feel like a twelve-year-old in a timed pud whacking contest. Grunting, I shoot my load, not giving a fuck where it lands. With my never-ending, torturous climax, I'm sure I'm impregnating the sheets, the walls, and the carpeting. I make a point to keep my flow from Ginny's cunt, though.

A violent wave of pleasure rolls me under in its unrelenting grip, starting at my groin to radiate throughout my body. Exhaustion blanketing me in a drug-like fog, I fall backward onto the bed. I've been fucked dirty: face slathered in Opal's pussy juice, as well as everything from my bellybutton to mid-thigh.

I close my eyes, refusing to move. "The odd bullshit I do for the sake of friendship," I grumble to myself. "There is no payoff big enough for a man to disengage mid-orgasm. It takes the pleasure out of it."

"Is he going to be okay?" I hear Ginny ask for the tenth time.

"Eh, let him pout. He's Robin Prynne," Opal says as example. "C'mere. I'm not done with you yet."

"Mmm…" Gin purrs a sound I wish I'd never heard. It's Ginny, but my cock doesn't care. He likes the sound of a horny woman. Freaking out, I jump from the bed before the lovers can start making love– for real this time.

Without me.

I can't help myself. My curiosity gets the better of me. I take a few peeks at the girls as they turn into a writhing ball of feminine arms and legs and luscious tits. Ginny does have a humungous rack. I should have motor-boated that bitch when I had the chance, but I freaked out because it was Ginny's tits that were getting me hotter than hell.

Shuddering, I lean down to wash my face off on Gin's whorehouse red sheets. Doesn't matter, they already smell like expensive cunt. This bedroom is like hotboxing pussy.

Speaking of hotboxing. Pot. That's what I need right now. Mary Prynne's finest. But first, I have to get the fuck out of here, and then shower at least a dozen times– maybe scrub my brain while I'm at it. Followed by a night of burning on the Widow's Watch, where I'll strategize on the best possible way to get my wayward partners to grow the fuck up and be happy.

Slowly dressing, I keep surreptitiously sneaking glances at the ladies. I finally understand why I couldn't force Opal to make that tone for me, because that siren song belongs solely to Ginny. Same as how I know there are noises Isis only makes for me, and some she only makes for Auggie, and the same holds true for Auggie and me. I'd pay a billion dollars to hear their song right this instant.

Slipping on my shoes, I understand with great clarity. Opal and Ginny are a couple. They belong together, and I'm an interloper in their bed. It's time I fused my relationship so that nothing can fracture it again, even if we lose a hundred unborn children.

On the brink of ecstasy, wrapped tightly around one another while crying out each other's names, I lean in to pay my end of the bargain. If my plan comes to fruition, I whisper the name of our baby's father. Kissing their foreheads goodbye, I snicker at how I've rendered them motionless and speechless.

CHAPTER SEVENTEEN

Opal Fischer

"Fancy meeting you here," Ginny purrs, wrapping her arm around my waist. I tug her closer, not caring about the flurry of whispers that surrounds us. Ginny and I will be the main topic of gossip in Fairport this evening.

Kissing Ginny squarely on the lips, in front of God and all of Fairport, I feel happier, more complete, than I ever have. "We seem to always meet at union-based functions," I murmur wryly.

Ginny and I may have met at the No-Name Diner, thanks to Malcolm Mason's naughty ways. But we got to know one another at a pre-wedding reception, hung out at a wedding, fooled around at a wedding after-party, and honeymooned with more passion than the bride and groom. Now we're celebrating two months of bliss-filled living, by showing off our exclusivity at Rory and Bethany's belated wedding reception at Rush.

"Someday…" Ginny trails off, not having the balls to say the words out loud so soon.

Someday, this could be about us, is what Ginny longs to say, as do I. But eight weeks is the blink of an eye, and anything could happen– anything. But I have great hope for our longevity.

Our passions run hot. Our sex is fierce. But our friendship is our strongest asset. Both Ginny and I are looking at our relationship from a mature, logical, and rational standpoint. We're trying to let go of the past, let go of our insecurities, and just take it day-by-day. But that doesn't mean we both don't want it to be more.

Rush is closed to the public, and it's teeming with everyone in our social circles. Clover's food is served, and Rush's bar is flowing booze like water. The music is ear-piercingly loud, but the excited chatter is even louder.

Every member of the Mason, Prynne, Webster, and Kline clans are in attendance. Clover and Malcolm are having a hard time keeping track of their children, who are all off getting into trouble. Willow and Ren are looking a fool on the dance floor. Rae just instigated a fistfight with Violet, because Violet accidentally-on-purpose danced with the in-demand Ozzy. Seth is trying his hardest to steal his relatives' drinks for shits 'n giggles, which makes me wonder what he's ultimately doing with them.

You can spot Devon Mason easily enough, by the swarm of brothers in blue making sure he's staying sober, much to the young man's great annoyance. Ozzy, smarter than the girls, has found refuge in the center of the swarm.

Tina Kline, fresh from rehab herself, is glaring hate-filled daggers at her brother, who is as drunk as a skunk at the bar, trying to avoid his mother and stepfather. Rob invited Lisa, Tina, and Patrick just to fuck with Auggie's head. Rob, being an even bigger ass than usual, keeps handing Isis a beer, only to shake his head *no* and steal it back– he does this repeatedly to stir the gossip shit-pot.

The grapevine is abuzz with the news that three women in Malcolm's family are knocked up, but no one knows which ones. Essie is the obvious choice, as she's the center of the cop swarm with her palm resting protectively on her huge belly. With Isis not drinking, despite Rob's taunts, all eyes are on the females in that family, checking to see if they take a drink or not. Making it difficult is the fact that some of the women are teetotalers or underage.

Ginny knows which three, but she's a proficient gossip. Trying to get a secret out of her is like cracking Fort Knox. I let it go after the thousandth time I asked her. After I gave up on my girlfriend, I started in on Rob, who's even more adept than Ginny. I guess I'll find out when the ladies are in labor at my hospital.

Draining her glass of wine, and then doing the same with mine, Ginny sets the glasses on the bar. She turns to me and asks, "Dance with me?"

"I'd love to, my lovely lady. But, do you see my son anywhere?" With my height, I should be able to spot Sage.

"Hmm… I have a better idea," Ginny says with a smirk. "Sage blends in because he's short. But someone else sticks out like a golden god, and he's also missing."

"Christ," I hiss, eyes seeking out Malcolm just to make sure. He's over at the bar relentlessly teasing Auggie, trying to make the guy act alive.

"Over there!" Ginny shouts, weaving through the crowd. I catch up with her, wrapping my hand around hers so I won't lose her again. "Oh…"

"Jesus Christ," I say for emphasis, or maybe it's a prayer to the Lord above.

My son is being a good boy, doing his damnedest, anyway. But Weston Mason is stronger, taller, and more determined. Sage is pressed up against the hallway wall, his arms outstretched, palms flattened on West's torso. But Weston is a foot taller, and he can bypass Sage's reach. West is also eclipsing my son with his body, head angled in such a way that you know West is kissing the hell out of Sage. Judging by Weston's enthusiasm, Sage is kissing him back just as fiercely.

My kid's legs are wiggling around like he's being fried alive. I don't want to think it's funny, but I can't help but laugh.

Ginny walks over like she owns the world, wraps her palm around the back of Weston's neck, and tugs sharply. "Do I need to hose your ass down, kid?" She flings the two hundred pound, six-foot-four, fourteen-year-old man-child like he's weightless.

Smirking, hitching up his pant leg, Weston Mason turns into the cockiest motherfucker I've ever seen. It's disturbingly fascinating to witness. He has the decency to blush, but that's about it. West wipes his damp lips with the back of his hand and just stands there expectantly.

My poor kid is slumped against the wall, hand covering his mouth, looking like he was just rode hard and caught red-handed. The heated look in Sage's eye is what frightens me senseless. He's been behaving, but who the hell could keep telling Weston *no* while holding onto their sanity.

Ginny flips around on Weston after giving Sage an apologetic look. "Do you want to get this nice young man arrested? Is that your goal, Weston? Because if it is, there are no less than ten cops at the end of the hallway, and they can assist you with your asinine efforts."

Cocky smirk disappearing, Weston breathes, "No. I checked first."

"You didn't see us coming," Ginny points out, "And Opal and I aren't exactly *tiny*."

Wrenching his fingers through his sandy hair, "We'll be more careful," Weston whines, finally looking like the child he is.

"No," Sage declares, stepping away from the wall. Pain flows from son, and I ache to take it away. "We're going back to how it was before ten minutes ago. You're my friend until you turn eighteen. Nothing more."

Blowing up, "You won't even be here when I turn eighteen, goddamnit!"

Ignoring Weston's outburst, Sage talks right over him, "We can only see each other if Rae's with you."

"NO!" Weston bellows, and in a flashing movement, he punches the cinderblock wall. The crack echoes with testosterone-fueled violence. Ginny goes to intervene but I yank her out of the way– my heart beating in my throat.

"That right there *is* why," Sage stresses. "You're better than that." He points at the blood blooming on Weston's hand.

"Are you really saying you'll wait for me until you're a senior at Berkeley?" Weston twists out, and then stalks away. Turning when he reaches the head of the hallway, he shouts back, "I don't fucking think so."

"I should go… do something," Ginny rasps out, but at a loss of what she should do.

"No," Sage sighs, slumping against the wall. "Let Weston cool off. He only gets this way after…" Blushing, my son avoids all eye contact. "Just don't ask me after what, because I refuse to answer that."

"Do you want a hug?" I ask, sounding silly. But I have my reasons for asking instead of bundling my son to my chest and squeezing the shit out of him.

Blushing deeper. "Um… No. Not yet, anyway. Yeah, I gotta go cool off myself." Pacing a few feet away, Sage says over his shoulder, "Don't worry about it. I'll go find Rae, and then we'll hang out with Weston."

"I can't believe that fucked up kid is my nephew," Ginny mumbles, tears in her eyes.

"Not fucked up," Sage says as he walks away, leaving me to finish his statement.

This person I can hug, not fearing whether or not they're aroused. I drag Ginny into my arms. "Weston is um… going through some serious hormonal bullshit, and my son is cock-blocking him. That punch was the best release he could think of."

Shuddering in my arms, Ginny breathes, "Gross."

"Disturbing," I add. "Enough teenaged angst for this forty-year-old. Let's go find the newlyweds and give them our salutations."

"Are the kids going to be okay?" Ginny asks me, and I just level her with a '*you're shitting me, right?*' look. "Yeah, Sage doesn't stand a chance of getting out of Fairport before Weston gets what he's after."

"Frankly, I don't give a shit either way. Your nephew is begging for it, but if he gets my son arrested…" We enter Rush's main floor, the crowd swallowing us, and I see something hopeful. "Kids are resilient."

"Thank God," Ginny agrees.

Distracting the overgrown child, Sage is dancing with Willow, Ren, Rae, and Weston. I say a little prayer Malcolm doesn't take a gander at the heated expressions on the boys' faces. The twins join the fray, bumping Weston out of Sage's orbit– on purpose by the looks of it. Two months as stepsiblings, and those kids have each other's backs.

The battle lines are drawn at the bar: Auggie on one side with Rob and Isis flanking him, and his family on the other side. Malcolm is in negotiator mode, and I have no idea what's going down. "You think you can get your girl to spill the gossip?"

Ginny laughs at me, glowing with pride. "You're getting as bad as me, Opal. Sage gets the gossip whore gene from his mother."

"Can you?" Since Rob left us all those weeks ago, we've distanced ourselves. We still communicate, but I can't get him to spill his secrets for anything. All I know, the more important it is, the closer to the vest Rob keeps it.

Smirking, Ginny eyes her best friend, who's hanging onto every word at the bar. "Clover will tell me…"

I cut Ginny off because I'm too excited to wait, "But, the question is, will you tell me?"

"Of course." Ginny tugs on my blouse, making it drag across my nipples. "But you have to make it worth my while."

Voice raspy with a flurry of potential payments, "What do I have to do to get the pregnant women's names?"

Eyebrow jacking up to her hairline, Ginny stares me down. "Why do you want to know?"

Grin splitting my face out of nowhere, I finally admit I'm a closeted gossip whore. "Curiosity is killing the fucking cat. M-E-O-W!"

Laughing, Ginny leans up to kiss me. Before she can pull away, my arms automatically wrap around her back. Imprisoning her, I attack Ginny's pouty lips, tongue dipping inside. Hands roughing up my hair, Ginny goes full-out bedroom mode, and it flashes heat through my veins.

"Whew," Rory whistles, causing Ginny and me to break apart. "I think these fine ladies are trying to burn Rush down to the ground tonight." Fanning in front of his reddened face with one hand, the big guy tugs his wife into view with the other.

"Thanks so much for the presents," Bethany gushes, drawing me into a hug. "But, seriously, what were you trying to say by getting us *Orange is the New Black* and *Shameless*?"

Pointing at her boobs, Ginny deadpans, "Convict." Poking me in the nipple, "My cellblock bitch."

Tipping my head to the side, "I thought you were *my* cellblock bitch?" I feign annoyance.

"Ladies," Rory drawls out, trying not to laugh. "I tried to explain to my lovely wife that you guys bought us *Orange is the New Black* and *Shameless* to spice up our evenings."

"It's true," I agree, nodding my head. "Nothing gets a hot-blood male going like lesbians. We have firsthand knowledge of this phenomenon."

"It is fact. Let it be known," Ginny chants, still stone-faced. "*Shameless* is for you, Beth. You'll heart Jimmy-Steve."

"I heart fantasies of Veronica and Fiona," I say pointedly to Rory. "Beth will love Jimmy-Steve because he's in sore need of a therapist. Frank, too."

My girlfriend holds her composure until the newlyweds are sucked back into the throng. Holding her side, Ginny busts out laughing. "They'll be fucking like bunnies before they get halfway through the first episode of *Shameless*."

"*Wife*, they'll be playing cellblock bitch by the end of the week," I tease.

"Mmm… my favorite game to play," Ginny purrs. "You ready to go home?"

I ask hesitantly, "Home?"

"*Home?*" Ginny says in a way that makes it means so much more than it sounds. As is our way, we don't bother with posturing. We say what we mean, what we need, and we trust that the other will not judge. In this case, instead of a long, drawn-out conversation, Ginny goes straight in for the kill.

"Let me grab the kid before he becomes someone's favorite cellblock bitch. Sage is too pretty to endure actual prison life."

"Home," Ginny decrees again, with the most beatific smile curling her lips. "My nephew isn't allowed to have any sleepovers until Sage goes to California. Chaperoning Rae, or not."

"Agreed," but I'm agreeing to so much more. A long life by Ginny's side. "Let's go home."

Thank you for reading **WANTON**. Don't miss out on what's to come…

GOOD GIRL, Willow's coming-of-age tale.

WILDLY WEDDED WIFE, Rory & Bethany's novella.

WIDOW, Malcolm & Clover's journey.

WANTON, Opal & Ginny's tasty treat.

WARPED, Devon, Essie, Kieren, & Willow's future.

COMING SOON.

WOVEN, a novellas with surprising narrators.

WICKED, a novella showcasing Auggie & Tina's parents.

WAYWARD, Auggie, Isis, and Robin's angsty emotional roller coaster ride.

…and many more to come.

ACKNOWLEDGEMENTS

A lot of work goes into writing a novel, and it isn't just by the writer herself. **My parents:** for their unconditional support. **My readers**: thank you for reading my twisted words and spreading my books to the masses. For without you, no one would've ever heard of my stories. My readers are my lifeblood. A shout out to the members of the **M&M of Restraint Group on Facebook**: thanks for the endless entertainment and inspiration. **Wicked Reads**: (in all its incarnations) **Angela G.**, thank you for taking over and making Wicked Reads better than I could have done by myself. & thank you for helping promote my work and the work of other authors. Angela? Have I told you lately how much I appreciate you? A huge thank you to the **Wicked Writer's Betas** for keeping me grounded and encouraging me to keep trudging along when I get frustrated. Your thoughts and observations are invaluable. ((Hugs)) Beta readers: **Kris | Suz | Darcy | Sandy | Di | Angela | Diane | Jacki | Linsey | Alexis | Billie Jo | Tassie | Caroline | Judith | Jodi Lynn | Jodi |** Someday, I'd love to meet you all in real life– it would be the experience of a lifetime.

ABOUT THE AUTHOR

Erica Chilson does not write in the 3rd person, wanting her readers to *be* her characters. Therefore, writing a bio about herself, is uncomfortable in the extreme.

Born, raised, and here to stay, the Wicked Writer is a stump-jumper, a ridge-runner. Hailing from North Central Pennsylvania, directly on the New York State border; she loves the changes in seasons, the humid air, all the mountainous forest, and the gloomy atmosphere. Introverted, but not socially awkward, Erica prides herself on thinking first and filtering her speech. There are days she doesn't speak at all. If it wasn't for the fact that she lives with her parents, giving her a sense of reality, she would be a hermit, where the delivery man finds her months after expiration.

Reading was an escape, a way to leave a not-so pleasant reality behind. Reading lent Erica the courage she gathered from the characters between the pages to long for a different life. Writing was an instrument of change, evolving Erica into the woman she is today– a better, more mature, more at peace thinker.

Erica has a wicked mind, one she pours out into her creations. Her filter doesn't allow all of it to erupt, much to her relief. Sarcastic, with a very dark, perverse sense of humor, Erica puts a bit of herself into every character she writes.

I love hearing from readers. If you would like more information on release dates, works in progress, teaser chapters, and random bits of madness, please visit my Facebook Fan Page:
https://www.facebook.com/thewickedwriter my website:
ericachilson.com or please contact me via email:
wickedwriter.ericachilson@gmail.com
DEVIANTS ONLY, if you'd like to join Erica Chilson's closed Facebook group, M&M of Restraint:
https://www.facebook.com/groups/MistressandMaster/